O9-AIC-656

BY JANET EVANOVICH

THE FOX AND O'HARE NOVELS
with Lee Goldberg

The Heist

THE STEPHANIE PLUM NOVELS

One for the Money
Two for the Dough
Three to Get Deadly
Four to Score
High Five
Hot Six
Seven Up
Hard Eight
To the Nines
Ten Big Ones
Eleven on Top
Twelve Sharp
Lean Mean Thirteen
Fearless Fourteen
Finger Lickin' Fifteen
Sizzling Sixteen
Smokin' Seventeen
Explosive Eighteen
Notorious Nineteen

THE BETWEEN THE NUMBERS NOVELS

Visions of Sugar Plums
Plum Lovin'
Plum Lucky
Plum Spooky

THE LIZZY AND DIESEL NOVELS

Wicked Appetite
Wicked Business

THE BARNABY AND HOOKER NOVELS

Metro Girl
Motor Mouth
Trouble Maker (graphic novel)

NONFICTION

How I Write

THE HEIST

THE HEIST

A NOVEL

JANET EVANOVICH

AND LEE GOLDBERG

BANTAM BOOKS NEW YORK

The Heist is a work of fiction. Names, characters, places, and incidents are the products of the authors' imaginations or are used fictitiously. Any resemblance to actual events, locales, or persons, living or dead, is entirely coincidental.

Published in the United States by Bantam Books, an imprint of
The Random House Publishing Group, a division of Random House, Inc., New York.

BANTAM BOOKS and the rooster colophon are registered trademarks of
Random House, Inc.

This book contains an excerpt from the forthcoming book *Takedown Twenty* by Janet Evanovich. This excerpt has been set for this edition only and may not reflect the final content of the forthcoming edition.

LIBRARY OF CONGRESS CATALOGING-IN-PUBLICATION DATA
Evanovich, Janet.
The heist: a novel / Janet Evanovich and Lee Goldberg.
pages cm
ISBN 978-0-345-54941-9
eBook ISBN 978-0-345-54306-6
I. Goldberg, Lee 1962– II. Title.
PS3555.V2126H35 2013 813'.54—dc23 2013005834

Printed in the United States of America on acid-free paper

www.bantamdell.com

2 4 6 8 9 7 5 3 1

Special Barnes & Noble Edition

ACKNOWLEDGMENTS

We would like to thank Vicki Hendricks for educating us about skydiving, and Twist Phelan, Jack Chapple, and Bill O'Meara for answering, in great detail, all of our questions about sailing the waters of Indonesia.

This is a work of fiction, and we've taken a few liberties with geography, among other things. Any mistakes, exaggerations, or instances of pure make-believe are entirely our fault. And yes, we know there aren't any female Navy SEALS. But we think there should be.

THE HEIST

1

Kate O'Hare's favorite outfit was her blue windbreaker with the letters FBI written in yellow on the back, worn over a basic black T-shirt and matching black Kevlar vest. The ensemble went well with everything, particularly when paired with jeans and accessorized with a Glock. Thirty-three-year-old Special Agent O'Hare didn't like feeling exposed and unarmed, especially on the job. That all but ruled her out for undercover work. Fine by her. She preferred a hard-charging style of law enforcement, which was exactly what she was practicing on that 96 degree winter afternoon in Las Vegas when she marched into the St. Cosmas Medical Center in her favorite outfit with a dozen similarly dressed agents behind her.

While the other agents fanned out to seal every exit in the building, Kate pushed past the security guards in the lobby and made her way like a guided missile to the first-floor office of Rufus Stott, the chief administrator of the hospital. She blew past Stott's stunned assistant without even acknowledging her existence and burst into Stott's office. The startled Stott yelped and nearly toppled out of his chrome-and-mesh ergonomic chair. He was a chubby, bottom-heavy little guy who looked like a turnip that some bored wizard had tapped with a magic wand and turned into a fifty-five-year-old bureaucrat. He had a spray tan, tortoiseshell glasses, and crotch wrinkles in his tan slacks. His hand was over his heart, and he was gasping for air.

"Don't shoot," he finally managed.

"I'm not going to shoot," Kate said. "I don't even have my gun drawn. Do you need water, or something? Are you okay?"

"No, I'm not okay," Stott said. "You just scared the bejeezus out of me. Who are you? What do you want?"

"I'm Special Agent Kate O'Hare, FBI." She slapped a piece of paper down on his desk. "This is a warrant giving us full access to your concierge wing."

"We don't have a concierge wing," Stott said.

Kate leaned in close, locking her intense blue eyes on him. "Six obscenely wealthy and desperate patients flew in today from all over the country. They were picked up from McCarran airport by limos and brought here. Upon arrival at your private concierge wing, they each wired one million dollars to St. Cosmas's offshore bank account and immediately jumped to the top of an organ waiting list."

"You can't be serious," Stott said. "We don't have any offshore bank accounts and we certainly can't afford to rent limos. We're teetering on bankruptcy."

"That's why you're conducting off-the-books transplant surgeries using illegally acquired organs that you bought on the black market. We know those patients are here and being prepped for surgery right now. We will lock this building down and search every single room and broom closet if we have to."

"Be my guest," Stott said, and handed the warrant back to her. "We aren't doing any transplant surgeries, and we don't have a concierge wing. We don't even have a gift shop."

Stott no longer looked scared, and he didn't look like he was lying. Not good signs, Kate thought. He should be in a cold sweat by now. He should be phoning his lawyer.

Eighteen hours earlier, Kate had been at her desk in L.A., tracking scattered intel on known associates of a wanted felon, when she'd stumbled on chatter about a certain financially strapped Las Vegas hospital offering organ transplants to the highest bidder. She dug deeper and discovered that the patients were already en route to Vegas for their surgeries, so she dropped everything and organized a rush operation.

"Take a look at this," she said, showing Stott a photo on her iPhone.

It was a medium close-up of a man about her age wearing a loose-fitting polo shirt, soft and faded from years of use. His brown hair was windblown. His face was alight with a boyish grin that brought out the laugh lines at the corners of his brown eyes.

"Do you know this man?" she asked.

"Sure I do," Stott replied. "That's Cliff Clavin, the engineer handling the asbestos removal from our old building."

Kate felt a dull ache in her stomach, and it wasn't from the Jack in the Box sausage-and-egg sandwich she'd had for breakfast. Her gut, flat and toned despite her terrible eating habits, was where her anxieties and her instincts resided and liked to communicate with her in a language of cramps, pains, queasiness, and general malaise.

"Cliff Clavin is a character on the television show *Cheers,*" she said.

"Yeah, crazy coincidence, right?"

"What old building?" she asked him.

He turned to the window and pointed at a five-story building on the other side of the parking lot. "That one."

The building was an architectural artifact from the swinging '60s with its lava rock accents, big tinted windows, and a lobby portico topped with white gravel.

"That was the original hospital," Stott said. "We moved out of there a year ago. We built this new one to handle the demand for beds that we wrongly anticipated would come from . . ."

Kate wasn't listening. She was already running out the door. The instant she saw the other building, she knew exactly how she and those six wealthy patients had been duped. The man in the photo on her iPhone wasn't Cliff Clavin, and he wasn't an engineer. He was Nicolas Fox, the man she'd been pursuing when she'd stumbled on the organ transplant scheme.

Fox was an international con man and thief, known for the sheer audacity of his high-risk swindles and heists and for the obvious joy he took in pulling them off. No matter how big his scores were, and he'd had some huge ones, he kept going back for more.

Kate had made it her mission at the FBI to nail him. She'd come close two years ago, when she'd discovered Nick's plot to plunder a venture capitalist's twentieth-story Chicago penthouse of all his cash and jewels at the same time that the self-proclaimed "King of Hostile Takeovers" was getting married in the living room.

It was a ballsy move, and pure Nick Fox. To pull it off, he somehow got himself hired as the wedding planner and brought in a motley crew of thieves as the caterers. When Kate crashed the wedding with a strike team, Nick's crew scattered like cockroaches when the lights go on, and Nick parachuted off the top of the building.

Choppers were called in, streets were closed, roadblocks were set up, and buildings were searched, but Nick slipped away. When Kate finally straggled into her hotel room at dawn, there was a bottle of champagne and a bouquet of roses waiting for her. All from Nick. And charged to her room, of course. The whole time she'd been hunting for Nick, he'd been relaxing in her room, watching pay-per-view movies, ordering room service, and helping himself to the Toblerones in her minibar. He'd even stolen the towels on his way out.

The bastard is having way too much fun at my expense, Kate thought as she bolted through the hospital lobby, out the door past two surprised agents, and charged across the parking lot.

When she reached the cyclone fence around the old hospital building, she was sweating and her heart was pounding so hard she could almost hear it. She drew her gun and slowly approached the entrance to the lobby. As she got closer, she saw a red carpet and a sign that had been obscured in the shadows of the alcove under the portico. The sign read:

Welcome to the St. Cosmas Concierge Medical Center.
Please excuse our dust as we remodel to give you more
privacy, luxury, and state-of-the art care.

Hugging the lava rock walls she made her way to the door, yanked it open, and spun into the open space in a firing stance. But there was no one to aim at. Kate faced an elegantly furnished lobby decked out with contemporary leather furniture, travertine floors, and lush plants. On the wall behind the empty reception desk were photos of the surgical staff. She looked at the photos and immediately recognized two of the faces. One of them belonged to Nick Fox, a stethoscope around his neck, exuding doctorly strength and confidence. The other one was her, with a dopey, drunken smile on her face. Her picture had been lifted, cropped, and photoshopped from the bridal party pictures taken years ago that were now on her sister Megan's Facebook page. "Dr. William Scholl" was written in bronze letters under Nick's photo, "Dr. Eunice Huffnagle" under hers.

Okay, so where was the "surgical staff" now? she asked herself. And what about the six rich patients who'd come from far and wide for organ transplants?

Kate headed for the double doors that were located to one side of the reception desk. She pushed them open and stepped into a foyer, ready to fire. But once again, there was no one there. Directly in front of her were three more sets of double doors. One was marked "Operating Room #1," the second "Post-Op #1," and the third "Pre-Op." An elevator was to her left. A stairwell door was to her right.

She eased open the door to the operating room and found a fully decked out surgical suite that took its design cues from an Apple Store. Everything was sleek and white. All the equipment gleamed like new cars on a showroom floor.

She closed the door and peeked into the post-op room. There was the standard hospital bed, the IV stand, and the usual monitoring devices, but the similarities to any other hospital room ended there. The room was luxuriously appointed with fancy French furniture, ornate shelves filled with leather-bound books, a flat-screen TV, and a wet bar stocked with assorted spirits.

He's smart, she thought. Posing as an asbestos removal company was the perfect cover for Nick's scam. It ensured that everyone at the hospital kept their distance from the old building while Nick and his crew were actually creating an elaborate set and staging their con.

Finally, she went to the pre-op room. The door opened onto a long ward with an abandoned nurses station and several curtained-off areas behind it. She stepped inside and cautiously slid open the first curtain. An unconscious middle-aged man in a hospital gown was stretched out on a gurney and hooked up to an IV drip. Kate checked his pulse. It was strong.

She made her way through the ward, yanking open curtains as she passed. All six of the men who'd come in that day from the airport were there, each of them sound asleep and, she assumed, a million dollars poorer.

The windows in the building vibrated, and she heard the unmistakable *thwap-thwap-thwap* of helicopter blades above her. Nick Fox was on the roof, she thought. *Again!*

She ran out of the room and to the stairwell, climbing the four flights as fast as she could, which was remarkably speedy for a woman whose most frequent dinner companions were Colonel Sanders, Long John Silver, Ronald McDonald, and the Five Guys.

Kate burst onto the roof ready to fire and saw a blue Las Vegas Aerial Tours chopper on the helipad, its side door open, several "doctors" and "nurses" inside.

Nick Fox was not among them. He stood casually midway between her and the helicopter with his hands in his pockets, the wind created by the chopper blades whipping at his hair and flaring his white lab coat like a superhero's cape.

Kate had created the man of her dreams when she was twelve,

and she'd hung on to the image. The dream man had soft brown hair, intelligent brown eyes, and a boyish grin. He was six feet tall with a slim agile body. He was smart and sexy and playful. So it was with terrible irony that over the course of the last couple years it dawned on Kate that Nick Fox was the living embodiment of her dream man.

"Dr. Scholl?" Kate yelled over the chopper noise. "Really?"

"It's a very respected name in medicine," Nick yelled back. "Glad to see you're wearing sensible shoes."

Nick knew she always wore Dr. Scholl's gels in her black Nikes. It was one of the many things he'd learned about her over the last couple years. Most of what he'd learned intrigued him. Some of it was downright scary. The scary part was offset by a physical attraction to her that he couldn't explain.

Her brown hair was pulled back in a ponytail, and her flawless skin had a slight sheen from her dash across the parking lot and up the stairs. Sexy, but he suspected the fantasy the sheen inspired was better than the reality. She was the job. Probably wore Kevlar to bed. End of story. Still, he did enjoy playing with her. He liked her big blue eyes, cute little nose, slim athletic body, and her earnest dedication to making the world a more law-abiding place. It made his dedication to crime much more interesting.

"You're under arrest," she shouted.

"How do you figure that?"

"Because I've got my gun on you, and I'm a great shot." She took a step toward him.

He took a step back. "I'm sure you are, but you're not going to shoot me."

"Frankly, I'm surprised I haven't shot you already." She took another step toward him.

"Still upset about those Toblerones?" He took another step back.

"Take one more step, and I'll put you down."

"You can't," he said.

"I can shoot the testicles off an eagle from a hundred yards."

"Eagles don't have testicles."

"I may suck when it comes to metaphors, but my aim is excellent."

"You can't shoot me because I am unarmed and not presenting any threat of physical harm."

"I can shoot the helicopter."

"And risk it crashing into a hospital full of children? I don't think so."

"The hospital isn't full of children."

"You're missing the point." He stole a glance down at the parking lot to see scores of FBI agents rushing toward the building and then looked back at her to see she'd advanced two steps closer. "It was really good seeing you again, Kate."

"It's Special Agent O'Hare to you," she said. "And you're not going anywhere."

He smiled and bolted for the chopper.

"Damn!" She holstered her gun and charged after him.

Even after racing up four flights of stairs she was still faster than he was, and she took a lot of pleasure in that. She was quickly closing the distance between them, and she was pretty certain that she'd get her hands on him before he could climb inside the chopper.

Apparently the pilot and Nick's crew shared her optimism, because the chopper suddenly lifted up and out over the edge of the building, leaving their ringleader behind. Nick picked up speed and kept running as if the rooftop extended another hundred yards instead of just a few more feet.

With mounting horror, Kate realized what he intended to do. He was going to jump. And this time, he didn't have a parachute.

"Don't!" she yelled, launching herself at him, hoping to take him down with a flying tackle before he could make a suicidal mistake. Too late. She missed him by inches, and hit the concrete hard just as Nick leapt off the building toward the hovering chopper. Her heart stopped for a couple beats while he was in midair, and resumed beating when he latched on to the helicopter's landing skid. He held on with one hand, blew her a kiss, and the chopper veered off toward the Las Vegas Strip.

Within seconds of his escape, Kate was on the radio, trying to get a police chopper into the air and patrol cars on the ground to chase Nick's helicopter. Kate knew it was a waste of time and effort, but she went through the motions anyway.

There were half a dozen identical Las Vegas Aerial Tours choppers in the airspace above the Strip, and even though only one of them had a man hanging from a landing skid, by the time she got the word out Nick's helicopter had disappeared. It didn't help that in all the excitement, she'd failed to note the chopper's tail number and had nothing to give to air traffic controllers so they could track its transponder. Not that it would have mattered. The helicopter wasn't actually part of the tour company's fleet. It had just been painted to appear as if it was.

Kate sped straight from the hospital back to the room she'd booked at Circus Circus, the least expensive hotel on the Strip. She approached her door quietly, one hand on her holstered gun. She slipped her key card into the lock and slowly eased open the door, hoping Nick Fox had been arrogant enough to pull the same stunt twice, hoping to catch him in the act.

No such luck. The room was empty and smelled like a freshly chlorinated swimming pool. She sat down on the edge of the bed and sighed. Not her best day. And she knew she'd catch a lot of crap for letting Nick get away instead of finding an excuse to shoot him. She certainly had plenty of them, the latest one being the picture of "Dr. Eunice Huffnagle" that she'd managed to snatch off the wall before anyone noticed it.

Kate stared glumly at her reflection in the mirror and started to take off her Kevlar vest. And that's when she noticed it. She didn't believe it at first, and had to look over her shoulder to confirm it, but there it was: a Toblerone bar on her pillow.

2

SIX MONTHS LATER . . .

When the average person accumulates more stuff than he can fit into his house, he'll haul everything to a rented cinder-block storage unit, stick a cheap padlock on the roll-up door, and immediately start buying more junk. If you're someone as old and rich as Roland Larsen Kibbee, you build a museum for it all, carve your name in marble out front, and charge admission so everybody can admire your stuff and, by extension, you.

Not only does opening a museum free up some room in your mansion, it has the added benefit of being a great status symbol, one that's hard to top even in an age when billionaires are launching rockets into space. Roland's collection of paintings, sculptures, and jewelry was acquired with the fortune he'd earned snatching up distressed California farms, kicking the owners off their properties, and harvesting their crops using the cheapest labor possible, thus becoming one of the state's largest employers of illegal immigrants and a pillar of Mexico's economy.

Of course he didn't build his museum in Mexico. He established the Roland Larsen Kibbee Art Collection in San Francisco, in a massive Pacific Heights mansion, modeled after a French château.

Roland's business practices clashed with the liberal ideals of his twenty-six-year-old curator Clarissa Hart, but her master's degree in fine arts wasn't getting her any work, she had $97,000 in student loans to pay off, and if she had to live another day with her parents, she'd smother them in their sleep. So she swallowed her ideals and took the paycheck each month from Roland. And while the Kibbee wasn't the Guggenheim or the Getty, and the artwork, most of it nudes, made Clarissa feel like she was a hostess at the Playboy Mansion, she took solace in the fact that she was still a museum curator.

The collection of paintings and objets d'art was displayed in hallways and intimate salons to make the visitors feel as if they were guests in Roland's home, though the eighty-five-year-old agribusiness magnate had never lived there. He lived in Palm Beach, Florida, with a twenty-two-year-old stripper named LaRhonda who was waiting for him to die. After he breathed his last agonizing breath she hoped to get her hands on the Crimson Teardrop, a rare two-carat red diamond that was his latest acquisition.

The Teardrop was also the Kibbee's best shot at wide recognition, and in anticipation of the Crimson Teardrop's opening-night display, the marble floors were being polished, the paneling was being restained, and the leather couches and armchairs were being replaced with new models. Clarissa was playing tour guide to SFPD Inspector Norman Peterson, who'd shown up to talk with her about traffic control during the exhibition and to make sure the museum had taken adequate security measures to protect the diamond.

"I've driven by this place a thousand times and never noticed there was a museum here," Peterson said, rubbing a mustache that looked like a very large caterpillar taking a nap under his bulbous nose.

He wore his badge on a lanyard around his neck in what Clarissa assumed was an unsuccessful attempt to cover his big belly and the mustard stain on his tie. She placed him in his mid-thirties, though he wouldn't see forty if he didn't change his eating habits.

She was right about the age, but wrong about everything else. Inspector Peterson was actually Nick Fox, padded to look fat, his face disguised by layers of expertly applied prosthetics and makeup.

"We're a boutique museum," Clarissa said as they made their way around the crew that was putting the new furniture into place.

"What's that mean?"

She could have said that it meant they were smaller, more intimate, and more carefully curated than larger museums, but something about him, and his absolute lack of pretension, changed her mind.

"It means that people drive by this place a thousand times and never notice us."

"That's a shame, because you've got some good stuff here." Nick stopped to look at a life-size five-hundred-year-old marble statue of a naked woman sitting on a tree stump and clutching her left breast. "You'd think she'd have brought a pillow or a blanket to sit on."

"She was beyond those kinds of concerns."

"Nobody wants to get a splinter in their butt. Who was she?"

"Aphrodite," Clarissa said.

"Don't know her," Nick said. "But keep in mind, you're talking to a guy who walks through the Wax Museum on Fisherman's Wharf and doesn't recognize half of the supposedly famous people on display."

Clarissa gave him a look, just to check if he was teasing her, and decided that his remark was genuine. She'd never visited the Wax Museum but knew they probably got more visitors in a day than the Kibbee got in a month.

"She's the Greek goddess of love, Inspector. Her origin story is interesting. The young and envious Titan Cronus wanted to dethrone his father, Uranus, ruler of the universe. So Cronus cut off his father's genitals with a scythe, threw them into the ocean, and Aphrodite rose up out of the frothy waves."

"And she symbolizes love?" Nick said. "That's brutal."

"You could say that's the theme behind every piece in the Kibbee collection," she said, though she doubted there was any theme at all to Roland's collecting of artwork, or wives, besides an obvious breast fixation. "The dark side of love. That's also the allure of the Crimson Teardrop."

"I thought it's because it's worth a gajillion dollars."

"Closer to fifteen million. It's an exquisite diamond, but as a piece of art its value comes from its history." She led him into the salon where the Crimson Teardrop was displayed in the center of the room, in a glass box, on top of an ornate marble pedestal. "It's named for all the love, death, and sadness that has surrounded it."

Nick was well aware of the diamond's history. The diamond had been discovered in 1912 by two young British naturalists hiking through South Africa. The couple were deeply in love, and intended to use the stone in a wedding ring, but when word got out about their find, they were hacked apart by machete-wielding thieves, and the diamond was stolen.

The stone somehow made its way to Russia, where it was fashioned into a necklace that Tsar Nicholas Romanov gave as a gift to his wife, Alexandra. She later passed it along to her daughter Anastasia, who was wearing it under her clothing, along with other heirloom jewelry, when the family was executed in July 1918.

The jewels pillaged from Anastasia's corpse, as well as those hidden on the other Romanovs and their servants, were sold and resold, and the necklace didn't appear again until November 3, 1929. That's when banker Dick Epperson and his wife, Dollie, left destitute by the stock market crash late the previous month, dressed in their finery, kissed each other, and then jumped hand in hand off the balcony of their Park Avenue apartment. The Crimson Teardrop was around Dollie's neck. No one knew how she'd come to possess it, but her heirs quickly sold it to pay off debts.

More owners and tragedies followed over the decades, none making news until, legend has it, the Crimson Teardrop was acquired by a secret admirer who supposedly gave it as a present to Marilyn Monroe shortly before her death in 1962. The diamond wasn't actually seen again until recently, when oil company heiress Victoria Burrows died at the age of eighty-seven in the Santa Barbara home she hadn't left since the death of her husband in 1965.

Roland Larson Kibbee snatched the diamond up at the Burrows estate sale, and now it's my turn to snatch it from Kibbee, Nick thought.

"They say the diamond is cursed," Clarissa said. "Especially for lovers."

"Somebody is going to want to steal it anyway. What's to stop them?"

"A state-of-the-art alarm system, magnetic fields around the doors and windows, and, in this room alone, motion detectors, heat sensors, and a half dozen wireless cameras, and that's just for starters," she said. "You'll notice there are no windows or doors in here."

"Of course I did," Nick said, looking around. "I am a trained detective." And thief.

"The room is essentially a nicely decorated open vault. There's only one way in, through the archway behind you. If any of the security systems are tripped, a recessed two-foot-thick reinforced steel door drops down, trapping the would-be thief inside and sending an instant alert directly to your police station. How fast do you think you can get here once the alarm is tripped?"

"You got the guy trapped, right?"

"Virtually entombed. The steel door is designed to withstand explosives and hours of concentrated assault by drills and blow-torches."

"So what's the rush?" Nick shrugged. "Maybe I'll stop by Star-bucks on the way just to make the guy sweat."

"Assuming he wasn't squashed under a half ton of steel before he even got inside the room."

"Then there's even less of a reason to hurry," Nick said. "Tell me now what your favorite coffee is and I'll pick you up one, too, if the situation ever arises."

"Cinnamon Dolce Latte, if you please." She smiled. The guy wasn't much to look at, but he had charm. "Would you like to see the rest of the museum?"

"Are there more naked women?"

"Yes," she said.

"Lead on."

"This is sort of awkward," she said, "but there was a Norm Peterson on *Cheers*."

"No relation," Nick said.

At 9:52 that same night, if you'd happened to be inside the Kibbee, you would have had the opportunity to see a most remarkable sight. Sadly for the two guards in the front office who were half-heartedly watching the surveillance camera feeds, the sight was not made available to them.

Earlier in the day, a leather armchair and a matching couch had been placed in the hallway outside the salon where the Crimson Teardrop was on display. There were cameras in the hallway aimed at the chair and couch, but one side of each piece of furniture was not visible to the cameras, and it was on those sides that the upholstery began to peel away and reveal two men. One of the men had been folded in a sitting position in the chair. The second man had been lying inside the couch. Both men were completely clad, from head to toe, in skintight green bodysuits.

If Spider-Man was entirely green, couldn't shoot webs from his wrists, wasn't ripped, and was self-conscious about the contours of his privates being so out there, these guys were what he'd look like.

Chair Man stood up and removed a folded green bedsheet and a small green gym bag from within the chair. Couch Man slid out and removed two thin boards wrapped in green fabric from within his couch. The lightweight boards were roughly the same size as his body and had handles on their backs, which allowed him to hold them like shields.

At that same moment, one of the two security guards looked at the monitor showing the camera feed from the hallway and saw nothing unusual. Chair Man and Couch Man and the contours of their privates and the things they carried were absolutely invisible on the camera feed.

Chair Man opened his bag, crouched in front of the archway, and took out a green aerosol can, which he sprayed in front of the archway walls, where he knew the heat and motion sensors were hidden. He and Couch Man waited for the mist to clear, then Couch Man handed one of the shields to Chair Man. The two green men, standing behind their boards, entered on either side of the archway. They each stopped in front of the archway frame, unfolded legs from the backs of the boards, and left them in place.

The half-ton steel door hidden above their heads didn't come crashing down, so they continued into the salon devoted to the Crimson Teardrop display. There was no corner of the room that was obscured from the view of the many hidden cameras, and yet none of them picked up the two men or what they carried.

Chair Man set the green gym bag and the green sheet on the floor in front of the pedestal holding the Teardrop. He picked up one edge of the sheet, Couch Man picked up the other, and they slowly lifted it up in unison and draped the fabric gently over the entire display. Chair Man slipped under the sheet with a glass-cutting tool and began to cut into the Teardrop's protective glass box. The cut was barely a scratch, hardly visible to the naked eye, but the instant the glass was breached, an alarm sounded and the steel door came crashing down in the archway, rocking the building like an earthquake and trapping the two green men inside the room.

3

Nick Fox, in his guise as Inspector Norman Peterson, arrived within twenty minutes of the alarm call, carrying two cups of coffee from Starbucks, one of which he handed to Clarissa Hart, who stood anxiously outside the steel door with the two security guards who'd been watching the monitors.

"One Cinnamon Dolce Latte, as promised, though I didn't expect I'd ever have to come through on it." Nick tipped his head toward the lanky young man in the corduroy jacket who'd arrived with him. "This is my partner, Inspector Ed Brown."

Brown nodded. It wasn't his real name, of course. Not even Nick knew what that was. Every time he'd worked with "Brown," the man had a different name and a different look.

"What set off the alarm?" Nick asked, taking a sip of his coffee, seeming to be in no hurry at all to apprehend the thieves trapped on the other side of the steel door.

"There's a sensor that monitors the air pressure inside the glass box that contains the Crimson Teardrop. It's tripped the instant the glass is breached. But here's what makes no sense, Inspector," she said, holding up her iPhone. "This is the feed from one of the security cameras. As you can see, there's nobody inside the room, but there's no way out and the image is definitely live. You can see the steel door in the archway."

"But you can't see pieces of this," Nick said, gesturing to the chunks of green Styrofoam on the floor from whatever had been crushed by the steel door.

Clarissa stared at the iPhone, then at Nick. "You're right. Are you saying this isn't a live feed?"

"No, it's live."

"Then I don't understand," she said.

"Are you familiar with Harry Potter?" Nick asked.

"Of course I am," she said.

"Then you know about his Cloak of Invisibility," Nick said, sipping his coffee again and getting a bit of foam in his mustache.

She smiled. "You think the thief is a wizard?"

"No, but he was working for one, who is long gone now and ran the whole show from a fake phone-company truck that was parked down the street."

"How do you know that?"

"We drove past it on our way here." Nick wiped the foam off his mustache with his finger, and wiped his finger on his pants.

"I meant, how do you know it's fake?"

"I didn't then, but I do now, because of this." Nick nudged a chunk of Styrofoam with his shoe. "That's green-colored Styrofoam wrapped in polyester."

"Sort of like you and your suit," Brown said with a grin, glancing at Clarissa to see if he'd scored a point with her. He hadn't, but he had with the two guards, which was no consolation.

"What's so significant about the polyester?" Clarissa asked.

"Polyester has very low thermal conductivity," Nick said.

Clarissa nodded with understanding. "So the thief used the polyester-wrapped board as a wall to block the heat sensors from picking him up as he entered the room."

"That's right."

Nick toasted her with his cup, she toasted him back, and Brown grimaced.

Clarissa regarded the inspector as if seeing him for the first time. Physically he wasn't much to look at, and after she'd had to explain to him who Aphrodite was, she'd dismissed him as an uneducated, though very likeable, oaf. Now she realized that she'd gotten him all wrong. This guy was no oaf. He was sharp, and comfortable in his own skin. The more he spoke, the more she liked him.

"I may have missed something, Inspector," she said, "but what does all of this have to do with why we can't see the thief in the room?"

"He's green," Nick said.

"He's done pretty well for an amateur," Brown said.

"I meant, Ed, that he's *wearing* green. The same color as these heat shields, which brings me back to Harry Potter and his Cloak of Invisibility," Nick said. "It's a movie special effect. The wizard behind this crime used the same technique that Hollywood uses to put actors on alien worlds that don't exist or in the cockpits of fighter jets that aren't actually in the air. They have the actors perform in front of a green screen and then they use a computer to replace the green background with something else, a still or moving image. But our wizard did the reverse."

"He put the thief and his tools in green," Clarissa said, getting it now. "The wizard, sitting with a laptop in that fake phone truck outside, tapped into our surveillance camera feeds to replace the thief, and anything else that was green, with video of whatever was behind them, making them appear invisible."

Nick nodded. "Then the thief draped a Cloak of Invisibility over the Crimson Teardrop display so he could steal the diamond without being seen."

"How did he do that?" Brown asked.

"He threw a green sheet over it, and the wizard composited a still image of the Crimson Teardrop display over that," Nick said. "What the guards saw was an empty room and the Crimson Teardrop safely on display."

"That's brilliant," Clarissa said. "The wizard is a genius."

"He's a complete screwup," Brown said. "You're forgetting that we're out here and the thief is in there with the diamond, ergo the plan didn't work."

"But he came close to pulling it off," Clarissa said. "You've got to give him credit for that."

Nick nodded in agreement. "A guy this smart has probably been at this awhile. The FBI might have some idea who he is, assuming the thief isn't kind enough to tell us. Speaking of which, I'd say it's time that we met our guest. Can you raise the curtain, please, Ms. Hart?"

Clarissa walked to a painting on the wall and moved it aside to reveal a hidden keypad.

Nick looked at the guards. "You two stand aside and keep your weapons in your holsters. We don't want any accidents."

Nick set down his coffee cup and drew his own weapon. He and Brown stood in firing stance and faced the steel door. Clarissa typed a code into the keypad. The steel door rose with a heavy groan to reveal two men in green bodysuits sitting glumly on the floor, their hands on their heads. The green sheet was in a clump at the base of the pedestal. The Crimson Teardrop shimmered untouched in its glass case.

"SFPD," Brown said. "You're under arrest."

"You took your damn time," Chair Man said. "I thought we were going to suffocate in here."

"Cuff 'em and read 'em their rights, Ed," Nick said, and tossed Brown his set of cuffs.

Clarissa stared at Nick with unabashed admiration. He was like a real-life Columbo, only much younger and without the glass eye.

"Are you single, Inspector?" she asked.

"Sadly, yes," he said.

"On the contrary," she said, slipping her card into his back pocket and giving it a pat.

The Crown Vic siren wailed as the car sped down Van Ness Avenue. Fog was spreading out from the bay and over the city, and the Vic's headlights fought through the thickening mist. Brown drove, and Nick sat beside him with the green gym bag on his lap. Chair Man and Couch Man were handcuffed in the backseat.

"Did you have to blather on and on for so long?" Couch Man asked.

"I was selling the con," Nick said.

The elaborate crime had gone down exactly like he'd laid it out to Clarissa, except that he'd been the wizard behind the camera trickery in the fake phone-company truck. And he'd left out that he'd intercepted the alarm signal from the Kibbee before it could reach the police department.

"You were showing off," Brown said. "You couldn't resist telling her just how brilliant you think you are."

"It was all part of the act. You can turn the siren off. People are trying to sleep."

"What's the point of driving a police car if you don't use the siren?"

"I have to hand it to you," Chair Man said to Nick. "Intentionally getting caught is the way to go. It really cuts down on the stress."

"I told you so," Nick said, opening the bag and taking out the Crimson Teardrop to admire it. "It's much easier to let the security system beat you than to try to beat it."

"It would have been even less stressful if I didn't have to wear something that showed everybody my junk," Couch Man said, tossing his handcuffs onto the floor.

"Don't be so self-conscious," Chair Man said, removing his green hood and running his hand through his sweat-soaked red hair. "You don't have anything everybody hasn't seen before."

"Easy for you to say," Couch Man replied, "you're hung like Godzilla's horse."

"Thanks," Chair Man said. "Spread the word to all the hot girls you know."

"Godzilla didn't ride a horse," Brown said.

Couch Man pulled off his green hood. "Well, if he did, the horse would be hung huge."

Nick dropped the diamond back into the bag and zipped it up. He wondered how long it would take before anybody spotted the fake they'd left at the Kibbee. He peeled off his mustache, which itched like poison ivy, and tossed it out the window. The fake nose was next to go.

"C'mon, turn off the siren. There's no sense drawing attention to ourselves," Nick said.

Brown did as he was told. "You're no fun, Nick."

"How can you say that?" Nick said. "You got to be a cop."

"The *dumb* cop," Brown said.

"It's better than being the ugly fat one," Nick said.

"You'd think so," Brown said. "But you still got the girl's number."

"He always does," Couch Man said with admiration.

Nick was too distracted to be flattered. He'd glanced at the street ahead and saw something in the fog, just beyond the next traffic light, that he wasn't expecting: a San Francisco Public Utilities Commission water crew was digging up the street. He could see a backhoe, a few workers wearing reflective suits and hard hats, and a big pile of dirt in the intersection blocking one of the two southbound lanes.

"What's wrong?" Brown asked.

"There wasn't any scheduled street maintenance on the books for tonight," Nick said. "I checked this morning."

"Maybe there was a power outage or a burst pipe," Brown said. "Things happen."

"All the lights in the neighborhood are on and I don't see any water on the street," Nick said. "Make a U-turn at the intersection."

"And go back the way we came?" Chair Man said. "That's not a good idea."

"You're being paranoid," Brown said.

"Just do it," Nick said, sitting up straight. He had a bad feeling.

Brown started to make a U-turn in the intersection. And that's when Nick looked out the passenger window and saw the headlights of a speeding Muni bus cutting through the fog like a freight train emerging from a dark tunnel. The bus T-boned their car, sending it rolling over and over and over before it finally came to rest wheels up on the sidewalk.

Nick was conscious but dazed, hanging upside down, belted into his seat, as the passenger-side airbag pressed against his face deflated with a hiss. The airbag, and the padding around his waist that he'd used to create his fake belly, had insulated him from injury. He heard the moans and groans of the other three men, which was good. It meant they were alive. His subconscious Scotty did an instantaneous full diagnostic and reported to his conscious mind, his inner Captain Kirk, that aye, they'd taken a beating, but all systems were functioning.

I can get you impulse power, Captain, but the warp drives are down. It will take me at least two days to repair 'em.

Make it two minutes, Scotty.

You're asking for the impossible!

That's what we're paid to do, Mister.

He closed his eyes, shook his head, and willed himself to focus. He opened his eyes again. Through the shattered windshield he could make out the SFPUC workers running toward the car, and he could see that they were carrying guns. So much for them being SFPUC workers.

Nick heard a crunch of glass shards under someone's shoes. He turned his head and looked out the open passenger window. He could see whoever it was only from the waist down. The guy was wearing jeans and black Nikes, walking slowly and deliberately toward the car and holding a Glock casually at his side.

Nick's first thought was that another crew was ripping them off. There was a whole class of predators who specialized in hijacking scores made by crooks more ingenious and industrious than they were. It was one of the risks of the profession, especially when several parties had their eye on the same high-profile prize. Let the best man get there first, then take it from him.

His second thought was more of a wish. He hoped whoever it was wouldn't put a bullet in his head before walking away with the Crimson Teardrop. But if the guy was smart, he *would* shoot him, because Nick vowed in that moment to follow the bastard to the ends of the earth and steal the jewel back in the most personally humiliating and financially devastating swindle he could devise.

The guy stopped at Nick's window, aimed his gun inside, and then crouched down to look at him.

"You're under arrest," FBI Special Agent Kate O'Hare said.

4

Kate hated the Federal Building on Mission and Seventh, which was designed not only to be environmentally friendly but also to promote healthy living among the people who worked in it. The main elevators stopped only on every third floor, ensuring that everyone had to walk up or down a flight or two of stairs every day. The only elevator that went to each floor was strictly reserved for deliveries and the disabled, so whenever a case brought Kate to San Francisco, she'd fake a debilitating limp. Sometimes she even brought a cane.

"Gunshot wound," she'd say when given a dubious look on the elevator by an agent in a wheelchair. "Tulsa, '06."

Or "IED, Kandahar. Damn shrapnel."

From this day forward, she hoped that the San Francisco Federal Building would take on special meaning for her. The sight of it would always remind her of the day she finally nailed Nick Fox. And not, as she feared now, of the forty-five minutes and counting she'd spent in the twelfth-floor women's bathroom, her stomach cramped with anxiety.

She'd taken an inordinate amount of time with her hair this morning, brushing it out and letting it fall to her shoulders, studying herself in the mirror. Everyone said she had her mother's hair. Deep chestnut, thick, and straight as a pin. Easy to manage unless it was confronted by humidity, and then it was a disaster. The brushed-out hair wasn't right, she decided. Too much of it. Too Saturday night. She tried wrapping it into a French braid and hated it. Too formal. So she pulled her hair into a ponytail, just like always.

She'd started out with makeup too. And it looked pretty good until she threw up. So now she was standing at the sink in her gray Ann Taylor pantsuit and white blouse, her face freshly scrubbed, her sleeves pushed up, her hands resting on the counter.

"Jeez Louise, get a grip!" she said to herself in the mirror. "This is supposed to be your finest hour. This is what you've worked for: to put him away. So do it. Finish the job." She popped open the third button of her blouse, applied fresh lipstick, and gave her lashes a swipe of mascara. "Eat your heart out, Nick Fox," she whispered to the mirror. "It'll be decades before you get up close and personal with a woman. Only one of many life experiences you can kiss goodbye."

Okay, so she felt a little stupid talking to herself like that, but she was getting into a frame of mind, right? She'd gotten rid of her breakfast burrito, and now she was going to walk into that interrogation room, and she'd own it. Nick Fox was a beaten man, and she'd remind him with every look, with every gesture, with every inflection of her voice, that she was the one who'd beaten him. She wouldn't let herself be manipulated by his charm. Nothing would distract her from her goal. It wasn't enough to get a conviction. There were millions of dollars in cash, jewelry, and art that he'd swindled and stolen that had never been recovered. He knew where it all was and she'd make him give it up. Without cleavage. She closed the third button of her blouse. She didn't need to use even a hint of her sexuality to crack him. That would be cheating. Not to mention, she wasn't down with the whole seduction thing. Truth is, it had been a while since she'd used her feminine charms. Maybe never.

She sucked in her stomach and stood military straight. She was ready to go. She had her mission. Time to go accomplish it.

The door opened and Agent in Charge Carl Jessup walked in. Jessup was her boss, up from Los Angeles just for the occasion. Jessup was a lean and sinewy Kentuckian in his fifties with a craggy face that looked like a crumpled road map, each line a rough road taken, or a detour that went nowhere, or a wrong turn that had sent him over a cliff. And from the looks of it, he'd been over a lot of cliffs.

"This is the women's room," Kate said. "You can't come in here."

"I infiltrated the Ku Klux Klan and lived with them for three years," he said. "I think I can walk through a door marked 'Women' and come out unscathed."

"It's a question of decency and respect for a woman's privacy."

"You hit Nick Fox with a bus."

"He was fleeing," she said.

"He wasn't being chased," Jessup said.

"He and another member of his crew had guns and therefore presented a credible threat to the safety and lives of others."

"The guns weren't loaded," he said. "There wasn't a single bullet in their possession."

"We didn't know that at the time," she said.

"Sounds to me like you're rehearsing your defense for a board of inquiry. Do I look like a board of inquiry?"

"Yes, in that they are typically made up entirely of men over the age of forty, even though nineteen percent of FBI special agents are women. But the board rarely convenes in women's bathrooms, so I'd have to go with no."

"Let me repeat myself. You hit Nick Fox with a bus!"

"I got a lot of flack from you and everybody else for letting him get away in Vegas, remember?"

"And that made you so angry, you wanted to hit him with a bus," Jessup said. "So you did."

"Yes," she said.

"Just so we're clear, you and I."

"We're clear," she said.

He nodded, satisfied. "How did it feel?"

"Great," she said, breaking into a smile. "*Unbelievably* great."

"I'd leave that part out when you meet with all those men on the board of inquiry," Jessup said. "But don't worry, I'll handle them. It took five long years of dogged pursuit and investigation, but you got your man. That's what the FBI is all about. Now put him away and claw back what he stole."

"Yes, sir."

"Sometime today would be nice."

"Yes, sir."

"Got some butterflies in your stomach?"

"Butterflies are awfully girlie for a woman who carries a Glock, don't you think?"

"Okay. African killer bees."

"That's more like it."

"Don't sweat it, O'Hare. I've stared into the eye of the porcelain god a few times after a big arrest. You're feeling the adrenaline, that's all." He looked around the room and frowned. "It smells nice, and there aren't any urinals, but other than that, this isn't any different than a men's room."

"What were you expecting?"

"A bowl of mints, maybe a tea service."

She turned and looked at him. "You spent three years undercover as a white supremacist?"

"Yeah," he said.

"How did you live with yourself?"

"I became an alcoholic," Jessup said, and left the room.

She gave herself another once-over, unbuttoned the third button of her blouse, and followed Jessup.

Nick Fox wore a white T-shirt and polyester slacks and sat at a gunmetal gray table. He was in a lopsided chair, his hands cuffed behind his back and the chain around his ankles locked into a steel eyelet on the floor. He faced the mirror that hid the agents watching him in the next room, but of course he knew that they were there. It was like he was starring in a play and the stage lights were so bright in his eyes that he couldn't see the audience in the darkness.

Kate came in carrying a fat, dog-eared file, her crisp white shirt unbuttoned enough to show cleavage. He knew the show of cleavage wasn't normal for her, and he appreciated the effort. He would have appreciated it even more if she'd popped a fourth button.

He smiled and Kate was almost blinded by the wattage. How does he do that? she wondered. She should have worn sunglasses, she thought, like those poker players on TV.

She sat down at the table, placed the file in front of her, opened it, and examined one of the pages. "You're in a lot of trouble," she said.

"I know," he said. "I was taken to an ER last night and I don't have medical insurance. It's going to cost me a fortune. Those crooks charge fifty dollars for a tongue depressor."

"Was your tongue depressed?"

"Thankfully, no. It's very well adjusted."

"Because it gets a lot of exercise. You've got to be a fast talker in your line of work."

"I'm a professional hand model."

"You're a con man and thief, wanted on three continents," she said. "That's how I knew you'd be at the Kibbee. It was the first time in decades that anyone knew exactly where to find the Crimson Teardrop and a rare window of opportunity to steal it. You couldn't resist. I was at the auction house in Santa Barbara, waiting for you to make your move before the diamond sold, but you didn't show."

"Sorry to have disappointed you," he said.

"It's okay," she said. "You're here now, that's what counts. And unless you can make a deal with me today, you'll be spending the rest of your life in prison."

He cocked his head, bewildered. "I don't see why."

"Well, for starters, we have you for impersonating a police officer, wiretapping, and possession of stolen property," she said. "And that's not even counting the outstanding charges on your last swindle."

"What swindle?"

"You bilked six men in Las Vegas out of a million dollars each for organ transplants that they didn't get."

"Really? There are people who've accused me of that?"

She shifted in her seat. She didn't know whether he'd guessed, or knew for a fact, that not one of the six men had ID'd his photo, or admitted to paying him a dime, or pressed any charges. They didn't want to confess to trying to buy their way to the top of the organ transplant lists and they didn't want him caught to contradict their story. So they claimed they'd come for face-lifts and had only seen a nurse. Each man gave a conflicting description of her.

"No," Kate said.

"Then I'm confused. What swindle are you talking about?"

"You trespassed on private property. You impersonated an engineer."

"Those are federal offenses?"

"You swindled a hospital for asbestos cleanup that you didn't do."

"Did they say they paid me?"

"No," she said, "but—"

"Is there asbestos in the hospital?"

"No," she said.

"I rest my case," he said, and smiled at her. "Can I go now?"

She wanted to hit him with a bus all over again. She was glad her back was to the mirror, to the agents who were watching, so they couldn't see the flush on her face and her frustration as the interrogation slipped away from her.

Kate leaned forward against the table. "There are dozens of other swindles and heists we haven't talked about yet. You've been doing this for a very a long time, Nick. Scotland Yard, the Sûreté, and the Russian Politsiya all want a piece of you. We're only just getting started."

He lifted his eyes to hers. "You must have me mistaken for someone else."

"Is that the best you can do?"

"You've misinterpreted everything that happened last night," he said. "You're making a terrible mistake."

"Then by all means, set me straight," she said, leaning back again. She needed a moment to regroup anyway, to collect her thoughts and regain control of the situation.

He looked past her, directing his appeal to the audience. "I'm a struggling performance artist. What happened at the Kibbee was a show."

"Like the Blue Man Group, only in green and with a diamond?" Kate said.

"In a sense, yes. Live theater on the stage of life. A big stunt that we hoped would go viral on YouTube. Obviously, it was a dumb thing to do. I'll gladly do my thousand hours of community service and pay restitution for the scratch we left in the glass display case."

"You drove away with a fifteen-million-dollar diamond," she said.

"No, I didn't," he said. "It was a cubic zirconia, a fifteen-dollar bauble just like the one we left behind in its place. So see, it was theater on both sides. No harm done."

It was another bold guess, but an educated one, Kate thought. She'd switched the real diamond before its arrival at the Kibbee, though only Roland knew that. And as the situation was playing out, her unwillingness to gamble with the real diamond would cost her in the courtroom. He wouldn't do much prison time for this heist. They'd have to nail him for all the swindles he'd pulled before, assuming they didn't end up having to stand in line behind the other countries that wanted to extradite him. Either way, though, he was going down. She had to show him how futile it was to fight the inevitable, that now was the time to make a deal.

"I know all about you, going back to when you were eighteen," Kate said. "I don't get it, either. You had such a bright future. You had the smarts to get yourself into Harvard, but you threw it all away by running a massive, multifaceted cheating operation for rich students. Your scams ran the gamut from hiring impostors to take tests to creating entirely fake transcripts that you planted in the registrar's office. When you were finally caught, you and a dozen students were expelled and seventy-eight of your other victims were quietly forced to repeat entire academic years."

"They weren't victims. They came to me to take advantage of the unique services that I offered so they could have more time for their leisurely pursuits," he said. "Harvard taught me how to be an enterprising entrepreneur in a global marketplace."

"What you learned was to target the rich and the venal, people who could afford to be swindled and would rarely report the crime or press charges because they wouldn't want to be seen as fools," she said. "That's what's kept you out of jail. Until now."

"It's odd to hear you talking to me about jail," Nick said.

"I don't see why," she said. "I'm an FBI agent and you're a crook."

"Your mother died when you were seven. Your father, a career soldier, took you and your younger sister with him from base to base, all over the world, so you lived the same regimented life that he did. Instead of escaping from the military life when you were eighteen, you joined up, becoming a Navy SEAL, until your commanding officer tried to cop a feel."

"He was a jerk."

Nick grinned. "You broke the jerk's nose, and the good ol' boy network made you settle for an honorable discharge instead of court-martial. You joined the FBI after that, which is like the army only there's no uniform and no saluting. You don't play well with others. You work alone, because you're too driven and emotionally distant for anyone to last as your partner, and you live alone for the same reason. So you're in your own kind of prison. Which is really a shame because you're very pretty, frighteningly competent, and compellingly complex."

Kate was momentarily speechless. She was shocked that he knew all those things about her. And she was gobstruck that he thought she was pretty.

"I usually look better," Kate said, "but I threw up."

"I hope it wasn't on my account."

"I'm pretty sure it was the breakfast burrito."

"You should take better care of yourself and stop eating all that fast food," he said.

"How do you know these things?"

"Facebook."

"I'm not on Facebook."

"But your sister is and so is everybody else in your family. I love the pictures from your thirteenth birthday party. What was with the braces on your teeth? I've never seen anything like it, all those wires, rubber bands, and headgear—"

"I had crooked teeth and an overbite, okay?"

"You were cute."

"I wasn't cute. I looked like a demented chipmunk."

Nick smiled wide. "I thought you looked cute."

Kate narrowed her eyes at him. "You're playing me."

"I'm not playing you. I'm serious. I'm attracted to you. You're sexy and exciting."

"That's it." She slapped the file shut, tucked it under her arm, and got up. "Forget about a deal. Let's see what your smile is like after ten years in prison."

Kate stormed out, slamming the door behind her. She squinched her eyes closed and slapped herself in the forehead hard enough to rattle things loose. "Ugh!" she said. "Crap, damn, phooey!" She threw the file against the wall, ran over to it, and kicked it twenty feet down the hall.

The door to the observation room opened, and Carl Jessup stepped out and eyeballed the file scattered over the floor.

"Feel better?" he asked.

"No. I'm sorry, sir. I let him get to me."

"He's a con man, it's what he does. But it doesn't matter. He's sitting in there in irons. You got him and he knows it," Jessup said. "He'll end up giving us what we want, every dollar that he stole, to avoid extradition and the possibility of ending up in a Russian gulag. So don't beat yourself up over this."

"I should have gone with the French braid," she said. "The ponytail isn't my power look."

5

Kate spent the next couple days back in Los Angeles, gathering all of her notes and files on Nick Fox and handing them over to the federal prosecutor who was leading the trial team. She offered to stick around, to do whatever additional investigation might be necessary, but the prosecutor thought it was best for the case if she stayed out of it until she was called to testify. So she was finally free of the investigation that had occupied most of her time and attention for years.

She enjoyed that freedom in the privacy of her cubicle for five whole minutes before marching into Jessup's office. It had a commanding view of the Santa Monica Mountains and the hilltop Getty Center museum, which she knew Nick Fox had twice tricked into buying fake paintings, not that she'd been able to prove it.

Jessup looked up from his desk. "Did you give the Justice Department everything?"

"I cleaned out my files," she said. "I even gave them my paper clips and the half-eaten turkey sandwich that's been in my desk drawer since January. What have you got for me?"

He handed her a thin file. "Pirates."

"You're sending me to Somalia?"

"There's a ring in Southern California that's been duping DVDs of movies and TV shows and posting the digital files on the Internet for people to download for free," Jessup said.

"We go after that stuff?"

"Haven't you seen the FBI warning at the beginning of every DVD?"

"Yeah, but I thought it was a joke."

"It's not," Jessup said.

"It is to me," Kate said. "I brought in Nick Fox. I should be going after the next Nick Fox."

"This is big-time crime, Kate. The ring has cost the studios millions of dollars," Jessup said. "One of the movies that they uploaded to a file-sharing site was downloaded twenty-seven thousand times in ninety days. And they've uploaded hundreds."

"I'm not feeling it," she said.

"The maximum penalty for conspiracy to commit copyright infringement is five years in prison, a two-hundred-fifty-thousand-dollar fine, and damages, which are computed by taking the sales price of the DVD and multiplying it by the number of times the digital file has been downloaded. On a twenty-five-dollar DVD downloaded twenty-seven thousand times, that's six hundred seventy-five thousand dollars. Now multiply that by hundreds of movies, and you get the picture. This is a huge case."

Kate shook her head and put the file down. "I should be going after someone in the same league as Nick Fox. What about Derek Griffin? That big-time investment guy who ran off with five hundred million dollars that he stole from his clients? I should find him."

"We've already got somebody on it," Jessup said. "An entire task force, in fact."

"There must be someone else on the Ten Most Wanted list I can have."

"They are all taken."

"All of them?"

"Believe it or not, while you were chasing Nick Fox, the rest of the Bureau was busy, too."

"Fine. I'll take number eleven on the list."

"You'll take this." Jessup tapped the file. "Oh, and you'll be working with an MPAA investigator on this one."

"MPAA?"

"Motion Picture Association of America," Jessup said.

"They have cops?"

"Yes," Jessup said. "They do."

"You're telling me to work with a make-believe cop."

"She's not make-believe," Jessup said. "She's real. It's what she's hired to protect that's not."

Kate looked Jessup in the eye. "Are you punishing me?"

"Not every case can be Nick Fox," Jessup said. "Get used to it."

"You have to take down your Facebook page," Kate told her sister, Megan.

It was clearly an order, but Megan wasn't the least bit intimidated. The two women were sitting at a table in the backyard of Megan's hillside home, one of the many red-tile-roofed Spanish Mediterranean McMansions in Calabasas, a suburb of guard-gated communities at the southwestern edge of the San Fernando

Valley. Megan was in shorts and a T-shirt, reading *Star* magazine and getting the latest news on the Real Housewives of Everywhere. While she was talking to Kate she was keeping an eye on her narrow lap pool, where her four-year-old son, Tyler, and six-year-old daughter, Sara, yellow floaties around their chubby, pale arms, were in a water cannon fight with Megan's husband, Roger. They were all splashing and shrieking, and their Jack Russell terrier, named Jack Russell, was running around the pool barking.

The air was rated "moderately unhealthful" by the Air Quality Management District, the fire hazard in the surrounding foothills was deemed "very high" by the Department of Forestry, and a SigAlert had been declared by the California Highway Patrol on the Ventura Freeway, meaning it would be an hour-long crawl to anywhere across the valley floor. In other words, it was a perfect Saturday afternoon in Southern California.

"Why would I want to take down my Facebook page?" Megan asked.

"Because it allows stalkers to mine personal information about you and your entire family," Kate told her.

"I don't have stalkers."

"You might." Kate was wearing a tank top, shorts, and flip-flops, and she felt naked without her Glock, which was in a lockbox in the trunk of her car. "You won't know until one of them kidnaps your daughter to be his sex slave."

Megan glared at her over the top of her *Star* magazine. "How can you say something awful like that about your adorable niece?"

"It's a fact of life." Kate gestured to the cover of the magazine. "It's right there. 'Teen Kidnapped by Hillbillies Reveals Ten-Year Ordeal as Sex Slave.'"

Megan put the magazine down on a stack of publications that

included *People, Us,* and the *National Enquirer,* all of which Kate had brought. Reading trashy gossip magazines and making fun of the celebrities was a traditional part of O'Hare family picnics. It was something they'd picked up from the mothers on the military bases when they were growing up.

"There are no hillbillies in Calabasas, and even if there were, nobody is going to kidnap my kids," Megan said. "You know why? Because my sister is an FBI agent, and my dad, an ex-marine who can kill a man sixteen different ways with an eyebrow tweezer, lives in the house."

"He lives in the garage," Kate said.

"It's a *casita,*" Megan said.

"What would Dad be doing with an eyebrow tweezer?"

"It's mine and it might be the only weapon handy when the hillbillies attack," Megan said. "We aren't taking down the Facebook page. The family loves it."

"So make it private," Kate said.

"It already is," Megan said. "Family and friends only."

"How many are there?"

Her sister reached for a handful of Doritos from one of the three big salad bowls of different chips in the center of the table. "One thousand three hundred and twelve."

"We don't have one thousand three hundred and twelve family and friends," Kate said.

"That includes family of family and friends of friends," Megan said.

Roger called out from the pool. "Easy on the Doritos, honey. You'll want to save room for my world famous cheeseburgers."

His burgers were simply ground beef patties sprinkled with Lawry's Seasoned Salt and topped with a slice of Kraft processed

American cheese. It wasn't like it was a recipe that his great-grandmother had smuggled over from the old country on a scrap of paper stuffed in her cleavage or a unique blend of spices that he'd refined over years of backyard barbecuing. But everybody in the family, Kate included, dutifully ooohed and aaahed over the burgers anyway.

"Fine, you can keep your Facebook page," Kate said. "But you have to remove all the pictures of me."

"I can't," Megan said. "They're family photos that you happen to be in. Everybody loves them. You are one part of a lot of great memories that we enjoy sharing. It's how we stay connected as a family. Well, all of us but you."

"Then photoshop my part out," Kate said. "Or at least erase my braces and zits."

"Oh, grow up, that was almost twenty years ago," Megan said. "Besides, you've never cared much what people think of how you look. So something else must be in play here."

"Thank you, Dr. Phil."

Megan studied her. "When was the last time you had a chitty-chitty-bang-bang?"

"Drove a flying car?"

Megan glanced over at her kids to make sure they weren't listening. "You know what I mean. How long has it been since you danced the horizontal mambo?"

Kate did know what Megan meant, but she was stalling for time. "What does that have to do with anything?"

"Because you're afraid of somebody seeing how geeky and awkward you were when you were a kid and finding you less attractive now as a result."

Megan was three years younger than Kate and had never been

geeky or awkward, so she didn't care about how she looked in old pictures. After birthing two kids she was carrying a few extra pounds but she wore the weight well, probably because she didn't give a damn about it, and half of beauty is attitude anyway. Or so they say in *Us Weekly*.

"Don't be ridiculous," Kate said.

"You want to know how often I have sex?"

"No!" Kate said.

"Three times a week," Megan said. "Mondays, Wednesdays, and Saturdays. How about you?"

"None of your business."

"So it's been at least six months," Megan said. "You need a love life. Heck, you need a life."

"I have one," Kate said.

"What you had was chasing Nick Fox. That's a case, not a life. Now it's time to reassess your goals and look ahead. Where do you want to be in five years? Who do you want to be? How many orgasms do you want to be having?"

"You plan your orgasms five years in advance?"

"You know how I got all of this?" Megan gestured to the house, the kids, and Jack Russell taking a crap on the lawn.

"Unprotected sex," Kate said.

Megan was twenty-four years old and six months pregnant when she married Roger, an accountant she'd met on a blind date.

Megan ignored the comment. "I imagined it. I saw myself as a wife and mother. And here it is, a dream come true. What's yours?"

Kate gave her a look and said, "Daniel Craig, a tropical island, a quart of Oreo cookie ice cream, and a pair of handcuffs."

"Who's wearing the cuffs?" Megan asked.

Kate ate another chip and let the question go unanswered.

Megan wagged a finger at her. "Your big problem is that you spend all of your time on the job, where the only men you meet are cops and crooks."

That comment worried Kate. She'd heard it before. It was Megan's excuse for creating an account under Kate's name at eHarmony and setting her up for dates.

"I'm serious about arresting you for identity theft if you sign me up for another online dating service," Kate said.

"I've been going to the gym twice a week, and as it happens I've met a terrific guy there. He's a pilot for one of the big airlines, flying international routes."

"You can stop right there."

"He's perfect for you. A man in uniform, only without a gun or a mailbag."

"I don't need you setting me up on blind dates."

"It's not blind, I've had a very good look at him. He's in his early thirties, has a fantastic body and a killer smile. He's so sexy and charming, I'm half tempted to leave Roger for him."

"Fine, you take him," Kate said.

They heard the clang of the wrought-iron gate closing on the side yard, and a moment later Jake O'Hare, their father, strode into the backyard. He was dressed in a golf shirt and slacks, and still wearing his cleats. He was square-jawed, square-shouldered, barrel-chested, and big-boned. His gray hair was buzzed to military specifications. He moved with a slight limp, the result of an injury he'd sustained on a mission that he still insisted was classified. It was his limp that Kate imitated when she used the disabled elevator at the San Francisco Federal Building.

"Dad, what have I told you about wearing your golf shoes around the house?" Megan said as Kate rose up to greet her father.

"I'm aerating the grass," Jake said, giving Kate a hug. "What brings you out here?"

"I brought the kids their Christmas presents," Kate said.

"Guns, of course," Megan said.

"Water cannons," Kate said.

"It's June," Jake said. "You're a little early."

"These were the gifts I was going to bring last Christmas, but then things got crazy at work," Kate said. "I had a strong lead on a case that I had to chase down. That's over now, so I'm catching up on some things that kind of fell through cracks during the investigation."

"That's right, you finally caught Nick Fox. Congratulations."

"Thanks," Kate said.

Jake gestured to her glass. "You feel like having something stronger than that Hawaiian Punch?"

"That'd be nice," Kate said.

"We're making my famous hamburgers in a half hour," Roger yelled from the pool.

"Wouldn't miss it," Kate said, and followed her father around the side yard to the front of the house, where there were two matching detached garages, one on either side of the driveway. Both had red-tiled roofs, of course. She'd parked her white Ford Crown Victoria, the police interceptor model, between the two garages. "Thank you for rescuing me."

"From what?" Jake said.

"From that," Kate said. "I don't know how you can take it here."

"It's a good life," Jake said.

"You live in the garage."

"It's a *casita*."

"It's a detached garage that they put a bathroom and kitchenette in," Kate said. "It still has the garage doors."

"They're nonworking. It's a garage door façade. We had to keep it to maintain conformity," Jake said. "The architectural committee in this neighborhood is stricter than the Taliban. But I still like it here."

"How can you?"

"It's sunny all the time. The streets are cleaner than Disneyland. We're right above the golf course and I get to be with my family. I get to tickle the grandkids and read 'em bedtime stories."

"Yeah, but there's Roger."

"He's a good man," Jake said.

"He's unbelievably dull."

"Nobody's asking him to open for Tony Bennett, just to be there for his wife and kids, and he is, more than I ever was for you and Megan."

"You don't have to be there to be there," Kate said.

"Yes, honey, you do." Jake went into his *casita* and came out a moment later with two cold Buds. Kate leaned against her car.

"So you're paying penance," Kate said. "That's why you're here."

"I told you, I like it here."

"You spent decades traveling to exotic locales, fighting wars. How can you like this?"

"I'm still fighting wars. We've got a real problem here with morning glories invading the common areas. I'm leading the landscaping committee's offensive to repel the invasion."

"You're depressing me, Dad."

He laughed and took a drink. "A new assignment will come along for you soon."

"I got one. It sucks."

"Not all of them can be Nick Fox."

"So everyone keeps telling me. To which I say, why not?"

They were quiet for a moment, looking at the view of the smog-covered valley and the community's front gate. There was a tiny guardhouse that looked like a miniature golf version of Megan's McMansion. The guard always greeted Kate when she arrived like they were colleagues, both servants of justice wearing badges, except hers wasn't a patch.

Her father took another drink of his beer. "I led a covert mission once to assist a ragtag group of rebels in liberating their country from a crazy, crack-addicted dictator and his corrupt army. I spent months in that jungle, fighting soldiers and mosquitos the size of Corollas. But we did it. Twenty years later, I was sent on another covert mission to help rebels liberate their country. Turned out to be the same damn country, same damn jungle. Different dictator."

Kate finished her beer and thought about what he said. "What's your point?"

"I have absolutely no idea," he said. "I just felt like telling the story. Maybe you'll find some deeper meaning in it later. If you do, give me a call and let me know what it was."

"How many ways could you kill a man with an eyebrow tweezer?"

"Sixteen," Jake said.

Kate looked at him in surprise. She'd thought her sister was just being a smart-ass, a quality they both shared. "Really?"

"Yeah," he said.

"Will you teach me?"

"Wouldn't be much of a father if I didn't," he said.

6

In the course of his fifteen-year career, U.S. Marshal Odell Morris had escorted all kinds of violent killers from their jail cells to the courtroom without any trouble, including a male model who'd strangled ten men, decapitated them, had sex with their corpses, then chopped them up and served them to the homeless in tuna casseroles. So Odell didn't get why his bosses insisted that he bring not one but *two* other marshals along to safely deliver Nick Fox to court. It made no sense at all.

Nick Fox wasn't some stone killer. He was a pretty-boy candy-ass con man who'd be in handcuffs and ankle chains the whole time. And even if Nick could do a Houdini with the chains, so what? Odell had a gun, a Taser, a baton, a can of Mace, a black belt in tae kwon do, and a very short fuse. Nick's only weapon was his mouth, something Odell could neutralize with one pop of his mighty fist. Not that he'd have to, because Nick was a total pussy, already teary-eyed and shaking when Odell and the two other marshals picked him up in his cell. By the time they drove up to the U.S. District Courthouse, Nick was so scared that he looked like he might soil his bright orange jailbird scrubs.

The four of them headed down the long corridor toward the courtroom. Odell walked beside Nick, gripping his arm so the scary criminal mastermind would move along and not trip over his ankle chain. One marshal walked ahead of them and the other trailed behind, just in case Nick hulked out, broke his chains, and flung Odell through a wall.

Yes, it was that stupid. In Odell's estimation, three guys on Nick Fox was overkill. So was wasting a man of Odell's skills on this. An elderly librarian could've guarded Nick, who was crumbling more and more with each step they took toward the courtroom. He was hunched over now, clutching his stomach and mewling like a baby, and this was just his preliminary hearing. By the time the trial started, Odell figured, he'd probably be catatonic.

"I'm going to be sick," Nick said.

Odell wasn't surprised by the news, just relieved that Nick had managed to hold it in until they got out of the car.

"There's a trash can over there." Odell started to lead him to it.

"Not that kind of sick," Nick said.

Odell spotted the men's room and, irritated, dragged Nick over and shoved him against the wall beside the door, pinning him in place with a hand to the chest.

"Watch him while I check the room out," Odell said to his fellow marshals.

This was not Odell's first dance, and he was savvy to the fact that Nick might be faking just to get into the restroom.

"Hurry," Nick whined.

Odell went inside and looked around. The restroom was windowless and empty. Only one way out. Odell was happy with that. There were urinals and sinks on one wall and three toilet stalls on the other. One stall, the farthest from the door and set against the back wall, had an "Out of Service" sign taped to its door. No surprise there. This wasn't exactly a restroom at the Ritz.

Odell went to the first stall and opened the door. There was a toilet paper holder and a toilet seat cover dispenser mounted on the partition between the stalls. He checked out the toilet, looking inside the tank and peering behind it, to make sure there wasn't a gun or a knife hidden there for Nick by some confederate. He did the same check in the center stall, then went to the third, the one that was out of service. There was no toilet inside the third stall, just a hole in the floor where it was supposed to go. Satisfied that the restroom was safe, Odell went back to the door, grabbed Nick by the shoulders, and yanked him inside.

"You two stay here," Odell said to the other marshals. "Nobody comes in. Even if the governor himself drops by to take a whiz. You got it?"

They nodded. Odell closed the door, dragged Nick to the center stall, and shoved him in.

"Make it quick," Odell said.

Nick held out his wrists. "Aren't you going to uncuff me?"

"Nope," Odell said.

"So how am I supposed to clean myself?"

"Should've thought of that before you broke the law," Odell said, and closed the door.

Technically, Odell probably should have left the door open, but the last thing he wanted was to watch Nick do his business. Turned out he'd made a wise decision, because barely an instant after the door closed, Odell heard a gastrointestinal explosion that sounded like it could kill a man.

Odell turned away and quickly put as much distance as he could between himself and the stall, which took him over to the urinals. Since he was there anyway, he decided to relieve himself. The "Theme from *Shaft*" played in his head as it always did whenever his zipper was opened. But the song wasn't loud enough to save Odell, no matter how high he cranked up his mental volume control. The noise coming from Nick's stall was epic. Odell wished he could walk out and wait with the other two marshals in the hall, but he knew he couldn't. He wasn't worried about Nick escaping from a windowless room with only one door, but what if he offed himself somehow?

Odell went to the sink, glancing at the stalls on his way. He could see Nick's feet, the orange scrub pants bunched around the chain on his ankles. The orchestra of intestinal distress continued, with special emphasis on the horns and percussion. It was sickening. Odell held his breath and washed his hands, then dried them with a paper towel and glanced at his watch. They were five minutes late for court already. But what could he do about it? Worse came to worst, he'd have one of the marshals go and notify the court. Maybe he should tell them to alert a HazMat team, too.

There was a new surge of digestive distress, as if Nick had found a second stomach within himself to disgorge. To Odell's horror, the disgusting melody was repeating itself all over again, from the top.

That last thought nagged at him. It *did* sound the same. Then again, he figured, it's not like there was a lot of variation to butt music. Even so, there was a disturbing familiarity to it. Like it was a loop. Odell risked a breath through his nose. There was no smell. How could that be? Odell glanced over at the stall and saw Nick's feet. He marched over and hammered his fist on the door.

"Open up," Odell said.

When Nick didn't respond, Odell took a deep breath and kicked the door open. Nick's shoes, chain, and pants were there, but Nick was gone. An ultrathin MP3 player rested on the toilet tank and played the intestinal soundtrack. Right beside the player was a pair of handcuffs. The MP3 player and the cuff keys must have been hidden in the toilet seat cover dispenser.

Odell pushed against the partition between the second and third stall, the partition pivoted on a support pole, and the opening allowed access to the third stall, the one without a toilet. There was a hole torn in the wall, revealing a closet that had been hidden by a layer of paper made to look like painted stucco. The sounds of gastrointestinal distress had covered the noise Nick made tearing open the sealed doorway.

Odell climbed through the center divider into the third stall, drew his gun, and went into the closet, which was full of mops, brooms, and cleaning supplies. He groaned at the sight of a second door, yanked it open, and found himself standing in the women's restroom. The two restrooms shared the same utility closet. He ran through the restroom and burst out the door into the courthouse hallway, much to the astonishment of the two other marshals, who were still standing guard outside the men's room.

"Hey, Odell, how'd you get over there?" one of them asked.

In that split second, Odell Morris saw his entire career pass before his eyes and even glimpsed his future working in mall security.

"Why me?" Odell asked, and grabbed his radio to raise the alarm.

There wasn't anything sexy, or even remotely interesting, to Kate about chasing down guys who copy movies and make them available for free on the Internet. Sure, the stakes were high. The studios were losing millions of dollars in revenue from movies and TV shows that wouldn't be purchased or rented because they were available for free. They'd probably cover those losses by cutting jobs, so it wouldn't just be people with fat stock portfolios who'd feel the pain, but average middle-class families struggling to pay their mortgages.

Kate understood all that, in an abstract way. Maybe if the pirate looked like Johnny Depp, or maybe if the guy they were chasing was actually stuffing those millions of dollars in cold hard cash into his pockets, then she could get into it. But this guy wasn't making a buck off his thievery or doing it for some greater evil purpose, like delivering a crippling blow to the American economy by making it possible to download every episode of *Will & Grace* for free. He was doing it because . . . well . . . Kate didn't know and didn't give a hoot. She just wanted this incredibly dull investigation to end before she put a gun into her mouth and pulled the trigger.

It wasn't hard for Sharon Cargill, the investigator from the Motion Picture Association of America, to pick up on Kate's discontent, mainly because Kate kept expressing it. The bulk of their investigation over the last five days had consisted of sitting together in the basement of the Federal Building on Wilshire, looking over the shoulder of a computer tech as he followed the cyber clues and devoured Hot Pockets.

The pirate was copying screeners—DVDs supplied to entertainment industry professionals for Oscar and Emmy award voting—and uploading them under the name Nanatastic74 to a file-sharing site. Digital watermarks in the files and Nanatastic74's IP address led them to Pete Debney, a forty-eight-year-old struggling screenwriter living in an apartment in Castaic.

Debney was a member of the Writers Guild of America, which explained how he got access to the screeners, but he didn't have any of them in his house, and there were no digital movie files on his computer. That's because he'd given all of his screeners to his mother, Janice, who lived in a retirement home in Ventura. He'd opened the broadband account for her and paid her bill.

So that's what brought Kate and Sharon to Sunny Vistas Active Senior Living Center. The lobby was like a hotel's, with a reception desk to the right and an open dining area to the left, a row of walkers parked like cars along the low wall. There were a dozen old folks sitting at tables, picking at plates of meat loaf and peas. A few of them were sleeping in their seats, their heads slumped onto their chests. Or maybe they were dead, Kate thought with a shudder.

Sharon went to the receptionist and asked where they could find Janice Debney.

"Down the hall in the community computer room," the receptionist said. "She's almost always there."

The computer room turned out to be a bank of four desktops in a room with shelves lined with DVDs. There were four seniors hunched over the computers, two men and two women, one of whom had an oxygen tank. Movies were playing silently on two of the flat screens as they were being encoded and converted from DVDs into digital files. Sharon went straight to the shelves of DVDs and started sorting through them.

"Excuse me," Kate said to the computer users, "I'm looking for Janice Debney."

The woman with the oxygen tank turned around. She was wearing a bad wig and fake eyelashes. Her skin looked like parchment paper. "That's me."

"FBI. We're here about the movies," Kate told her.

"What movies?"

"These," Sharon said, holding out a DVD. "They're all Academy screeners."

"They're mine," Janice said.

"Actually, they belong to the studios and are loaned to Academy members for screening purposes only. You are not an Academy member."

"My son gave them to me. He's so sweet. We show them here on Saturday nights."

"And you copy them and post them on the Internet," Sharon said.

"So other people our age can see them without having to go to a movie theater," Janice said.

"It's a crime," Sharon said.

"It certainly is," Janice said. "Movie theaters are horrible. The ticket prices are outrageous and the movies are way too loud."

"Or they aren't loud enough," one of the men said.

"You have to climb a bunch of stairs to get to your seats now," the other man said. "Whose brilliant idea was that? I have a hip replacement."

Kate squelched a grimace. Her life was over. As long as she was here, she might as well see if they had any vacancies.

"You could buy DVDs," Sharon said. "Or rent downloads."

"I'm on Social Security, honey," Janice said. "It barely covers the price of cigarettes."

"You're still smoking?" Sharon said. "You're using an oxygen tank."

"Oh, relax," Janice said. "You don't have to make a federal case out of it."

"*This* is the federal case," Sharon said, holding up a DVD. "What you're doing is criminal copyright infringement."

Janice dismissed Sharon with a wave of her bony hand. "That movie sucked."

The other woman spoke up. "I wish they'd make more musicals."

Kate's phone rang. The caller was Jessup.

"Nick Fox escaped on his way to court," he said.

Thank God, Kate thought.

"Damn," she said, trying to sound suitably angry, which she knew she should be, instead of joyously relieved. "Un-friggin'-believable. How could that have happened?"

"Smoke and mirrors," Jessup said. "I'll fill you in on the details later."

"I'll be back in the office in an hour."

"There's no rush," Jessup said. "I just didn't want you hearing about the escape on the news. Special Agent Ryerson is handling the case."

"Ryerson? He couldn't find the fortune in a fortune cookie," Kate said. "Nobody knows Nick Fox better than I do."

"The feeling upstairs is that we need a fresh perspective."

"By the time someone else gets up to speed on Nick Fox, the *Mona Lisa* will be gone and Donald Trump will be broke, and everybody will be wondering how the heck he did it."

"You think Fox is going after the *Mona Lisa* and Donald Trump?"

"I don't know what he's going after," Kate said. "But I know I'm the only one who can catch him."

"You had your shot," Jessup said.

"And I got him," Kate said. "Someone else lost him."

"I'm sorry," Jessup said. "But this is the way it's got to be."

7

Kate had several weeks of vacation time banked, so two days after her conversation with Jessup she cashed her days in and showed up at the door of her father's *casita*. It was lunchtime, and she'd brought her MacBook, a six-pack of beer, and a bucket of Kentucky Fried Chicken. She knew that her sister would be at a Mommy and Me gym class with her kids and that Roger would be at work.

Her father greeted her in a polo shirt and chinos and immediately relieved her of the bucket and the six-pack.

"You are the perfect daughter," Jake said, stepping aside and beckoning her in. "But I will deny it if you ever tell Megan."

His *casita* was like a large hotel room and just about as clean and impersonal. There was one bedroom, Jake's bed always made up as tight as a sarcophagus, and a tiny bath and a kitchenette that opened onto a front room barely large enough for a small table, a love seat, and a flat-screen TV. Jake hadn't kept any mementos from his career and world travels, except for his medals, which included a Purple Heart, a Bronze Star, and a Silver Star. He kept the medals tucked away in his nightstand drawer with his spare change and antacids. The only personal items on display were pictures of Kate, Megan, and their mother in small frames on the nightstand.

Kate put her laptop on the table. "I'm sure you tell Megan the same thing."

"Don't be ridiculous," Jake said, pulling plates from the cupboard and setting them on the table.

"She says you tell her that she's the perfect daughter all the time."

"That's absolutely not true," Jake said, opening the bucket and helping himself to the biggest, greasiest piece of chicken he could find.

"That's a pro forma denial." Kate got a piece of chicken for herself and cracked open a beer. "I bet she's never brought you a bucket of chicken."

"She's worried about my heart," Jake said.

"Your heart is fine. It's cast-iron and wrapped in Kevlar. Just like mine."

"I'm not sure that's such a good thing for you. Have you heard about the pilot Megan met? He's traveling half the time, so if you're worried about some guy clinging to you, then he's perfect."

"Please, not you too," Kate said. "The last thing I need is my family meddling in my love life."

"We just want you to be happy."

"I am."

"Really?" He studied his enormous chicken breast, as if trying to determine the best angle of attack. "It's great that you're here, but it's the last thing I expected, not with Nick Fox on the loose again."

Of course Jake knew all about that. Everybody did. Nick's bold escape from the U.S. Courthouse was all over the news an hour after it happened and had immediately vaulted him to the top of the FBI's Ten Most Wanted list. That was two days ago. Now he was on Interpol's global hot list as well.

"They want a fresh perspective on the case," Kate told Jake as she analyzed her piece of chicken. Was it a thigh? A breast portion? Or a rat that had fallen into the deep fryer? She decided it didn't matter and took a bite. "So I'm on vacation, which I've started by sharing a bucket of chicken and a few beers with my dad."

"And you expect me to believe that you're happy."

"Of course I am," she said. "I'm with you."

"I'm touched. And if you were still sixteen, this is where you'd be asking me for the keys to my Jeep and twenty bucks."

"Trust me, Dad. I couldn't be happier than I am right now."

If she'd been a more introspective person, the kind who enjoys exploring her understanding of herself, she'd have wanted to examine that assertion in more depth.

"I'm here because I don't spend nearly enough time with you," Kate said. "I've got a big trip planned and I want your advice. You're the world traveler in our family."

"I'm impressed that you've taken being sidelined so well. I don't mean to rub salt in your wound or anything, but the curiosity is killing me. How did Fox escape from three marshals on his way to court?"

She gave her father the broad-stroke details of Nick's escape from the men's room while under guard. "He had one of his cronies build a fake stall with a swiveling center partition right in front of the closet door and then paper over it."

"How'd they do it without anyone noticing?"

"By being completely out in the open about it. There was a crew in there for a week remodeling the restrooms. People in the courthouse had wanted those restrooms spruced up for years, so they were glad to see it finally getting done and didn't question it."

"So Fox slipped out dressed as a woman?"

"Nope, there was a hiding place built in the closet. Once the marshals raised the alarm and went looking for him, he walked out of the men's room dressed as a judge. We've got that much on security camera footage. How he slipped out of the building after that is a mystery."

Jake looked at Kate skeptically over his beer can as he took a sip. "One that you aren't the least bit interested in solving."

"It's not my problem."

"That's the right attitude," he said. "You caught him, they lost him, let them deal with it. So where are you going on your trip?"

"Greece." She opened her laptop and hit a few keys, bringing up on the screen a detailed map of the country.

"I've been there many times. It's a breathtaking place. What part are you visiting?"

"Mount Athos," she said.

He finished his beer and set the can down. "It's the oldest monastic settlement on earth, going back to the seventh century A.D., built within a mountainous, inhospitable, rocky peninsula that is thirty miles long, ranging from four to eight miles wide, and pounded by the Aegean Sea on three sides. It's technically part of Greece, but it's actually an autonomous state where two thousand devout bearded monks and hermits live in centuries-old fortified monasteries, ancient stone huts, and caves. They abide by the laws of the Byzantine Empire, even though it fell five hundred sixty years ago, and they still mark their days by the Julian liturgical calendar. But you know all about that, right?"

"Of course," she said. "It sounds charming."

"Then you also know that females have been forbidden on Athos for nearly a thousand years. That prohibition is so strict that it extends to all female creatures, including cows, horses, and hens. They'd ban female reptiles and birds, too, if they could find a way to do it."

"And that's why I think Nick Fox is there," Kate said. "Because it's the one place on earth that I can't go."

"That's a big reach, Kate."

"There's more. I know that a few months ago he applied for a visa from Athos under the alias 'Father Dowling,' and under the guise of doing research on Byzantine monastic architecture. The visa was granted. I'd assumed he did it as part of some larger scheme to steal some of their priceless and poorly protected artifacts, holy relics, ancient manuscripts, and icons. But now I realize he might have just been taking out an insurance policy against his eventual capture and escape."

Her father opened another beer. "Or not. He could be anywhere or purposely leading you astray. It's still a big jump to make that he's there."

"That's why I scanned hours of surveillance footage of the customs area at the Athens airport, and I spotted Nick in disguise as a priest, the cocky bastard. I pulled up the customs records. 'Father Dowling' flew from Athens to Thessaloniki, then took a bus to

Ouranoupoli, the ramshackle seaside village that happens to be the only spot on the western side of the peninsula where you can pick up the Athos ferry."

"And you want to go after him."

"Of course."

"Well, if you disregard the law banning women—"

"And I do," she said.

"The other big problem is that Athos is virtually inaccessible by land. There aren't any roads leading to it. But even on foot it's damn near impossible," he said, pointing out on the map that the narrow peninsula was dominated by a mountain range, with peaks ranging from 1,600 feet high to 6,600 atop the snowcapped Mount Athos itself.

The rest of the peninsula's geography was hardly more hospitable, with impassable gorges and deep ravines, dense forests, and a coastline of jagged cliffs, with imposing medieval monasteries rising from them as if they were natural extensions of the rock. Amid those formidable obstacles, however, were crop fields and olive groves from which the monks sustained themselves nutritionally and economically. They grew their own fruits and vegetables and produced olive oil and wine.

"The only way in is by boat, but even then, each visitor must be male and obtain a permit, written in Greek and following the Julian calendar, from the leaders of at least four of the monasteries," Jake said. "That process is complex, tricky, and takes forever. Even if the permit is granted, getting to Athos by ferry from Ouranoupoli can be treacherous. The sea is historically, and notoriously, unpredictable and dangerous."

"How do you know so much about Mount Athos?"

"I'm a student of military history. I try to learn from past mistakes," Jake said. "In 492 B.C., Mardonius, the great Persian general, lost his entire fleet of three hundred ships and twenty thousand men off the storm-tossed coast of Athos. In 411 B.C., the Spartan admiral Epicleas lost fifty ships."

"That's because they couldn't fly," she said. "I'm going to parachute onto Athos at night."

"You are," he said.

"Athos doesn't have radar or air defenses, and it certainly doesn't have security patrols or other perimeter defenses on the ground. So how hard can it be? All I've got to do is fly into Athens, catch another flight to Thessaloniki, then charter a small plane from there to take me over Athos."

"That's all? Tell me, how many pilots do you know in Central Macedonia who'd be willing to defy centuries of Byzantine tradition and violate current Greek law to drop you over Athos?"

"None," she said. "But I'm sure that you do."

"You expect me to use my covert assets in Greece, calling in favors I earned through my blood and sweat during decades of military service, so you can chase a fugitive into a sovereign monastic state that you are forbidden by law, and some would say God, to enter."

"Can you think of a better vacation than that?"

Jake had to use every ounce of his military training, everything he'd learned about withstanding brutal physical and mental torture at the hands of our most ruthless enemies, not to smile. He almost succeeded.

"Dad, I'm not going to hit the ground, let down my hair, and stroll around the monasteries in a bikini," she said. "I'm going to pass myself off as a man, one of the pilgrims visiting Athos to study."

"You think you can do that?"

"Barbra Streisand did it in *Yentl.* I'll cut my hair, tape down my boobs, and belch a lot. Nobody will suspect a thing. It's not like they have a lot of experience recognizing women."

"Even if you're right about Fox being in Athos, there are twenty monasteries and countless remote huts and caves," he said. "How are you going to find him?"

"Because Nick Fox is not a hermit or a monk. There's no television or radio on Athos, and only limited electricity and phone service. He will want to be in constant contact with the outside world. So he will have a satellite phone, and I have a device that can pick up its unique electronic signature. Or something like that. I don't know exactly how it works, just that it will."

"Okay, assuming you are able to apprehend him, how are you going to get him off Athos without revealing yourself and causing an international incident that could have devastating consequences for U.S. foreign policy?"

"I'll alert Interpol by satellite phone that I've apprehended a fugitive hiding out in Ouranoupoli, and they'll send agents there to meet us. In the meantime, we'll leave Athos for Ouranoupoli on the same ferry that the other authorized visitors do, except that Nick will be doing so at gunpoint and wearing handcuffs under his robes."

"He'll be wearing robes?"

"Isn't that what monks and hermits wear? It's not like they have a Tommy Bahama outlet up there."

"This is a terrible plan," Jake said. "There are a hundred ways it could fail."

Kate shrugged. "So I'll have to do it the one way it can go right."

"*We* will," he said.

"No way," Kate said. "You're retired and in your sixties."

"I'm not talking about jumping out of the plane and tracking Fox. I *am* too old for that. I'll go to Greece with you and coordinate the op."

"I can do this on my own," she said.

"No, you can't."

"I'm an ex–Navy SEAL, a crack FBI special agent, and Jake O'Hare's daughter. I can handle myself."

"I'm sure you can. But that's only one small part of the mission. Logistics and resources are the key. The people you'll need to pull this off are mercenaries and criminals who will participate because they owe me something. They won't help you without me. Besides, I know a few things about extraordinary rendition."

"You mean kidnapping," she said.

He ignored the comment. "You'll parachute in on a moonlit night, and if you succeed in capturing Fox, instead of calling Interpol or taking the ferry, you'll call me and make your way to a prearranged extraction point on Athos, where I will pick you up by chopper. We'll go back to Thessaloniki, where we will stash Fox someplace remote and abandoned. That's when you will call Interpol with an anonymous tip that will lead them to Fox, who will be gift-wrapped for them."

"But I won't get any credit for the arrest that way."

"Oh, forgive me. I was working under the assumption that you wanted to keep your job and stay out of prison yourself."

He had a good point. Her bosses at the FBI were unlikely to be pleased that she'd captured Nick Fox after she'd been thrown off the case, or that she'd engaged in an unsanctioned apprehension on foreign soil where she had absolutely no jurisdiction, or that she'd failed to notify the FBI or local law enforcement of her intentions. And there was the little matter of kidnapping Nick, which was technically a criminal offense in Greece, whether he was a fugitive or not.

Kate sighed with resignation. "Okay, fine, I guess I'll just have to be satisfied knowing that I was the one that got him."

"Welcome to my life. Most of my career was made up of missions like that. To this day, very few people know what I've done."

She opened a beer and took a sip. "You'd really go all the way to Greece, and run a covert operation again, just so I can have the satisfaction of capturing Nick Fox?"

"Sure," he said. "We don't get nearly enough quality father-daughter time."

8

The Greek smuggler's 1978 Cessna 182 Skylane had three seats salvaged from an old Volvo, an instrument panel held together with duct tape, and a single propeller on its rusty nose. The smuggler's name was Spiro. No last name given. He was a crusty old man in a moth-eaten sweater, a worn-out leather bomber jacket, and stained cargo shorts. Jake and Kate kept him company at dinner, during which time Spiro had barely touched the platter of salted fish, olives, hard-boiled eggs, feta cheese, and pita that he'd laid out in his drafty hangar. The hangar doubled as Spiro's home and barn and was located on a private airfield outside of Thessaloniki. Jake had enlisted Spiro to fly them to Mount Athos, and in preparation for the hundred-mile flight, Spiro had chosen to forsake the food and instead guzzle an entire bottle of ouzo.

"We have to scrub the mission," Kate said to her father when Spiro stepped out to relieve himself on the side of the hangar. "Spiro's too drunk to fly."

"He's a better pilot drunk than most pilots are sober."

That didn't give Kate much comfort, but it wasn't like she had any choice. It had to be tonight. She had to jump during a full moon so she could see where she was landing. And there weren't many pilots who were willing to drop her over Athos, and probably none who'd do it for nothing. But Spiro was grudgingly repaying a debt to her father, and neither one of them would tell her what it was. All she needed to know, her father insisted, was that Spiro had a plane and two choppers and could fly them, even if he couldn't pass a field sobriety test.

Spiro returned to the table, drained the last drop from the ouzo bottle, and chased a flock of roosting hens out of his plane. He said something in Greek and made some hand motions that Kate interpreted as *Let's get this stupid mission over and done so I can crack open another bottle of ouzo.*

So here she was, flying twelve thousand feet above the Halkidiki peninsula at midnight, a mere two weeks after laying out her plan to her father. Her hair was cut pixie-style under her helmet, and her breasts were minimalized by a compression sports bra. She had her Glock and a pair of handcuffs in special pockets on the thighs of her jumpsuit, an altimeter strapped to her left wrist, gloves on her hands, and the tracking device for Nick's satellite phone in a pack on her stomach.

Judging from the smile on her father's face, Kate was guessing this was definitely more fun than another round of golf at the Calabasas Country Club.

Kate gave her father a kiss on the cheek, and he put his arm around her.

"You're going to be fine," he said.

"I know that," she said. "I'm just glad you're here."

"So am I," he said. "We should do this more often."

Spiro peed into the coffee can at his feet, and Kate couldn't help seeing it as an expression of his feelings about their conversation.

Jake checked his handheld GPS. "We're at the drop point," he said, turning to Kate. "Are you ready?"

"I can't wait."

Kate stood up, adjusted her goggles, and opened the door. A blast of air roared through the plane, making it shake and rattle.

"Good luck," Jake yelled, and Kate jumped into the darkness.

She stretched out into the box position, belly to the earth, her arms out at her sides, her legs bent. Although she was dropping at 120 miles per hour, she didn't feel like she was falling. She felt like she was flying. Kate moved through the air as if she'd been born with wings. It had been two years since her last skydive, and she'd forgotten how exhilarating and liberating it could be.

She flew over fortresslike monasteries rising dramatically out of the sea mist, and over honeycombs of earthen hermitages clinging like mud dauber nests to the jagged faces of gorges and cliffs, and over the stone huts that blended into the meadows and forests. It was like no landscape she'd ever seen before. She felt as if she'd traveled into the past, not as it ever existed but as imagined by the Brothers Grimm.

At three thousand feet she reached down with her right hand and yanked the small leather strap behind her, releasing her canopy. The chute caught the air and yanked her up, feet to the earth, so she was now dropping in a standing position.

Kate headed into the wind to slow her descent and steered toward a clearing that was a safe distance from the monasteries and far from the dangers posed by the cliffs and dense chestnut forests. She'd been trained to land within a ten-foot square on a drop zone, so she knew she could be precise.

The drop was smooth, fast, and silent. She landed on her feet, quickly gathered up her chute, and dragged it into an olive grove that bordered the clearing. Kate stood for a moment to get her bearings. It was so quiet that the silence was unsettling, as if the volume of the entire world had been shut off. She saw lights coming from within the fortified walls of an imposing monastery on the nearest peak, but she wasn't concerned about that. The monks were already deep into hours of prayer. She wasn't likely to run into any of them as she made her trek, unless Nick was hiding in the monastery, but she doubted that.

She took the tracking device out of her pocket, hoping she'd made a good choice in landing on the western side of the peninsula. If Nick was on the eastern edge she'd face an arduous journey on foot, over a mountain pass. The tracker looked like a standard handheld GPS, but was designed to pick up a signal from a satellite phone. If it turned out Nick didn't have a satellite phone or didn't have it powered up, she was screwed. She turned the tracker on and nearly collapsed with relief when, almost immediately, a red dot began pulsating on the map of Athos. There was a satellite phone emitting a signal a few miles north of her present position. The good news was that there was a satellite phone nearby. The bad news was that its location appeared to be on the edge of a cliff, and she hadn't brought any rappelling gear.

She headed north and had only walked a short distance when she came upon a collection of primitive huts arranged around a lopsided church no bigger than a double-wide mobile home. In the front yard of one of the huts was a small vegetable garden, a pile of cut wood, and a clothesline strung between two crooked chestnut trees from which several pairs of pants and shirts had been hung to dry. The clothes looked as if they'd been sewn together from gunny cloth and old potato sacks.

Kate snatched a shirt and a pair of pants that seemed to be about her size and slipped them on over her jumpsuit. She crept out of the village, following the course set by her tracking device. She hiked along a narrow footpath through the dense woods, across a crystal-clear creek, and then up a steep, rocky hillside that had a rope strung through bolts hammered into the stone to use as a handrail.

After about an hour of climbing she came to a centuries-old stone and earthen hut built out from the mouth of a cave. A curl of smoke rose from its chimney. A stream originating from the wooded peak high above spilled down from a wide crevice beside the hut and turned a paddle wheel. She assumed that the paddle wheel powered the steady light that glowed warmly behind the single small window. The setting had such a storybook quality to it that she half expected the Seven Dwarfs to pop out, singing as they headed off to work.

Kate doubled-checked the tracker. The satellite phone was inside the hut, and it was on. Her gut told her she'd found Nick Fox's hideaway, and judging by the light and the smoke, he was awake. She put the tracker back into the stomach pocket of her jumpsuit and removed the Glock from the pocket on her thigh. She tiptoed slowly up to the large wooden door and pressed her ear to it. She could hear the crackle of the fire, the burbling of the stream, and the churn of the paddle wheel.

Pressing her left side against the door, she carefully tested the latch and decided it wasn't locked. She took a deep breath, threw her entire weight against the door, and burst into the room.

Nick Fox smiled at her from across a small table. He was wearing an aloha shirt, board shorts, and flip-flops. And he was eating a sandwich and drinking tsipouro, a clear liquor made on Athos from the residue of the wine presses. He didn't seem especially surprised to see her or alarmed that she had a gun pointed at him.

"You're under arrest," she said.

"Is that how you greet everyone?"

"Only international fugitives."

She kicked the door closed and looked around the tiny room. It was a bleak hermit's cell, built for quiet spiritual contemplation and little else. A small fire burned in the stone hearth behind Nick, and a ragged curtain was drawn across an archway leading back to the cave.

"You really ought to try 'Hello, Nick, it's nice to see you' as a greeting one of these days."

"I'll try it the first time I visit you in prison."

Nick's eyebrows raised a fraction of an inch. "You'd visit me in prison?"

"No," she said. "I lied."

Nick smiled, and Kate sank her teeth into her bottom lip to keep from smiling with him. The man was irresistible. What's with that? she thought. It was like wanting to bake cookies for the spawn of Satan.

"Would you like some wine?" he asked her. "Why don't you sit down and relax?"

She kept her gun trained on him. "This is how I relax."

"Okay, that's just scary. Would you like half of my corned beef sandwich?" he asked. "It's direct from the Carnegie Deli in New York."

"Meat is forbidden on Athos."

"So are women," Nick said. "But here you are."

"Did you really think a thousand years of sexist doctrine would keep me from getting you?"

"No, I didn't. In fact, you might ask yourself how this corned beef got here." He took a bite of the sandwich. "Or how I did."

"You had help from whoever is behind that curtain." She gestured to it with her gun. "How many men are there?"

"Two," Nick said. "I was getting a little midnight snack while they slept, but thanks to you slamming the door they're probably awake now."

"Are they armed?"

"I don't think so, but unlike you I don't make a practice of patting down everyone I meet."

Kate aimed her gun squarely at Nick and faced the curtain. "Both of you come out nice and slow, because if you startle me, I might accidentally splatter the wall with Nick's head."

A man's hand reached out from behind the curtain, grabbed the edge, and slowly lifted it to one side. Kate gaped at the man and felt all the air leave her lungs in a single *whoosh*. It was Carl Jessup, her boss. He stood there in a cable-knit sweater and old jeans and he didn't seem all that worried at being discovered.

The sting of betrayal that Kate felt was every bit as sharp as a physical slap and raised the same red tint on her cheeks that his hand would have. Now she knew how Nick was able to slip out of the courthouse, and the country, so easily and without leaving a trace. He had help at the highest level of law enforcement.

"Well, now I know why you wanted me off the case and put a boob like Ryerson on it," Kate said to Jessup. "You engineered Nick's escape, and you knew if I was on the hunt I'd get him. Your mistake was that you believed I'd actually sit on the sidelines if you assigned the case to someone else. You should have known me better. Then again, I guess I hardly knew you either, did I?"

"It's not what you think," Jessup said.

"You're here, aren't you?"

"Yeah, but I'm not alone."

Jessup stepped aside to allow the man behind him to come out.

The second man behind the curtain was gray-haired, ten years younger than Jessup, and looked like he'd been born wearing a tie. He was in his casual wear, a cardigan sweater that would have made Mister Rogers proud, a long-sleeved blue dress shirt buttoned at the cuffs, a pair of khaki pants, and shiny loafers. He was Fletcher Bolton, deputy director of the FBI, the highest position an agent could reach within the agency without being appointed by the president of the United States.

Kate glanced at Nick, who clearly thought this was a lot of fun. He poured a glass of tsipouro, and slid it toward her.

"You're going to need this," he said.

Kate looked back at Jessup and Bolton. "The Bureau set this idiot free?"

"Officially, no," Bolton said. "He's a fugitive from justice and wanted on three continents. He's being actively pursued by dozens of law enforcement agencies, including the FBI."

"And unofficially?" Kate asked.

"He works for us now."

Nick held up his drink in a toast to Kate. "Welcome to the team."

"Sit," Bolton said to Kate, motioning to a chair.

Kate took a seat at the table, arms folded over her chest, the expression on her face saying *ex–Navy SEAL in kill mode.*

"First, I wanted this meeting to take place somewhere so

remote that there was virtually no chance anyone besides the four of us would ever know that it had occurred," Bolton said. "Second, it was the ideal audition. I wanted to see how far you were willing to bend the law to enforce it."

"I wanted to see how far you'd go to see me," Nick said, smiling.

"To *arrest* you, or shoot you," Kate said. "Or if I was really lucky, both."

Bolton took a chair and leaned forward, elbows on the table. "My feeling was that if you showed up here, halfway around the world and in a place where women have been forbidden for a thousand years, then there was no question that you're the right person for this job."

"And clearly you're game for anything, especially if it seems impossible," Nick said. "Just like me."

"Believe it or not," Kate said, "the whole world doesn't revolve around you."

"Your world does," he said.

"Don't flatter yourself."

"You're here, aren't you?"

In her mind, Kate briefly relived the glorious moment when she'd hit his car with a bus. Channel the bus, she thought. *Be* the bus.

She turned to Bolton. "Where is this going?"

"We want you to do the same thing you're doing now. Catch the bad guys."

"Like this one sitting across from me?" Kate took the half of the corned beef sandwich that Nick had offered her earlier and ate it.

"Bigger," Jessup said.

"But only half as charming," Nick said.

"As effective as we are at what we do," Bolton said, "there's still a class of criminals that operates outside of our reach, people so rich and powerful that they can manipulate the legal system so they never have to answer for their crimes, assuming that they are ever caught at all. We're going to change that."

"By letting Nick Fox go free?" Kate said, and looked at Jessup. "Am I the only one who sees the contradiction here?"

"He's not free," Jessup said. "Nick Fox escaped from custody and is a fugitive. If he's caught, he will go back to prison. But in the meantime, it's the perfect cover."

"It's not a cover," Kate said. "It's who he is."

"That's why it's perfect," Bolton said. "Nick Fox is going to do what he does best. Only now he will be doing it for us, for the next five years, while remaining a fugitive. After that, you'll capture him, but then he'll be set free, and all charges will be dropped, when prosecutors discover that the case you put together was fatally flawed and won't stand up in court."

"Yes, it will," she said.

"I think you're missing the big picture here," Nick said.

"I think I'm the only one in this hut who isn't," she said, turning to Jessup. "If I understand you right, you broke Nick Fox out of prison so he could swindle and steal for you."

"For the FBI and the greater good," Bolton said sternly. "He's going to help us bring down criminals we can't catch by conventional methods."

"By that you mean the legal ones," Kate said.

"That's one way to look it at," Bolton said.

"It must be the only way, or we wouldn't be meeting in a cave on Mount Athos."

"We aren't meeting," Jessup said.

"This is fun already," Nick said, pouring himself another drink.

"This is surreal," Kate said. "Am I dreaming? Am I being punked?"

"To bankroll Nick's scams, swindles, and heists against the targets we select, and to finance his requisite glamorous lifestyle, we'll be tapping a secret fund made up entirely of money and assets confiscated from convicted criminals," Bolton said. "I consider it poetic justice."

"What happens if he gets caught by a mark or by some law enforcement agency?" Kate said.

"He's on his own," Jessup said.

"Even if he's apprehended by the FBI," Bolton said.

"Okay, now I am really confused," Kate said. "*We're* going to be chasing him?"

"Of course," Bolton said. "He's a federal fugitive."

"But we're the ones who set him free," Kate said. "He'll be out there doing missions for us."

"We don't know that," Jessup said.

"Yes, we do," Kate said. "That's the deputy director of the FBI sitting next to you."

"It was worth getting arrested just for this moment," Nick said.

"Fox is still going to be on our Most Wanted list," Bolton said to Kate, "and every agent except you will be on the lookout for him."

"What will I be doing?" she asked.

"Keeping him from getting caught," Bolton said. "While pretending to be pursuing him, of course."

"Of course," Kate said, and she finally knocked back her glass of tsipouro. "What happens if I get caught covering for him or helping him in one of his schemes?"

"You will be arrested and prosecuted," Bolton said.

"That's nice," Kate said. "That makes me feel all warm inside."

"Probably that's the tsipouro," Nick said.

Kate turned to Bolton. "What's to stop him from stealing that secret slush fund from us or using it to pull off scams and heists of his own?"

"You," Bolton said.

"What's to stop him from ditching us and *really* going on the run?"

"You," Bolton said.

She nodded. "I see a fatal flaw in your plan."

"What's that?" Bolton said.

She pointed at Nick. "Him."

9

Bolton wanted Kate's decision in the morning, though she had no idea what he would do, or what she would do, or what would happen to Nick Fox, if she refused to participate in their operation.

Bolton and Jessup chose to sleep on the cots behind the curtain. Kate opted to sleep on a bench in the main room. She liked the hard wood under her back and head. It kept her aware of her location and her bizarre situation. In fact her situation was so bizarre, she wasn't sure it was real. Maybe she only *thought* she'd had a perfect landing when she parachuted in. Maybe she'd hit her head and she was hallucinating.

"Out of curiosity," Kate asked, staring at the aged beams holding up the pitched ceiling, "how long have Jessup and Bolton been here?"

"They came in yesterday when it was clear you were making your move."

"And who came up with this insane plan?"

"I did," Nick said. "I thought it was a win-win for everybody."

"Except for me," Kate said.

"Especially for you."

"How do you figure that?" she asked.

"You like chasing after me, traveling all over the place, kicking down doors, jumping out of airplanes, smashing into cars with buses," he said. "There aren't a lot of cases that are going to have the same excitement, danger, and fun. Not to mention you're living in a box and this gives you a chance to get out."

"I like the box."

"It's still a box."

"And what's in it for you, Nick, besides staying out of a cell for the time being?"

"Time being?"

She propped herself up on an elbow and looked at him. "You're a crook. Your fate is inevitable. Even if you honor this deal, which I doubt, in five years you'll walk away a free man and immediately pull off another big swindle and it will start all over again. I will come after you, and when I catch you there will be no deals. You'll do hard time."

"I might emerge from this a changed man. Or you might become an entirely different woman. You might not want to catch me anymore."

"Yeah, right, that's all not gonna happen."

He shrugged. "We'll see."

Kate wanted to punch him, wanted to wipe the smug smile off his face. Then she wanted to punch Bolton and Jessup.

"Honestly," she said, "this just isn't fair. I'm a team player, but this is too much. This is wrong."

"It's the chance of a lifetime," Nick said.

"For you."

"Yes, but it comes with a price. I'm going to be stuck with you for five long years. And if you want to know the ugly truth, it's not my idea of the good life. True, I find you strangely attractive, but that doesn't mean you're not a huge pain in the ass."

Kate perked up at that. She liked the possibility that she could make his life a living hell. And while she was raining on Nick Fox's parade she might be able to catch some bad guys. Sure there was some risk involved, but risk was always present. Look at Nick Fox: He was driving home from work one day, and he got hit by a bus. Who would have thought?

Nick stayed awake long after Kate fell asleep. There were practical problems he had to face. To mount his cons and heists, he'd need a crew. He rarely used the same crew twice, but he was loyal to everyone who'd been loyal to him. He wouldn't betray them by involving them in a hustle that he was secretly running for the FBI.

And he didn't trust the FBI much more than they trusted him. If he introduced the feds to his network of fellow con artists and thieves, he'd be exposing them all to law enforcement scrutiny, revealing not only who they were but their methods of operation. The FBI might turn around one day and use that knowledge to arrest them. Nick couldn't live with himself if that happened. Not to mention if his clever cohorts discovered he was working with Kate instead of running from her, his cover would be blown and his life would be in jeopardy. Nobody in his field liked a rat, which is what they would naturally assume he was even if he wasn't. And they would justifiably begin to wonder what he'd divulged about his past scores, and his past colleagues, and if he'd tipped the FBI off to the Crimson Teardrop job, even though he'd arranged with Bolton for the release of his crew on a sketchy legal technicality as a condition of his participation in this operation.

So to mount the cons against the big fish targeted by the FBI he'd have to assemble a crew from scratch, recruiting entirely new people and never letting them know who they were actually working for. He already had some people in mind, since he was always on the lookout for new talent, but he knew that bringing in an entirely inexperienced crew introduced a level of risk and uncertainty that could swiftly derail a con and get everybody killed. And no one was more of a wild card in the deck than Kate O'Hare. She was 5' 5" of trouble, and he was going to have a hard time keeping his hands off her, torn as he was between wanting to wring her neck and wanting to sweet-talk her out of her Kevlar vest.

Kate woke up with a stiff back. She stood and stretched and checked to make sure her cuffs and gun were still in her pockets. Nick was at the fireplace, stirring a big pot suspended over the fire.

He glanced at her over his shoulder. "You were expecting me to steal your gun?"

"You're a thief," she said. "I expect you to steal everything. What are you making?"

"Hermit's stew. Basically, a lentil soup. I've also got some fresh bread, some salted fish, and red wine, all produced here on Athos."

"Wine for breakfast?"

"It's what the monks drink."

Jessup and Bolton joined them. Bolton looked like he'd spent the last few hours in cryogenic freeze. There wasn't a wrinkle on his clothes and his hair was perfect. Jessup looked like an unmade bed.

"Have you reached a decision, Agent O'Hare?" Bolton asked.

Kate gave him a single nod. "I'm in. But I want a few things clear from the get-go. I'm in charge of this partnership."

"You obviously don't understand the meaning of 'partnership,'" Nick said.

"I'm the cop, you're the crook," Kate said to Nick. "If I think something is too risky, or too crooked, or too anything, I can shut it down." She turned to Bolton. "That goes for you, too, sir. Once we have an assignment, I have the absolute authority to change the play or call the whole thing off."

"I don't know if I'm comfortable with that," Bolton said.

"It's not your comfort I'm worried about," she said. "I'm the one who could end up dead or in a prison cell if one of our operations falls apart. This is nonnegotiable."

Jessup looked at Bolton. "I have to back O'Hare on this. I've been undercover. I know what it's like being out there on your knees in the muck, with your neck on a chopping block over an open latrine while a psycho in overalls stands over you with a roaring chainsaw."

Bolton mentally chewed on that for a moment. "Very well."

Nick smiled, poured four glasses of wine, and held his up for a toast. "To our grand adventure."

"This is not an adventure," Kate said. "It's a job. We aren't doing it for fun or for profit."

"Speak for yourself," Nick said.

"I am speaking for both of us," she said.

Nick glanced at Jessup. "Is she always this irritable in the morning?"

"I wouldn't know," Jessup said.

"Okay, let's try this again," Nick said, and raised his glass for a new toast. "To a long and fruitful relationship."

"This isn't a relationship," Kate said. "It's strictly professional. Don't you forget that for one second."

Nick sighed and held up his glass again, eyeing her warily as he said, "May misfortune follow us the rest of our lives, but never catch up."

Before Kate could object, he tapped her glass with his and the other men jumped in to do the same and everyone chugged their wine.

"Now that we've settled that," Bolton said, setting down his glass, "here's the protocol. Jessup will be your primary. He will release the funds necessary to complete each mission to an offshore account that we've set up in O'Hare's name."

"Yadda-yadda-yadda," Nick said. "Save the bureaucracy for the bureaucrats. Just tell me who we're going after."

Bolton smiled. "Derek Griffin."

Griffin was a high-flying, charming playboy investment banker whose name was mentioned as often in *Vanity Fair,* for the lavish parties he attended and the charities he supported, as it was in *Forbes,* for the audacious deals he made and the big money he earned for his elite clients. He got even more headlines when he abruptly disappeared with $500 million of his company's money mere hours before he was about to be arrested by the FBI for running a massive pyramid scheme.

Nick whistled. "Not bad. I have to hand it to you, Bolt, you think big."

"It's 'Bolton.' Or 'sir.'"

"There's been an FBI task force looking for him for almost a year," Kate said. "Nick is a con man and a thief, not a fugitive tracker. What can he do for us?"

"There's one person who knows where Griffin is, and perhaps all of that money, and that's Neal Burnside, his lawyer," Bolton said. "He's protected by attorney-client privilege from being forced to talk."

"I know about Burnside," Nick said. "I was tempted to hire him when you arrested me. The guy is brilliant."

"He's scum," Bolton said.

"You didn't think so when he was a Justice Department prosecutor," Nick said.

"He uses what he learned about our tactics and our personnel to get scores of high-profile crooks and murderers off the hook and make the FBI look inept in the process," Bolton said. "There's a word for men like him."

"Expensive," Nick said.

"Traitor," Bolton said.

"So you want the two of us to use Burnside to find Griffin, bring him to justice, and recover the half a billion that he stole," Kate said.

"Yes," Bolton said.

"No problem," Nick said.

"Huge problem," Kate said. "How are we going to get Burnside to give up Griffin without resorting to torture?"

"I'll come up with something," Nick said.

"And even if Burnside does betray his client," Kate said, "what makes you think Griffin will tell us where his money is?"

"I'll figure out a way," Nick said.

Kate stared at him. "That's it?"

Nick shrugged. "It's a start."

"It's nothing," she said.

"Let's get together four days from now, at four P.M., at the Schokoladen-Café in Berlin," Nick said. "And I'll tell you how we're going to do it."

"No way. I'm not letting you out of my sight."

"So you want us to live together?"

"No, of course not," she said.

"Then how did you think this was going to work? Did you assume you'd just lock me up in a dungeon somewhere each night?"

"I like the sound of that." Kate glanced at Bolton and Jessup for backup on this key point, but she could see from the looks on their faces that she wasn't going to get it. "C'mon, guys, help me out here."

"He's a free man," Jessup said. "With restrictions."

Nick smiled. "Is speaking in contradictions some secret language they teach you at Quantico? Because you and Bolt are both very good at it."

"It's 'Bolton,'" the deputy director said again.

"He could be captured by some other law enforcement agency in the meantime," Kate said. "And there is nothing to stop him from committing his own scams between assignments."

"That's a risk we have to take," Jessup said.

Kate looked at Bolton, who was obviously in agreement with Jessup. She looked at Nick, who was way too pleased with it all.

"So what am I supposed to do for four days?" Kate asked.

"Enjoy your vacation," Jessup said.

She had been, right up until the time Bolton and Jessup stepped out from behind that curtain.

. . .

It was decided that the four of them would leave Athos separately, to avoid any chance of them all being seen together, and that Kate would go first, since there were others awaiting word from her.

She stepped outside the hut and called her father on the satellite phone. She told him that the mission was a bust, that Nick Fox wasn't on Athos, and that she'd take the ferry to Ouranoupoli and then the bus back to Thessaloniki, where she would meet him later that day at their hotel.

"You're lying about Fox," Jake said. "But I can respect that."

"You respect lying?"

"Sometimes it's necessary," he said. "I only hope that you made the right decision."

"So do I," she said.

10

Nick had to admit there were some undeniable benefits to working for the FBI instead of hiding from them. They made it easier to move around and look legitimate, and even better, he was now operating on someone else's dime. Bolton had supplied Nick with a new alias, Nicolas Raider. Raider had a U.S. passport, a platinum AmEx card, a bank account, and detailed histories in the IRS, the DMV, Experian, and other major government and private sector databases. The flip side, of course, was that every time Nick used the alias a blip popped up on Bolton's computer telling him exactly where Nick was located. No problem, Nick thought. I can deal. It's a new game.

Nick swiped his brand-new credit card through the machine at the airport, flashed his brand-new passport, and flew from Greece to his three-hundred-year-old stone farmhouse in Bois-le-Roi, France. Bois-le-Roi was a small village on the Seine just outside of Fontainebleau. It was one of Nick's many properties, and it had been chosen primarily for the solitude it offered.

The rambling single-story house, and the two acres it sat on, were surrounded by a stone wall that could be easily scaled but at least shielded the grounds from prying eyes. The former barn housed a beautifully restored red 1966 Jaguar E-type convertible and a three-year-old Mercedes GLK. The house and grounds were tended during his long absences by his neighbor, a gregarious horse trainer by trade who, in his free time, built ships in a bottle and gave them away. There were probably twenty bottled ships around Nick's house.

Nick arrived in Bois-le-Roi, checked in with his neighbor/groundskeeper, got briefed on all the local gossip he cared nothing about, then stopped by the baker, the butcher, and the grocer. For dinner he made himself a thick steak, fresh vegetables, and a warmed-up baguette, and he washed it down with a bottle of wine from his well-stocked cellar.

While he ate he opened his laptop and did some basic research into Burnside and Griffin. Most of what he read he already knew. Neither man was a shrinking violet, and their private lives were public record. Their professional lives were legend. Nick finished his steak, sipped his wine, and logged in to his encrypted cloud account, where he browsed through the files he'd been compiling of potential new crew members. His late-night diversion was online poker, where he targeted someone calling himself "Le Chiffre," handily winning $15,000 from him. By the morning of his third day in Bois-le-Rois, Nick had come up with the broad strokes of his plan.

Jake O'Hare knew how to keep a secret, so three days after Kate's return from Athos, she shared hers with him. She needed some-one she could turn to for advice and support as the operation unfolded, someone who didn't have any hidden agendas. She didn't trust Nick or her own bosses. They were all looking out for themselves. Her father was the one person she could always depend upon to look out for her.

They were sitting at a café in the airport in Athens, waiting for his flight back to the States and hers to Berlin, when she finally told him about the outrageous scheme Nick had sold to Fletcher Bolton.

"I think it's brilliant," Jake said.

"You're being sarcastic."

"I'm being straight. For once, your hands won't be tied by bureaucracy, civil rights, and the law."

"Oh, *those* pesky things," she said.

"You'll be able to bring down a lot of bad guys who've played the system to their advantage."

"But I'll be teamed up with a criminal."

"The pilot who flew you to Athos was a criminal, but you didn't seem to mind. Sometimes a criminal is exactly who you need to get a job done. But I don't have to convince you, you've already signed on. So what are we really talking about here, Kate?"

"I'm technically in charge, but I know ultimately it's Nick who'll be running the cons. I can't count on him to tell me everything he's doing and what the dangers might actually be. I'm going to need a safety net of my own, a plan B he doesn't need to know about," Kate said. "I'm hoping it can be you."

"It's always been me, didn't you know that?" Jake said. "That's what fathers are for."

"What I am asking could be above and beyond."

"Hell, Kate, that was my profession for forty years," he said. "It also happens to be my motto."

"You have a motto?"

"I do now. It's 'Above and Beyond.' "

Kate hadn't ever been to Berlin, nor had she ever had the desire to visit. Her image of the city was shaped by cold war spy movies where everything was in shades of gray, the streets were frosty and bleak, the trees were spindly and bare, and the people were pale, oppressed, and haunted. So she was unprepared for how colorful, vibrant, and energetic Berlin appeared to be as her taxi driver took a long, roundabout, fare-inflating route from the airport to the Hyatt in Potsdamer Platz.

They drove through the lush, sprawling Tiergarten, a forest within the city that made Central Park look like a vacant lot, and cruised by the iconic Brandenburg Gate and a skyline of bold, edgy architecture that embraced the old while also breaking with the past. That architectural philosophy was epitomized by the Reichstag. Built in the late nineteenth century and virtually destroyed in World War II, the Reichstag was restored in the 1990s to its original grandeur as the seat of the German parliament, but its Neo-Baroque dome was replaced with a steel-and-glass version, with a dazzling spiral of 360 mirrors in its center, that looked like it had fallen onto the building from outer space. Kate thought it was a real-life Tomorrowland, without the rides.

She checked in to her room with two hours to kill before her meeting with Nick Fox. So she did the tourist thing, and walked over to Checkpoint Charlie and the replica of the guard shack that once stood on the western side of the Berlin Wall on Friedrichstrasse. Kate was wearing black slacks and a white sweater, but she didn't have her usual fashion accessories. She'd given her gun and handcuffs to her father to spirit back to the States, using whatever black bag method he'd employed to get them to Greece. She didn't have Mace, a Taser, or a telescoping baton. This made her purse about fifteen pounds lighter, and she felt like the strap practically floated off her shoulder.

There was a double line of cobblestones in the street that marked where the Berlin Wall had once stood. She followed the line, which ran under parked cars and along sidewalks as it meandered over several streets. Nobody but her seemed to notice it. The memorial to a wall that once divided a country, that was the bloody front line of the cold war, got less attention than Jack Webb's star on the Hollywood Walk of Fame. Eventually she found her way to the Fassbender & Rausch Schokoladen-Café at the Gendarmenmarkt, an eighteenth-century market square with ornate cathedrals at either end.

Fassbender & Rausch, Berlin's oldest and most renowned chocolatier, occupied the first two floors of a corner building that faced the Gendarmenmarkt. There was an enormous chocolate sculpture of the Reichstag in one of the first-floor windows, and beyond it Kate could see a burbling chocolate volcano in the center of a store filled with an astonishing assortment of handmade chocolate delicacies that would have made Willy Wonka mess his pants.

Kate was afraid she'd lose control in the store, racing up and down the aisles, stuffing her mouth with candy. For sure a good time, but not an attractive picture if she ran into Nick Fox. It might be hard to establish authority after he saw her with chocolate dribbling out of her mouth and running down her chin. So she skipped the store entirely and went straight to the elevator, which took her to the second-floor café. She was expecting an ice cream shop like Ghirardelli in San Francisco, but the café at Fassbender & Rausch was an elegant wood-paneled space that had the feel of a private club.

Nick was already seated at a corner table, overlooking the Gendarmenmarkt. There weren't many other people in the café: a young couple in their twenties, two businessmen in suits, a guy in a leather jacket reading *Der Spiegel,* and a family of tourists with four excited kids.

Nick rose when she came to the table. "I took the liberty of ordering when I saw you walk up the street," he said.

"What did you get?"

"Everything."

A waiter in a crisp white shirt, gray vest, and red tie approached, wheeling a cart. He set down four cups of hot chocolate and a platter of chocolate pastries and candies.

The Mokka-Creme-Sinfonie had chocolate musical notes atop layers of mocha cream, chocolate ganache, and biscuits. The Mousse au Chocolat-Törtchen was a dome of smooth, dark chocolate filled with chocolate mousse and crowned with gold leaf. And that was only the beginning. Kate got a hot flash just looking at it. It was sex on a platter. She glanced up at Nick and saw that he was watching her. His expression was pleasantly bland, but she knew that somewhere deep in the murky crevices of his diabolical brain he was plotting against her. He was luring her into stupefied complacency with chocolate. The man was pure evil.

"I know what you're up to," Kate said, popping a Törtchen into her mouth. "You're trying to drug me with chocolate."

"Guilty as charged."

She did a test drive on the hot chocolate. "Do you have any other reasons for being here?"

"I thought we should talk."

"Yes, but why Berlin?"

"For the symbolism," he said. "A wall used to divide this city, two bitter enemies on either side. After decades of conflict, the wall came down almost overnight to jubilation on both sides."

"I'm not jubilant." That wasn't entirely true. Her taste buds were ecstatic. She'd never be able to drink Swiss Miss instant cocoa again.

"The point I'm making is that people from two very different worlds put their deep distrust of one another aside and worked together. And now the city is thriving. That could be us."

"What you're trying to do is smooth-talk me," she said.

"How's it working?"

"I'm not one of your marks. You want to impress me? Tell me your plan for getting Burnside to reveal where Griffin is and retrieving the half a billion dollars that he embezzled."

"It's simple," Nick said, breaking into a warm chocolate cake with his fork. "As long as you don't mind getting killed."

Nick watched Kate eat chocolates while she listened to him explain the con. She didn't interrupt him with questions and objections, as he'd been expecting, and he worried that her focus was more on the dessert display than on him. The woman could really pack it away. An ordinary woman would be having a chocolate-induced seizure by now, but Kate looked fresh as a daisy.

"And?" Kate said. "Why did you stop talking?"

"I wasn't sure you were listening."

"Of course I'm listening. Where do we go from here?"

"I've got to put my crew together."

"*Our* crew," she said.

"Right. Our crew. Then we have to gather our resources, scout locations, build our sets, and select our wardrobe."

"It sounds like we're putting on a show."

"We are," he said. "For an audience of one."

He relaxed back into his seat while Kate polished off a plate of petits fours. This was the first time they'd met face-to-face, outside of that one encounter in the interrogation room, that didn't begin with her pointing a gun at him. They were actually sitting at a table, like two old friends, not like the hunter and the hunted. And it wasn't especially awkward. They were comfortable together, despite the fact that they didn't trust each other or that she'd hit him with a bus. Maybe his scheme would work.

11

They left the café and walked side by side out of the Gendarmenmarkt and up Markgrafenstrasse in the general direction of Unter den Linden, the wide, tree-lined boulevard that ran from the Brandenburg Gate to the Spree River. As they walked, Nick briefed Kate on the potential crew members he'd found, what their skills were, where they were now, and what he and Kate would have to do to recruit them.

Three of the four prospects were civilians with no serious brushes with the law in their pasts. But they all had problems, pressing needs, or unfulfilled desires that Nick could exploit to make them receptive to participating in their con.

Kate shook her head. "I don't like it. We're enticing innocent people into participating in a crime. It's entrapment."

"You have to stop thinking like an FBI agent. It's only entrapment if you intend to arrest them," Nick said. "Besides, what we're doing isn't a crime. I'd say it's more like an elaborate practical joke."

"That could get us all ten to twenty years in prison."

"You worry too much," Nick said. "If there wasn't any risk, it wouldn't be any fun."

Markgrafenstrasse ended at a T-junction with Behrenstrasse. The buildings there were all the same height, clad in polished stone and glass, and flush with one another, creating an unbroken roofline that made the structures seem to blend into one solid wall. It made Nick feel like a rat trapped in a labyrinth, and he didn't like it because he was pretty sure they were being followed. He quickly went to their right, where Behrenstrasse spilled into the Bebelplatz, a wide-open square that was bordered on three sides by the monumental Baroque and Neoclassical architecture of the Old Palace, Saint Hedwig's Cathedral, the Old Royal Library, and the State Opera House. Unter den Linden ran on the fourth side.

They'd just stepped into the square when Kate slipped her arm around his, drew him against her side, and laid her head gently against his shoulder. She did it as smoothly and naturally as if she'd sought the warmth and comfort of his closeness a hundred times before.

Nick would have been less shocked if she'd shot him. Just moments ago she was worried about going to jail, and now she was cuddling up to him. Never underestimate the power of chocolate, he thought. And, he had to admit, he liked the feel of her breast pressed against his arm. Still, it would be awkward if she thought he was boyfriend material. Sure, he was attracted to her, but women always had to go beyond that. Women got nesting fantasies. It wasn't long before they were redecorating your apartment and criticizing your choice of mustard. He was hooked up to Kate for five long years. He wouldn't be able to simply walk away from her when he couldn't tolerate another day of having bright yellow mustard in his refrigerator.

Kate raised her face and surreptitiously glanced over Nick's shoulder. "I make three of them, how about you?" she asked softly.

POP! The nesting fantasy bubble burst in Nick's head.

"I spotted two," Nick said, relieved that he wouldn't have to engage in a mustard war anytime soon. "I'll take your word for the third."

Kate led them to a crowd of tourists standing around a clear pane of Plexiglas embedded in the plaza floor. The tourists were all hunched over, taking pictures through the Plexiglas of a deep, subterranean room full of empty white bookshelves, an artistic memorial to the twenty-five thousand books burned by the Nazis in the Bebelplatz on a single night in 1933.

"Excuse me," Kate said, taking her iPhone from her pocket and approaching a young man with a Berlin guidebook under his arm. "Could you take a picture of us?"

"I would be glad to," the man said with a thick Swedish accent.

Kate maneuvered Nick so their backs were to Behrenstrasse and Saint Hedwig's Cathedral. "Be sure to get the cathedral. We just love that dome."

Nick put his arm around Kate, and the tourist clicked a picture. Before he could hand the camera back, Kate hustled Nick over so their backs were now to the Old Royal Library. "Can you get us with the library and palace behind us, too?"

After several more pictures Kate took possession of her phone and huddled with Nick to look at the shots.

Kate enlarged the photo and pointed to a man in the background. "Gray suit, white shirt, and red tie. He was in the restaurant, reading a newspaper."

"What a cliché," Nick said.

"He followed us out." Kate swiped her finger across the screen, bringing up the next photo with the Old Palace as their backdrop and two other men in the background. "This guy started shadowing us when we crossed the Gendarmenmarkt, and this one just pulled up in a car on the other side of Behrenstrasse as we were coming into the square. They're too far away to see their faces, but they're all wearing gray suits and white shirts." She swept the photo away and brought up the one of them against the backdrop of Unter den Linden. "There's a fourth guy here, leaning against the Audi, looking right at us. They have us boxed in. Do you know these guys?"

"Not personally, but a year ago, maybe two, I might have tricked a German shipping mogul out of a few million euros for the purchase of a stolen Vermeer that wasn't actually a stolen Vermeer."

"And you came back to Berlin?"

"If I stayed away from every place where I've done business or had a little fun, I'd never leave my igloo in Antarctica."

Nick knew that Heiko Balz carried a grudge, but he didn't think that he'd go to the considerable expense of keeping people on alert for him at airports, train stations, restaurants, and hotels after all this time. Obviously, he was wrong.

Kate and Nick mixed in with a tourist group that was leaving the Bebelplatz and making their way across Unter den Linden to the German Historical Museum. The museum sat alongside the Spree River by the ornate Palace Bridge. Nick glanced across the bridge and saw a van with dark tinted windows pull up to the curb beside the Berlin Cathedral.

Kate stole a look over her shoulder. The three men behind them were moving in and not bothering to hide their intent any longer. The fourth man was getting back into his Audi.

"They're closing in on all sides," she said. "How good are they? Are they likely to be trained operatives or just garden-variety bone crackers?"

"Hired muscle with anger management issues, lousy childhoods, and some street fighting experience," Nick said, breaking off from the tourists and heading toward the bridge. "The good news is, they want me alive."

"How do you know that?"

"Because Heiko Balz wants his money back," Nick said. "So that gives us some wiggle room."

"To do what?"

"Wiggle," Nick said, and gestured to his left as they passed the edge of the German Historical Museum. The weekend flea market stretched along the banks of the Spree, from the Palace Bridge to the next crossing, which went to Museum Island. "Can you buy me some time?"

Kate looked over her shoulder at the three men as they dashed across Unter den Linden. The van was crossing the bridge toward them. It would park at the curb in front of the flea market to block any chance of Kate and Nick making a retreat. The Audi made a sharp U-turn on Unter den Linden and sped away, probably to the other end of the flea market to cut them off.

"Sure," Kate said, and the two of them ambled into the flea market as if they didn't have a care in the world.

"Thanks. I'll see you at the Stony Peak Lodge in Cape Girardeau, Missouri, in two days."

She stopped to browse at a booth selling vintage jewelry. "If you don't show up, I'll find you."

"I wouldn't want it any other way," Nick said.

Nick disappeared into the crowd and Kate picked up a necklace, held it to her throat, and looked at her reflection in a mirror hanging from one of the booth posts. She wasn't looking at herself, of course, but at the three men hurrying her way. She sized them up and decided on a direct approach. She put the necklace down, stepped into the center of the path, and turned to face the three men, cutting them off. She named them Moe, Larry, and Curly. They were all doing their best to look mean.

"I don't like being followed," she said. "So I'd appreciate it if you'd turn around and go back where you came from."

Moe shared a look with Larry and then said something to Curly in German. She didn't speak the language, but from his gestures she figured he'd said something along the lines of "You grab the girl, we'll take care of Fox."

When Moe moved to pass her, she kicked him in the groin, and as he bent over in pain, she elbowed him in the back of the neck, knocking him out and putting him on the ground.

Larry took a swing at her that he telegraphed so early, and so obviously, he might as well have sent his intentions to her in a postcard three weeks ago. She calmly ducked under the swing, hammered him in the stomach with her fist, then kneed him in the face as he bent over, smashing his nose like a tomato and putting him on the ground beside Moe.

The whole skirmish was over in less than thirty seconds, and Kate was feeling good about herself. Okay, maybe she wasn't so great with the finer points of landing a boyfriend, but she could dropkick a two-hundred-pound man without breaking a sweat.

People were backing away from her, giving her plenty of room. She looked at Curly, who appeared dumbfounded, as if an immutable law of nature had just been broken. The sun rises in the morning and sets at night, two plus two equals four, and women are supposed to be helpless.

"I know this didn't work out the way you planned," she said to Curly, "but I'm okay with how it went down. I've got nothing against you. We're cool. You can walk away from this and take your friends with you."

Even if he didn't understand English, she hoped that the tone of her voice, her body language, and the two guys on the ground would get the point across. But Curly decided to up the stakes, even with witnesses all around. He pulled a knife and rushed at her.

She waited until the last possible second, turned sideways, grabbed his knife hand, and held it as he passed, yanking his arm behind him and using his own weight and forward momentum to dislocate his shoulder with an audible crack. He yelped in agony and went to the ground. Kate looked back toward Unter den Linden and saw the van speeding off. Scared away by the police sirens one street over, she thought. She hurried in the direction of Museum Island, the people around her giving her a wide berth. She didn't see the Audi at the next street. She hoped that was because he'd gotten scared off, too, and not because he'd managed to capture Nick. The irony of that thought made her smile. She'd never rooted for Nick Fox to escape before.

A flash of something cream-colored caught her eye, and she realized it was Nick's shirt hanging on a rack in a booth selling vintage clothes. She did a 360 degree scan of the area and spotted Nick on a tour boat moving down the Spree canal. He was standing at the railing wearing a blue watch cap, sunglasses, and a gray East German army shirt with double-buttoned breast pockets and elastic bands at the sides of the waist. He gave her a little nod and Kate nodded back.

Two green Polizei patrol cars pulled up on Unter den Linden and people pointed in Kate's direction, so she made a quick exit down a side street and didn't stop moving until she got to her hotel.

12

Kate was done with Berlin. She'd seen everything she wanted to see. She'd had her meeting with Nick. She'd pigged out at the Fassbender & Rausch café. She was ready to get on with it. So she checked out of her hotel, paying for the day without spending the night. She went back to the airport, where she booked the first available flight to London, an evening flight out of Heathrow to New York, and an early morning flight from New York to Cape Girardeau, Missouri.

Kate crashed in an airport hotel close to JFK for the night, and rushed out first thing in the morning only to find that her flight was indefinitely delayed. She roamed the airport and finally napped in a chair, coming awake when her flight to Cape Girardeau was announced. She hoisted her tote bag onto her shoulder and shuffled her way to the gate, jet-lagged and not in a happy place. She'd had a fast food burger and fries at JFK. By the time she boarded she was wearing most of her ketchup, her short hair was a mess, and her eyes were red and puffy. They were right to boot her out of the SEALs, she thought. She was a wimp. She couldn't even manage commercial air travel.

She Googled Cape Girardeau while the plane was still loading and found that it was a big town in the middle of nowhere, midway between St. Louis and Memphis, on the banks of the Mississippi. It was known for having a picturesque old hilltop courthouse and a floodwall covered in murals, and for being the birthplace of conservative radio host Rush Limbaugh. She could give a hoot about any of it. She wanted a real burger and ten hours of sleep.

She landed in Girardeau, picked up a rental car, and drove to the Stony Peak Lodge, which wasn't on a peak and wasn't stony. It was a '60s-era motel beside a freeway that a regional hotel chain had renovated by building a two-story A-frame lobby between two of the wings. It was like putting antlers on a dog and calling it a reindeer.

Kate parked in the lot and staggered into the lobby, dragging her suitcase on wheels up to the front desk. The lobby reeked of popcorn from a movie-style popper stuck in a far corner. There was a big stone fireplace with a roaring gas fire, the flames licking at concrete logs. The walls were decorated with mounted animal heads, all fakes that made it look like somebody had slaughtered a lot of Disney characters. The desk clerk standing under the dismembered heads of Tigger and Bambi was blond, rail thin, and in her early twenties.

"I'd like a room," Kate said, sliding across her credit card. "As far away from the freeway as possible, nonsmoking, with two double beds."

"How long will you be staying?"

"Two nights," she said.

The clerk ran Kate's credit card, Kate got her key, and as she turned to leave she crashed into Nick.

"What the heck?" Kate said, taking a step back, shocked to see him standing there.

He was wearing a V-neck pullover, jeans, and Vans. No ketchup stains. No airplane hair. He was looking relaxed and as handsome as ever. And he was smiling. Looking like he was having fun. She had no clue how he did it, but the guy always looked like he was having fun. Even now that he was working for the government he looked like he was having fun, and no one was supposed to have fun working for the government.

"How did you get here so fast?" Kate asked, her voice barely above a whisper.

"Private jet," Nick said.

"You have a private jet?"

"No, but billionaire Count Lippe of Lisbon is in the market to lease two or three of them, so the sales staff of UniJet Global in London were eager to give him a demonstration flight to the U.S. to show off their amenities and services," Nick said. "The lobster was excellent and the masseuse was a nice touch that I hadn't expected."

Kate's amenities and services were an economy class chair that reclined 2 degrees, a flat can of Coke, and a bag of stale pretzels.

"Is there really a Count Lippe?" she asked.

"Of course, and he cherishes his privacy, which is why there are so few photos of him around and instances of mistaken identity are bound to arise."

"Only if someone goes around calling himself Count Lippe and leasing airplanes," Kate said. "This is how you keep a low profile?

How many counts do you think fly into Cape Girardeau in private jets?"

"You think I was putting our operation at risk just to indulge myself in extravagance," Nick said.

"You had lobster and a midair massage."

"You are missing the practical aspects."

"I certainly am," she said, stopping outside the door to her first-floor room, which was conveniently located next to the ice maker and the vending machines. She was certain that if Stony Peak Lodge had a presidential suite, Nick was in it.

"I flew straight into St. Louis on a private jet, thus avoiding an international commercial flight and the chance of being recognized at customs in New York, where they are on heightened alert for terrorists and felons. Things go much smoother on a private VIP level, especially in smaller international airports in midwestern cities. I rented a car as Nicolas Raider and drove here. So Count Lippe, in essence, disappeared upon arrival in St. Louis. And by using the Raider alias, I quietly checked us in with Bolton, who certainly knows by now that we're both back home and on the job."

Kate couldn't argue with the practicality or logic behind his choices, though she really wished that she could. His reasoning demonstrated to her why he'd evaded arrest for so long. There was more going on beneath the surface of his actions, even the ones that seemed frivolous or indulgent, than she'd ever realized. She appreciated the knowledge. It would make it easier to catch him next time.

Nick checked his watch. "We have two tickets to the seven P.M. show of *Death of Salesman*, so you'd better get ready."

"Tonight?"

"We aren't on vacation here," he said. "We have a job to do. I thought you were indefatigable." He looked at her chest. "Is that ketchup?"

"Yes."

"It's a good color on you. You should wear red more often."

"I'll keep that in mind. What's the dress code tonight?"

"Missouri black tie," Nick said. "No shirt, no shoes, no service."

Country Mama's Buffet & Theater was located next door to the Stony Peak Lodge. The hostess who seated Kate and Nick told them to help themselves to the buffet, enjoy the show, and have a blessed meal.

Kate didn't think a blessing was going to be nearly enough to save them from what they were facing. Everything at Country Mama's was fried, breaded, cheesed, and noodled, including the desserts. She thought it was no wonder most of the diners prayed before they ate. What the buffet really needed wasn't blessings or prayers but a team of paramedics on standby and a priest on hand to perform last rites. And Kate couldn't wait to dig in.

"Yum," Kate said, "this looks fantastic."

Nick grinned. "Go for it."

She came back to their table with a mountain of fried chicken, broccoli noodle casserole, hash brown casserole, fried corn bread, buttermilk biscuits, fried shrimp, an oozing glob of grits, fried okra, and dumplings. All smothered in gravy.

"That looks like the artery-clogging special," Nick said to Kate.

"I have excellent genes," Kate said. "No one in my family has ever had heart disease. We all die from unfortunate circumstance. Like my Uncle Stump got run over by a cement truck. And my Aunt Jean was struck by lightning."

"That didn't turn up in my research on you."

Kate glanced at his plate. No food. "You obviously didn't bring me here because you like the cuisine," she said. "So why *are* we here?"

"We're here for the show."

Kate dug in to her broccoli noodle casserole and looked over at the makeshift stage set up against the far wall of the huge dining room. Someone had hung a crudely painted canvas backdrop of a living room and placed a couple pieces of worn-out furniture on the wood riser.

Halfway into the dessert course Kate paused to listen to the cast introductions. Boyd Capwell, as Willy Loman, was the headliner. All the others were local amateurs. As far as Kate could tell, none of the diners had much interest in the production. Conversation continued after the show started, and the actors were frequently obscured by people passing the stage to make trips to the buffet line.

"This is horrible," Kate whispered to Nick, wishing she had the nerve to scuttle in front of the stage for another piece of pie. "This is the worst acting *ever*."

"Concentrate on Boyd Capwell. I stumbled on Boyd performing three roles in *Equus* in a hotel dinner theater in Billings, Montana, after some cast members were sidelined with food poisoning. Boyd actually managed to pull it off, delivering three distinct performances, even when he was the only one on stage. I've kept my eye out for Boyd's shows during my travels and ended up seeing him in productions all over the country. He has a broad range, as well as an ability to perform in the worst possible circumstances. I once saw Boyd hold the audience spellbound in a dinner theater production of *One Flew Over the Cuckoo's Nest* in El Paso, and in the middle of a key dramatic scene he performed the Heimlich maneuver on a woman choking on a buffalo wing without breaking character."

"Good to know in case I get a chunk of apple pie stuck in my throat tonight."

"You scoff, but at the rate you're shoveling the food in you might need his help. Do you ever chew anything?"

"Excuse me, but I'm starving. I didn't have caviar and hot fudge sundaes on my flight." She cut her eyes to Boyd. "So how did this amazing actor end up exiled to the dinner theater circuit?"

"He's a nut. He won't compromise on his artistic vision. Early in his career he was offered a big break, the chance to be the new voice of Casper the Friendly Ghost, but he got fired when he insisted on playing the character in anguish and misery. He told the director that Casper was a dead child, for God's sake, what does he have to be happy-go-lucky about? More recently, he was hired for a beer commercial, and he said he needed to know the background of his character. Did he graduate from college? Was he married? What was his ethnic background? The director screamed at him to just drink the freaking beer, and Boyd walked off the set. He said he couldn't create under the existing circumstances."

"Now he's here as Willy Loman, in Cape Girardeau," Kate said.

"Yep," Nick said. "Check him out."

Kate pushed aside thoughts of more lemon meringue pie and found herself completely captivated by Boyd's performance. It was as if he was infusing Willy Loman with his own lifetime of disappointments, unfulfilled dreams, and unmet potential. It was a genuinely moving performance.

"You're right," Kate said when the play was over. "He's good."

"He's better than that," Nick said. "He's a natural grifter, he just doesn't know it yet. He's going to join our band of merry men."

Kate felt the gravy and grits slide around in her stomach. This was the first step on the road to hell. Kate's original assignment from Jessup had been to watch over Nick and make sure he was kept out of harm's way. Now, as the con was beginning to unfold, she realized she was going to have to play a role in it. There was no room for an observer in the con. There was only room for participants. She was going to help Nick persuade this poor schmuck to enter a life of crime. And she shuddered to think what she'd be called upon to do in the future. Not that she hadn't done some morally questionable things in the past, depending on how you felt about shooting at people and home invasion in foreign countries. Granted they were all legal military operations, but some people (and even possibly God) might find them unsavory. And then there were smaller transgressions, like cheating on her final algebra exam in tenth grade and wearing a push-up bra for Megan's wedding so her breasts could compete with her sister's.

Nick intercepted Boyd as he was leaving the stage and asked him to join them to discuss Boyd's possible participation in a new production in Los Angeles.

"You bet. Give me five minutes," Boyd said. "I need to get out of character."

Boyd joined Nick and Kate after he'd removed his makeup and made a pass through the buffet line. His plate was loaded, and Kate was pretty sure he had a few rolls stuffed into his pockets. He was good-looking, she thought, but in a slightly dated way, like last year's model of a sports car immediately after the sleeker, redesigned model has come out. And he moved as if there was a spotlight following him. Even his littlest gestures, whether it was putting his napkin into his lap or reaching for his silverware, had flamboyance, as though he was aware, or at least hoping, that people were watching his every move. Not entirely attractive in a man, but oddly compelling to watch.

Nick introduced himself without giving a last name. "And this is my associate, Kate," he said.

"What did you think of my performance?" Boyd asked Kate. "I was a little worried I might have played the ending with too much intensity."

"No way," Kate said. "You were great. I don't know how you were able to keep focused with all those people walking in front of the stage on their way to the buffet."

Boyd pulled a roll and two pats of butter out of his pocket and set them beside his plate. "You have to be a bit delusional to be an actor. In my mind, I wasn't in a restaurant performing on a plywood stage with grocery store cashiers, car salesmen, and college students," he said. "I was Willy Loman, desperately trying to hold on to a life that was coming unglued. That was my world and I totally believed it."

"I did, too," Kate said.

"I couldn't ask for a better review," he said, buttering the roll, "particularly from a Hollywood producer."

"We aren't Hollywood producers," Nick said.

Boyd looked up from his buttering. "I thought you said you were producing a show in Los Angeles."

"We are, but it's not like anything you've been involved with before," Nick told him. "We are operatives with Intertect, a private security and detective agency, and we're on the trail of an international fugitive who has stolen a great deal of money that we want to recover for our client."

"What do you need an actor for?"

"To find this man we have to make one of his accomplices talk, and to do that we have to make him an actor in a play, only he'll be the only one on the stage who doesn't have a script."

"He won't even know it's a show," Kate said.

Boyd set his roll aside and took up a drumstick. "You're talking about running a con."

"You're very perceptive," Nick said.

"I did six weeks as Harold Hill in *The Music Man* at the Loon Lake Casino," he said. "The thing is, cons are usually illegal."

"Think of this as an elaborate practical joke," Nick said.

"Exactly," Kate said. "A practical joke that is sort of illegal but not entirely. We've been asked to do what the police can't, and that's catch a man who has robbed thousands of people out of their homes, their savings, and their retirements. We're using kidnapping and fraud to accomplish that goal. If we don't fool the mark, and he goes to the police, we could all get arrested."

"But it's highly unlikely that he will," Nick said.

Boyd gnawed on his drumstick. "What's in it for me?"

"Fifty thousand dollars," Nick said. "And the role of a lifetime, an acting challenge greater than any Oscar, Emmy, or Tony award winner has ever dared or attempted."

"Because the Oscar, Emmy, and Tony award winners don't have to," Boyd said.

"But we both know that they wouldn't because they don't have the guts or the skills, and you will because you do," Nick said. "And this will prove it."

Boyd sat back and looked at them. "And nobody will ever know."

"You will," Nick said.

"There won't be any reviews, no film to put on my reel," he said. "It won't get me more work."

"It might from us," Kate said.

"But if I am not utterly convincing in my performance, or another actor lets me down, or a set falls, or some other calamity happens that I can't act my way out of, I could get thrown in jail."

"Or worse," Nick said, "you could spend another night performing here."

Boyd met his gaze. "How big is my trailer?"

"You won't have a trailer," Nick said. "But you will have a mansion."

"I'm in," Boyd said. "I don't think I caught your last names."

"We're on a first-name basis," Nick said. "Last names are cumbersome."

13

Wilma Owens could drive, steer, or pilot just about anything that moved people from one point to another—cars, planes, boats, Zambonis, motorcycles, bulldozers, helicopters, steamrollers—with the possible exception of the Space Shuttle, not that she wasn't game to give it a try. She'd grown up in Alvin, Texas, living in a double-wide next to her daddy's auto body shop. She raced motocross and dirt track stock cars, and got a job straight out of high school driving a dump truck for Owens Excavating. Two years down the road she married the owner's son, Buster Owens, and since they didn't have any luck getting Wilma pregnant, she kept driving the dump truck. After twenty-six years of marriage and dump truck driving, Wilma divorced Buster, citing terminal boredom. She got a couple double-D implants that perked up her boobs, joined a spin class, and set out on what she'd named The Big Adventure.

Nine years into The Big Adventure, Wilma was finding it hard to get a job driving heavy equipment what with the economy in the toilet and her not belonging to a union. She'd had a short stint flying tourists over the Everglades until she crashed her plane in the swamp and it was discovered she wasn't licensed to fly. Ditto the job she wrangled flying a helicopter, spraying toxic chemicals over mosquito-infested Port Charlotte.

It was while Wilma was recovering from the helicopter crash that she got the idea to be a contestant on *The Amazing Race.* She figured she was a cinch to win, since she'd be good as new as soon as they took the pins out of her broken ankle. She'd win *The Amazing Race,* and she'd be rich and famous. She'd buy a sweet piece of land somewhere with her winnings, and maybe she'd buy a backhoe to drive around. And it might have happened too if Wilma hadn't had a stroke of bad luck.

Wilma and her best friend, Loretta Sue, were inches from making the last cut for *The Amazing Race* when it was discovered that Wilma had "borrowed" a freight train to make the tryouts on time when her Ford crapped out. Loretta Sue was let go on a technicality, being she wasn't the one driving the borrowed train. Wilma was arraigned in Solano County court, where she was represented by a public defender. Bail was set at $35,000, but it might as well have been $350,000. There was no way Wilma could raise the cash, so she was remanded to a cell at the Solano County jail in Fairfield to await trial. It would be an enormous understatement to say that she was stunned when a deputy came to her cell, where she'd been sitting for six weeks, and told her that her bail had been posted and she was free to go.

Two days before, Nick had been in Cape Girardeau. Now here he was on a bench outside Solano County's Romanesque courthouse, which was set back from the palm-lined street behind a large crabgrass lawn. He watched Wilma walk out of the courthouse and knew he'd made a good choice. She'd be perfect for his purposes. She was another natural grifter. She was fearless. She had talent. She was desperate.

He recognized her from her picture in the paper. Average height and average weight except for the boobs. The boobs weren't average. She was wearing skintight jeans, a poison-green tank top, and platform raffia-wrapped wedge sandals that had about a five-inch heel. She had bleached-out blond hair pulled into a haystack ponytail. She was in her mid-fifties, but thanks to her boob job and either good genes or some nip and tuck she looked younger. If the light was dim enough and her date was drunk enough, she might even pass for late thirties.

Nick stood and waved to her, and she walked over to him.

"Hey, hon," she said. "Were you waving at me? And is that a bag of candy you're holding? Isn't that kind of a cliché?"

"They're jelly beans fresh from the Jelly Belly factory here in town. While I was waiting for your bail to be processed, I took the tour. They've got a portrait of Ronald Reagan made out of jelly beans. Just think, if jelly beans had been around in Leonardo da Vinci's time, the *Mona Lisa* might look very different today."

She looked him up and down. "So you're the one who bailed me out?"

"Yep."

"Well, you're cute as a button and you got a bag of jelly beans. A girl couldn't ask for much more. I'm guessing you're a Hollywood producer sent by *The Amazing Race*. They changed their minds, right?"

"Wrong."

"Then what's the deal?"

"I want you to drive cars and fly airplanes for a project I'm putting together."

"My driver's license was revoked and I don't have a pilot's license," she said.

"A license is just a piece of paper. It means nothing to me. What I care about is that you're a quick learner, you can steer anything, and you're willing to take chances."

"And I'd want to drive these cars and airplanes for you why?"

"I got you out of jail, and I can make the criminal charges against you go away."

"How can you do that?"

"I have friends in very high places in law enforcement," Nick said.

"What if I decide to walk away right now?"

"I lose thirty-five thousand dollars," Nick said.

"And I'll have you chasing me? Not that I'd mind, being you're a little hottie, but still . . ."

Nick shook his head. "I don't chase people. I do, however, swindle them. That's what this is all about. I want you to help me trick a man into telling me where to find an international fugitive who has stolen half a billion dollars."

"So you can take the money?"

"So I can give it back to the people he took it from," he said.

"What are you, one of those Robin Hood do-gooders?"

"No. It's a job."

He took a key out of his pocket and aimed it at a red Ferrari F12 Berlinetta, the most powerful car ever built by the Italian automaker, capable of going from zero to 120 miles per hour in 8.5

seconds, thanks to a 730 horsepower V12 engine and 509 pound-feet of torque. The car chirped and Wilma sucked in air.

He dangled the keys in front of her. "Want to drive?"

She snatched them from his hand. "I'm in. And you can call me Willie."

While Nick Fox was handing the keys to a $375,000 car to Willie Owens, the zombie apocalypse was beginning in the desert outside of Gallup, New Mexico. It was a very low-budget nonunion apocalypse, written and directed by a twenty-seven-year-old whose prior filmmaking experience was a series of viral videos of drunk girls taking their tops off at Lake Havasu during spring break.

The job of making the two dozen amateur actors look like decaying zombies hell-bent on eating human flesh fell to Chet Kershaw, a big bear of a man who, at thirty-eight years old, had come to the sobering conclusion that he was an aging dinosaur facing imminent extinction.

It was cruel and ironic that he was having this epiphany while sitting in the western-themed bar at the El Rancho Motel. The motel had been built in Gallup in 1937 by the brother of director D. W. Griffith to cater to all the big-name Hollywood directors and actors who were flocking to this dramatically photogenic patch of desert to shoot westerns. Perhaps Chet's realization of his bleak future was hitting him with such force because Chet was sitting exactly where Errol Flynn, John Wayne, Kirk Douglas, and John Ford had once washed the sand out of their throats.

Among the many filmmakers who came to Gallup in those early days was Chet's grandfather Cleveland Kershaw. He was one of the greats in the art of movie makeup and related special effects. Cleveland passed along the experience, skills, and tricks that he knew to his son, Carson, who carried on the family business in film and TV well into the 1980s.

But by the time Chet took over the family business in the 1990s, his art was quickly becoming a software application. More and more makeup effects, and virtually everything that was once considered a "special effect," including simple gunshots and bullet hits, were being done in postproduction using computer graphics.

Even location shooting and the fake streets on studio back lots were becoming a thing of the past. A director didn't have to go to New Mexico to get the desert look. He could shoot in Calgary in the dead of winter. All he needed was a green screen and a digital effects company. Now if directors came to New Mexico to shoot, it was because of the generous production tax credits and rebates, known in Hollywood as "free money," offered by a state government desperate to stimulate the local economy. Which was one reason why *Revolt of the Zombie Strippers* was being shot in Gallup and not in a warehouse in Van Nuys. The other reason was that the producers of the film were so incredibly cheap, they couldn't afford even the simplest digital effects.

But, sadly, they could afford Chet, who was finding it harder and harder to get work that took advantage of his many skills. So he'd schlepped from L.A. to the hellhole of Gallup just for the pleasure of plying his trade. He didn't want to spend his days in a trailer powdering noses and applying concealer to the Botoxed faces of aging actresses for shit wages. Instead, he was out in the blazing desert sun making a bunch of young strippers look like decomposing brain-hungry corpses for even worse wages.

The usually jovial Chet might have found the decomposing

strippers amusing if he wasn't so miserably depressed. And then he looked up from the bottom of his fourth beer and noticed Kate sitting on the bar stool next to him. He had no idea how long she'd been there, studying him with undisguised curiosity.

"Can I buy you another beer?" she asked, gesturing to his empty glass.

It was an unbelievable question. No woman in a bar had ever offered to buy him a drink before, and while he wasn't painful to the eyes, he knew he wasn't Sam Worthington or Chris Hemsworth either. "Are you a hooker?"

"I don't think hookers buy men drinks," Kate said. "I think it works the other way around."

"I haven't got a lot of experience with hookers."

"Me neither. Do you want the beer?"

"Sure," he said. "Thanks."

They sat in awkward silence until two fresh mugs of beer were set in front of them.

"Cheers," Kate said, hoisting her mug.

They clinked glasses and Chet chugged his down. "I meant no offense."

"None taken," Kate said.

Chet wiped his mouth with the back of his hand. "I'm recently divorced and I guess I've forgotten how to talk to women. Then again, seeing how things went with my ex, maybe I've never known. What brings you to Gallup?"

"You," she said, and told him basically the same story they'd given Boyd Capwell two days before. "We need your makeup and special effects skills to convince our mark that what is happening is real."

"I'm in," he said.

"Wait a minute," she said, startled. "You don't even know what we're willing to pay."

"Has to be more than what I'm getting now," he said. "Plus you bought me a beer."

"Has it occurred to you that what we are proposing is most likely illegal, and if things go wrong you could be arrested?"

"Lady, jail can't be any worse than this hellhole I'm in now."

14

If George Pogue had a mustache, he would have been twirling it like a silent-film villain. In the absence of a mustache, the pale, balding banker sat behind his desk, tapping his pen on a bulging file folder, looking at Tom Underhill as if he was an unpleasant smudge on his calendar. To Tom, the tapping of the pen sounded like the ticking of a stopwatch, counting down the seconds until his home was taken away from him, his wife, and their three children.

"I'm not asking for a free ride," said Tom, dressed in his best suit and tie. He wanted to impress the banker with his professionalism, but he felt like a kid trying to pretend he was a grown-up. "I am willing to make payments."

"How gracious of you," Pogue said.

"All I ask is that you adjust the principal to take into account the reality of the marketplace. We both know that the house isn't worth much more than half what I paid for it."

When Tom bought the house in 2006, it was at the height of the Southern California housing market, and $557,000 seemed like a steal for four bedrooms and two baths in Rancho Cucamonga, a rapidly expanding suburban community in San Bernardino County. Thousands of houses were spreading across the valley and creeping up the hillsides toward Mount Baldy. But then the housing bubble burst, the market took a dive, and jobs in the area evaporated. Entire housing tracts became ghost towns.

"But the fact remains, five hundred fifty-seven thousand dollars is what we paid the builder on your behalf," Pogue said. "That is cash that is now gone. I fail to see why the bank should take the loss."

"Because I was stuck in a subprime loan with an adjustable interest rate that skyrocketed. Every six months it jumped up, even as my income was going down. I repeatedly tried to renegotiate the terms, but you wouldn't let me."

Pogue held up his hand in a halting gesture. "I don't need to hear the litany of excuses or your version of events. The fact is, you have fallen woefully behind in your mortgage payments."

"I've sent you a check every month, but you haven't cashed the last four of them."

"Because the amount you are sending doesn't meet the minimum payment due."

"It's what I can afford," he said. "It's what my payments were before you kept jacking up the interest rate."

Pogue waved off the remark. "It has come to the point that we have no choice but to exercise our right to seize the property and auction it off to recoup our losses."

Tom took a deep breath, trying to control his anger. He didn't want to be on the eleven o'clock news that night, depicted as the angry black man who threw himself across a desk and strangled a white banker.

"Instead of listing the house for half what I paid for it, and then letting it sit vacant for years while squatters and vandals strip the place," Tom said, "wouldn't it make more sense to just lower the loan amount to that same figure so that I can afford to stay in my home, maintain the property, and provide you with cash flow?"

"It's more complex than that," Pogue said.

"It certainly is," Nick Fox said, taking the seat beside Tom and directing his remark to Pogue. Nick was dressed in a navy blue blazer, an open-collared shirt, jeans, and loafers, and he seemed to have appeared out of thin air. "What Tom doesn't realize is that you talked him out of making a down payment, making him ineligible for a more attractive interest rate, and steered him into a subprime loan back in 2006, even though he had a FICO score of 690 and a forty-five percent debt-to-loan ratio, because you personally earned a two percent higher commission from those loans over prime mortgages. You also got bonuses, and all-expenses-paid trips to Hawaii, from the bank based on how many subprime mortgages you moved."

"I don't know what kind of crackpot activist you are, or what kind of stunt this is, but if you don't leave right now, I'll have security drag you out," Pogue said.

Nick calmly continued. "Not only that, you gouged him on fees. Shame on you, George. Or would you prefer I called you 'Le Chiffre'?"

Pogue went pale. "Who are you?"

"I'm the man you've lost nearly forty-five thousand dollars to over the last few months playing online poker," Nick said. His most recent win against Le Chiffre had come during his short stay in Bois-le-Roi.

Pogue stared at Nick as if he had risen from the dead. "You're Bret Maverick."

"At the online poker table, yes, that's me. But right now, you can call me your conscience. Because here's what else I know, George. You covered those gambling losses, and others totaling another twenty-three thousand dollars, by embezzling funds from this bank."

"What do you want?" George whispered, waving at Nick to keep his voice down.

"You're going to modify Tom's loan to reflect the true market value of his home and offer him the lowest available interest rate with no refinancing charges whatsoever. You're going to credit him for making all of his payments to date and you will erase any penalties. And you're going to repair his credit rating, all by this time tomorrow when he comes back in to sign the papers, or I will turn you in to the authorities."

George glanced around again, and then whispered, "What about the other matter?"

"It'll be our little secret. My advice would be to put back what you took and hope nobody ever finds out what you did. If you're thinking about making a run for it, that's fine, but you'd better make things right for Tom before you go, because I will find you and I won't be as understanding next time." Nick turned to Tom, who was staring at him in shock. "Can I buy you a cup of coffee?"

Tom was so dumbfounded by this unexpected turn of events that all he could do was nod. Nick ushered Tom out and led him to the Starbucks next door. They got their coffees and took a table outside. A number of the properties in the strip mall were vacant, and the parking lot was mostly empty, but Starbucks was busy. The sun was shining in a brilliant blue sky, and Tom was grateful for the warmth soaking into his shirt after the frigid air in Pogue's office.

When Tom Underhill was a kid, he'd lived in a place not unlike this, a seemingly ever-expanding suburban housing tract that gobbled up the walnut orchards that gave his hometown of Walnut Creek its name. He'd been fascinated by the construction, especially since nobody in his family worked with their hands. The family business was insurance. So each day Tom climbed the walnut tree in his backyard and spent hours watching the houses go up, making detailed drawings of every stage of construction. He salvaged scrap wood, borrowed some basic tools, and built a rambling multilevel treehouse in his backyard.

Tom's friends went on to college after high school, but Tom kept building treehouses. He moved to Southern California, and the treehouses turned profitable. He added playhouses to his repertoire and his business boomed. He was famous for his miniature Victorian houses and Swiss Family Robinson tree forts, and for his ability to replicate virtually anything in reduced size. Unfortunately the playhouses weren't cheap, and the playhouse bubble burst when the housing bubble burst and the global economy took a nosedive. Now Tom scrounged up work as a handyman while his wife took care of their kids, ages two, eight, and ten. What Nick had just done for him was a miracle, but it didn't solve all of his problems. And his fear was that he might have fallen into an even bigger, more awful problem.

"I don't mean to seem ungrateful," Tom said, "but who are you, and why did you just do that?"

"I stepped in because you're a magician with a hammer, nails, and a pile of wood and I want to convince you to work for me," Nick said.

"I'm not that hard to convince and there are easier ways to hire someone."

"This is not a typical job. For starters, I need someone who can transform a Palm Springs vacation home into a drug lord's fortified compound in Mexico."

"Okay, that's a little off the map."

Nick gave him the short-form explanation.

"You saved my house from being taken by a sleazy banker who tricked me into a crap loan, and now you're asking me if I'll help you take down an even bigger, sleazier banker who ran off with people's life savings?"

"You don't owe me anything," Nick said. "You can walk away right now, and maybe you should, because there are people who'd call what I'm proposing illegal."

"Don't care," Tom said. "I'm going to love taking that son of a bitch down. Count me in."

Two days after Nick enlisted Tom Underhill, Kate stopped by her sister's place at midafternoon. She'd hoped to catch her father while Megan was away, but her timing wasn't perfect. Kate pulled up just as Megan was leaving in her huge Toyota Sienna for a Costco run with the kids. They rolled down their windows and talked to each other from their driver's seats.

"Good news," Megan said. "The hunky airline pilot is back in town. I told him all about you and he's very interested."

"I'm not."

"He didn't even blink when I told him you're an FBI agent," Megan said. "Usually that sends them running."

"Usually?" Kate said. "How many men have you talked to about me?"

"It doesn't matter. Can I give him your number?"

"No!"

"Your loss. What are you doing here?"

"I'm taking Dad to the shooting range," Kate said.

"This is his nap time."

"He takes naps?"

"In case you haven't noticed, he's a senior citizen and he's still recovering from the sport fishing trip to Mexico he took with his army buddies."

Kate knew that was his cover for going to Greece with her. "It's okay, I'm sure that shooting at things relaxes him almost as much as a nap."

Megan drove off and Kate pulled into the driveway. Kate hadn't planned on taking her dad shooting, but since that was the excuse she'd given her sister, they went to the range together anyway. It was very relaxing for them both. Afterward, she ran the broad outlines of the con and her misgivings about it past him over a couple beers at a bar on Ventura Boulevard in Woodland Hills.

"Sounds like a winner to me," Jake said. "And even if it goes to hell, it's not like you're going to be backed against a wall in some third-world country and executed by an army of illiterate rapists that the bozos at the CIA, in their infinite wisdom, armed with U.S. weapons."

"But I could end up in prison."

He waved off her concern. "I'd break you out."

"You'd do that for me?"

"You're my daughter, aren't you?"

Kate smiled. Sure, he'd missed a lot of Christmases and birthdays during her childhood, but not many fathers could be counted on to mount a prison break.

15

When Neal Burnside was a kid, he wanted to be Superman. Over the years, especially those he'd spent as a federal prosecutor, he decided that fighting a never-ending battle for truth, justice, and the American way was a lousy line of work if you weren't born on Krypton. By Burnside's thinking, the Man of Steel could afford to be the all-American hero because his overhead was low. He didn't have to pay a mortgage, property taxes, or even utilities on his Fortress of Solitude. He also didn't have to deal with any crap. He could leap tall buildings in a single bound, change the course of mighty rivers, and bend steel with his bare hands without having to worry about FAA regulations, environmental impact reports, or union contracts. And at the end of the day, he could be satisfied going home with Clark Kent's paltry paycheck because he knew he'd won clear, unambiguous victories.

Burnside never reached the Clark Kent level of satisfaction as a federal prosecutor, because after a couple cases Burnside realized he didn't so much care about the clear, unambiguous victories. Burnside cared about the money. And federal prosecutors didn't make much money. So Burnside had no regrets or moral qualms about leaving the Justice Department and becoming a criminal defense attorney, trading his Men's Wearhouse suits for Tom Ford, his Chevy Malibu for a Maserati Quattroporte, and his two-bedroom Culver City apartment for a secluded Bel Air mansion.

As far as truth and justice goes, he'd decided those were flexible concepts that depended entirely on a person's social and political standing, and how much money they earned. That's why he didn't represent accused murderers, child molesters, kidnappers, or rapists unless they happened to be movie stars, major sports figures, or CEOs of Fortune 500 companies.

Burnside's sleep aid of choice was a big steak dinner washed down by a bottle of excellent wine with a chaser of sex. Tonight he was presently about to move on to the chaser stage. He was at Mastro's in Beverly Hills with a woman he'd "friended" on Facebook and was seeing in the flesh for the first time. And there was a lot of flesh to see because she was wearing a skintight, very low cut, slit-sleeve little black dress that might as well have been painted on her knockout body. She'd devoured her steak, lobster mashed potatoes, and a whole side of mushrooms like a mountain man and hadn't gone slinking away to the bathroom to cough it back up, which Burnside took as a very good sign. In his experience, a woman with a voracious appetite for food also had one for sex. Okay, maybe she was a little older than he'd expected, but she was hot all the same, and he wasn't in the mood to start over searching out a good time at this hour.

The older woman happened to be Wilma Owens, off and running on her first assignment. Willie was full of steak and lobster and looking forward to rounding out her night by getting behind the wheel of Burnside's Maserati and delivering Burnside to Nick.

"Well, my goodness, will you look at this car," Willie said, jiggling her double-Ds in the excitement of the moment, almost giving Burnside an on-the-spot stiffy, as the restaurant valet pulled up with Burnside's Maserati Quattroporte. "I'd do anything to drive this car," Willie told Burnside. "*Anything.*"

"Sounds like a good deal to me," Burnside said, taking the shotgun seat. "Just be careful. This is a high-powered car."

"Sugar, I'm a high-powered kind of girl. Hold on to your hat. We're gonna have fun."

Willie put the pedal to the floor and Burnside sucked air as she blasted through the streets of Beverly Hills, down Sunset Boulevard, and up into Bel Air like she was racing in the Monaco Grand Prix, hugging the curves, weaving through traffic, and never slowing for anything.

"Sweetie, this is just like being back on the dirt tracks in Texas," she said to Burnside. "I'm lovin' this. I'm downright moist."

Burnside was approaching moist too, but he was trying to control himself. By the time the car came to a screeching, sudden halt at the end of the long circular driveway in front of his house, he felt like he'd already run the bases and was ready to slide home. Apparently his date felt the same way, because she turned, grabbed his face in her hands, and gave him a kiss that nearly set his clothes on fire.

"I like the way you drive," he said.

"I'm just getting started."

Burnside would have dragged her across the console and done the deed without even unbuckling his seat belt, but Willie was already halfway to his front door.

"Come on, hot stuff," she said. "I can't wait much longer. If you don't hurry up and get out of the car, I'm gonna have to start without you."

Burnside's sprawling one-story home, with its white-gravel roof, floor-to-ceiling windows, and Jet Age angles, was set back far from the street. Designed by some once-beloved, now-dead architect, it was considered a classic example of early 1960s modernism. Burnside had bought the house and saved it from the wrecking ball not because he believed in the preservation of historic architecture but for the publicity and the stature of living in a famous property. The truth was, he hated the house, which was dated and poorly designed, and he often regretted not leveling it when he had the chance. Tonight his thoughts weren't of the house when he punched his code into the security panel and unlocked the front door. His thoughts were about burying his face in the double-Ds.

He led Willie inside and slammed the door shut, and she grabbed him again and pulled him into a kiss. Burnside pressed her back against the wall and was hiking up her dress when he felt her suddenly stiffen, and not in a good way. She was looking at something over his shoulder. He was just registering that when someone yanked him away from her and backhanded him across the face.

He staggered back, momentarily stunned at the sight of two men with black ski masks over their faces, holding him at gunpoint. His first reaction wasn't fear but anger, and not toward the armed intruders but at the high-end security company that had installed his outrageously expensive, and supposedly state-of-the art, alarm system. I will sue them into oblivion, he thought.

Willie was frozen against the wall, staring at the man nearest Burnside in wide-eyed terror.

"What do you want?" Burnside asked.

The man pointed his gun at Willie and shot her in the forehead, killing her instantly. Burnside's gasp of horror was louder than the muffled gunshot, which had a deceptively gentle, pneumatic sound. Willie's head slammed back against the wall with a *thunk*, and she slid lifelessly to the floor, leaving a wide streak of blood.

Burnside stared at her and backed away, holding his hands up in front of him and waving them as if that simple gesture would, like shaking an Etch A Sketch, just make it all go away. "No, no, no."

His attention was so focused on the shooter who'd blithely killed Willie that he wasn't aware of the other man next to him until he was jabbed with a stun gun. And then he wasn't aware of much at all because fifty thousand volts coursed through him. He felt heat, heard something go *zing* in his brain, and he was on the floor staring up at the ceiling. His mind made an attempt to reboot, but his body lagged behind, and his first clear thought in that helpless moment was the hope that his sphincters had held.

He was dragged outside as a black panel van roared up his circular driveway and slid to a stop on the far side of his car, just past his front steps. One of the hooded men opened the back doors of the van, and Burnside was about to get tossed inside when a woman shouted at them:

"Halt, FBI."

While the scene that was unfolding was a fake, the FBI part was true, because the FBI agent was Kate.

The two men dropped Burnside, whirled around, and exchanged

gunfire with Kate. The shooter nearest to Burnside took a hit and was blasted clear off his feet and into the side of the van, his chest covered in blood. Scrambled neurons notwithstanding, Burnside made a feeble, uncoordinated attempt to crawl for cover. Car doors slammed, more shots were fired, and the van sped away.

Kate looked down at Burnside. "If you want to live you'll do exactly what I say."

She pulled him to his feet and dragged him down the driveway toward the street, where her Crown Victoria was parked, the engine running. She opened the door to the backseat. "Get on the floor."

"What?"

"On the floor!"

Kate shoved him into the car and slammed the door shut. She ran around to the driver's side, jumped behind the wheel, and floored it, the tires burning rubber and the rear fishtailing as she fled the scene.

"Who are you?" Burnside asked.

"FBI. Are you okay?"

He did a quick check of his body. There were no injuries, and he hadn't peed his pants. His body and his dignity were intact. Thank God for that.

"Yes, I'm fine, but they killed my date."

"Of course they did. They never leave witnesses. Anything with a pulse gets put down. If you had a goldfish, they would have killed that, too. Do you have a cell phone on you?"

He felt around in his pockets and found his phone. "Yes."

"Toss it onto the front passenger seat," she said.

He flipped the phone over the seat and Kate threw it out her open window.

"What? Why?" he said.

"Do you want to live?"

"Yes, of course," Burnside said.

"Then do as I tell you. If they are tracking your cell phone, then another hit squad is closing in on us right now, so we only have a few minutes head start. Give me your shoes."

"My shoes?"

"You heard me. Your shoes. And your jacket, too. Make it fast."

He slipped them all off and handed them to her, and she tossed the whole bundle out the window.

"What did you do that for?" he asked. "What was the point to that?"

"In case they slipped a tracking device into your shoes or the lining of your jacket." She shook her head. "Have you forgotten everything you learned as a prosecutor?"

He fought back the bile rising up in his throat. It wasn't the horror of what he'd witnessed or delayed anxiety that was making him sick—it was her driving. She was no Wilma.

"Who are they?" he asked.

"The Viboras."

Burnside felt like he'd been jabbed with a stun gun again. One that delivered fifty thousand volts of raw, primal fear. He knew all about the Viboras. They'd started out as a dozen Mexican soldiers trained by the U.S. Army to be elite narco-commandos. But the dirty dozen went rogue in 1998 to become protectors and enforcers for the Gulf Cartel, then turned on their masters. They used their U.S. military training and the tricks of the drug trade that they'd learned from the cartel to create their own criminal organization and declare war on their competitors. They quickly amassed ten thousand soldiers and became known for the horrific scale of their atrocities, like decapitating dozens of their rivals and putting their heads on stakes along a popular smuggling route, and their willingness to blithely kill civilians, massacring entire villages with any ties to rival cartels.

The Viboras' influence, and their terrifying use of violence, spread beyond Mexico's borders into the United States, where they made inroads by recruiting, arming, and training urban street gangs.

The Viboras were like rabid dogs, but Neal Burnside had no idea how they'd picked up his scent. He'd never gone after the Viboras when he was a federal prosecutor, and he'd never represented one of them—or, worse, one of their rivals—in his years as a criminal defense attorney.

"This is a big mistake," he said. "I haven't had any dealings with any of the Mexican drug cartels. What do they want with me?"

"They want their money back," she said.

"I don't have it."

"But Derek Griffin does," she said.

16

While Burnside was cowering behind his car for cover and Kate was shooting blanks at Nick and Chet, Willie slipped around the corner of the house and replaced Tom Underhill in the driver's seat of the van.

Nick jumped into the van beside Chet, who was the gunman who'd pretended to be blown off his feet by Kate's shot, and closed the door. Willie put the van in gear and drove off.

"This is a real step down after that Maserati," she said. "It's like driving a lawn mower."

"Good, you won't be tempted to speed," Nick said, sitting down on the floor across from a grinning Chet Kershaw.

"That was awesome," Chet said.

Nick relaxed back against the side of the van. "Thanks to your Hollywood magic."

"Bullet hits and exploding blood packs are old school," Chet said. "My granddaddy was doing them before I was born. This was easy."

Nick had designed it to be easy. He was working with an amateur civilian crew and had no idea how they'd react once the hustle was in play. He'd purposely devised the moves so he wouldn't push the crew too far beyond their comfortable fields of expertise, and that included Kate. All he'd asked them to do was what they already did well. The only one outside his element now was Tom Underhill, but he'd simply been required to drive the van into the driveway, park it at the right angle to mask Willie's escape, and position it for a quick exit to the street. With a wife and three kids, Tom had plenty of practice driving an SUV and dealing with distractions. Everything else, at least from Nick's perspective, had been basic. He hadn't bothered trying to hack Burnside's alarm system. He'd simply bumped the locks on the back door, waited for Burnside to disarm the system himself, and then, while Willie was groping Burnside, he and Chet rushed in.

Tom turned up the police band radio under the dash, tuning in to the constant stream of dispatch orders and cop chatter. "Are you listening to the police band?" he asked Nick. "They're after us. One of the neighbors reported gunshots and gave a description of the van to the police. Black-and-whites and a chopper are on their way."

"It's okay," Nick said. "We have an escape plan."

"I've never been chased by the police before," Tom said.

"You aren't being chased," Nick said. "The van is."

"I'm in the van," Tom said.

"They don't know that," Nick told him.

Willie drove west on Sunset, skirting the northern perimeter of the UCLA campus, and Chet pulled off his bloodied shirt and removed the exploded blood bags that were taped to his chest. They were crossing the intersection of Sunset and Stone Canyon Road when they heard the dispatcher notifying patrol cars in the area that a van matching the description of the one reported by Burnside's neighbor had been spotted by the chopper heading west on Sunset toward Westwood Plaza Drive. Willie made a hard left into the UCLA campus and sped down the long ramp into the parking structure beneath the athletic field. A soccer game was going on and there were thousands of fans in the stands.

No one was talking now. Tom and Chet were hanging on to their seats with white knuckles, listening to the dispatcher announce that patrol cars were seconds away. Willie was in the zone, concentrating on executing turns in the cumbersome van. Nick was watching his crew, confident in the outcome, knowing they would sail through the garage entrance because he'd purchased a parking permit in advance.

Willie parked at an angle in a loading zone. It was a spot Nick picked so the van would block the surveillance camera aimed at the elevator and stairwell. Everyone grabbed a gym bag, burst out of the van, ran to the stairwell, and stuffed themselves into UCLA Bruins shirts, sweats, and hats. They dumped the bags in the trash, bolted up the stairs, split up, and disappeared into the crowd watching the game just as police cars drove into the parking structure and the chopper circled overhead.

Topanga Canyon runs through the Santa Monica Mountains between the San Fernando Valley and the beach. It's a secluded, deeply wooded enclave that became known in the 1960s as a bohemian hideaway for artists, poets, actors, beatniks, hippies, lesbians, communists, and anyone else who delighted in being cast as a rebel, radical, or outsider. And for the most part, that was how Topanga Canyon had remained, a place where the sound of tinkling wind chimes drowned out the birds, where the air was redolent with incense, and where you could still find braless women wearing tie-dye shirts and flowers in their hair driving VW Beetles.

Kate drove Burnside deep into the canyon toward a cabin that was at the end of a dirt trail, far from any neighbors, even farther from a paved road, and surrounded by tall trees and dry, overgrown brush.

The one-bedroom cabin was a fire waiting to happen. And if it did, it would be history repeating itself. The cabin had been badly damaged in the Malibu fire a decade ago and abandoned ever since, mired in a complicated legal dispute among the owners, the bank, and the insurance company. It was perfect for Nick's needs. He had Tom Underhill fix it up, patch the roof, install a generator, and make sure the water, electrical, and septic systems were working.

Kate's Crown Vic wasn't made to be driven hard over unpaved roads and it bounced like a boat on a stormy sea, but Burnside didn't complain. He'd been silent ever since their discussion about the Viboras and Derek Griffin. She was glad for that, but knew the questions would be coming soon. He was a former prosecutor and she expected to be grilled like a hostile witness on the stand.

Okay by her. She was ready for it. Nick and the crew had spent the last eight weeks prepping for the con, acquiring the resources, building the sets, finding the properties they needed, and rehearsing their parts.

She turned off the ignition and headlights and sat in the car for a moment, listening and observing, making sure there was no one around. The cabin was dark, the drapes drawn. The generator hummed in the otherwise quiet area.

Burnside sat up slowly. His hair was mussed, his face pale. "Where are we?"

"One of our safe houses," she said. "It's totally off the grid."

Kate got out of the car, gun and flashlight in hand, and checked the perimeter of the cabin. Burnside opened his door, leaned out, and vomited up everything he'd eaten at Mastro's.

Kate returned to Burnside, her feet crunching on the gravel and dry twigs. "It's all clear."

"Do you have shoes for me?"

"No, but you don't need them," she said. "You're not going on any walks." She'd taken his shoes to make sure of that.

"How am I supposed to get to the cabin?"

"Man up, for God's sake," she said, turning her back on him.

Burnside closed the door, slid across the backseat to the other door, and got out, walking gingerly in his stocking feet across the dirt as if it was covered with thorns.

Kate unlocked the cabin door, reached inside to flip on the light switch, and beckoned him in. "Make yourself at home."

17

The air inside the cabin smelled stale, and there was a fine layer of dust on everything. The small kitchen had chipped Formica countertops, a stove-and-oven combo that was older than Kate, and a refrigerator with a brick under one corner to keep it level. The furnishings consisted of a table and four mismatched chairs, a cracked vinyl couch, a rocking chair, and a couple dusty rugs on the hardwood floor. There were a few framed prints on the wall that Nick had bought at Walmart for five dollars apiece. The bedroom was just about big enough to hold a full-size mattress on a creaky bed frame and a nightstand. The bathroom was barely larger than a Porta-Potty, with slightly better ambience. There were some yellowed, dog-eared paperbacks on a three-shelf bookcase against one wall.

Burnside went to the kitchen sink, opened the faucet, and stuck his face into the stream of water, sucking in a mouthful of water.

He gargled with the water, spit it out, and repeated the action, before shutting the faucet off and facing Kate.

"We weren't expecting guests, so there isn't much in the way of food," she said. "But we've got enough for the first few days."

Burnside held up his hand. "You're getting way ahead of yourself. I'm not sure I'll be staying in this shack for five more minutes."

"Go ahead, walk out the door. I already regret saving your life. My entire weekend is shot now."

"What were you doing at my house in the first place?"

"We picked up some chatter that Derek Griffin had helped the Viboras launder millions of dollars in profits from the drug trade."

"That's not true," Burnside said. "He's never engaged in any illegal activity."

"Word was they were furious that he'd run off with it, along with all the cash he stole from his other clients. Since you're the only one who knows where he is, my boss thought they might come looking for you."

"Mr. Griffin hasn't stolen money from anyone."

"Does this look like a courtroom to you? I know he stole the money, you know he stole it, and so do the Viboras."

"What did you hope to gain from watching me?"

"To save you from getting killed."

"I didn't know the FBI was so concerned about my safety."

"We don't like Mexican cartels killing American citizens, even the ones we loathe."

Burnside took a seat at the table. "You have no reason to dislike me. Everyone is entitled to legal counsel and a strong defense. It's the bedrock of our legal system."

"You set criminals free."

"It's the fault of law enforcement, not me, when an accused individual is found innocent. If your case is solid, it should be able to withstand even the strongest defense, or the charges shouldn't be brought in the first place." He did a fast scan of the room. "Now what?"

"You're in protective custody until my boss says otherwise."

"That should be my decision, not his."

"The Viboras are ruthless and relentless. They aren't going to stop until they get you. They won't think twice about walking into your office with automatic weapons, spraying the place with bullets, and dragging you out over the dead bodies of all of your co-workers. Do you really think you can protect yourself, and everyone around you, from these guys?"

He thought about what had happened to Willie and shuddered. He'd never seen anyone killed before and was just thankful it wasn't someone he'd known better and deeply cared about. Not to mention, when he saw her slide down the wall he realized she was much older than he'd originally thought. He was going to have to be more careful who he picked up online.

"I am not going to stay in hiding for an indefinite period of time," Burnside said.

"You don't have to. It's not you they really want, it's Griffin. Give him up to us and your troubles are over."

"And so is my career as a defense attorney, and that's assuming that I know where he is, which I don't."

"What kind of career are you going to have in a coffin? The only thing that's going to get the Viboras to give up on you is if Griffin comes out of hiding."

"There has to be another way," Burnside said.

"If you think of one, let me know. I'll pass it along."

"Shouldn't you be calling this in? Getting us some backup?"

Kate set her iPhone on the table and punched in her audio recorder app. "We have protocol. I need to file a report before I call anybody."

"I can't tell you much. They were on us as soon as we came in the door. Willie was shot, and I was zapped, and there was the shootout in the driveway."

"What do you know about Willie?"

"She had big tits," Burnside said. "That's about it. I picked her up on Facebook. This was our first date."

"Did the men say anything?"

"Not a word. They were cold and efficient. The whole thing was over in a few seconds."

"Can you describe them? Did you see anything that could help identify them?"

Burnside shook his head. "They were wearing ski masks and gloves. I can't tell you anything about them."

That was good news, Kate thought. She stopped the recording and called Carl Jessup, filling him in.

"I want to talk with him," Burnside said.

She handed the phone to him, knowing this was a key moment in the con, the one that would sell it. Burnside knew Carl Jessup, and hearing the man's voice on the other end of the line would reinforce her authority and the "reality" of the situation he was in. Talking Jessup into doing it hadn't been easy.

"I'm not going into hiding, Carl," Burnside said. "I've got professional obligations, cases on the docket, and bills to pay."

Kate couldn't hear Jessup's side of the conversation, but she knew he was reiterating what she'd already told Burnside, adding that they'd soon be turning him over to the U.S. Marshals Service, the pros at witness protection. The FBI's expertise wasn't in babysitting.

"I expect you to be proactive," Burnside said. "Round up these Vibora guys, get them off the playing field so I don't need protection."

It was an absurd demand. There were thousands of Viboras, and countless gang members under their thumbs. If this was a real situation instead of an elaborate deception, the Viboras would keep sending waves of shooters after Burnside unless Griffin showed up, and then they'd shift their efforts to getting the man who actually had their money.

Jessup was undoubtedly telling Burnside all of that. She could see the frustration building on Burnside's face as he listened.

"Going into witness protection until such time as Derek Griffin returns and makes himself a target is not an option for him or for me," Burnside said. "There has to be some back-channel way to get word to the Viboras that I don't know where he is and that my client is innocent."

Jessup's laughter was so loud that Kate could hear it. She didn't hear what Jessup said next, but she could feel the anger rolling off Burnside.

"We'll talk tomorrow," Burnside said. "I expect to hear some other options."

He was in no position to make demands, and on some level he had to know that, but Burnside didn't want to appear as powerless as he felt, Kate thought.

Burnside handed the phone to her. "He wants to talk to you."

"I know you don't have TV reception out there, but the news media have already picked up that gunshots were reported at

Burnside's house and that he's missing," Jessup said to Kate. "The LAPD is on it, not that they have anything to go on, but stay on your toes anyway."

"Will do, sir." She disconnected the call and turned to Burnside. "Another agent will take over for me in the morning."

"Just one?"

"I'll still be here, but he'll be taking the day watch while I get some sleep. We're only babysitting you until the U.S. Marshals can take over, which hopefully will be tomorrow night."

He gestured for the phone. "I need to make some calls."

"Sorry, that's not allowed."

"I have pending cases. I need to talk with my team, let them know I'm okay and how they can reach me."

She stared at him. "Were you really a federal prosecutor?"

"For five years," he said. "One of the best."

"Then what happened? Did you sustain a serious head injury?"

His eyes narrowed. "Because I left the Justice Department to become a defense attorney?"

"Because you should know better than anyone that you can't contact anybody."

"It's my life, my decision."

"No, now it's also *my* life. I will not let you put me, or my loved ones, in danger because of your arrogance and stupidity. If you use my cell phone to contact anyone, then ten minutes later the Viboras could know where we are or who I am. And then maybe the next thing that happens is they come here and kill us. Game over. Or maybe they show up at my sister's house, shoot one of her kids to prove that they're serious, and then use her as leverage to get me to give you up. And I will."

"You wouldn't."

"In a nanosecond," Kate said. "You either play by my rules, or you can walk out that door right now and take your own chances."

"You threw away my shoes," he said.

She tossed her car keys onto the kitchen table. "What's your excuse now?"

He scowled at the keys and then at her. He wasn't going anywhere. "This sucks. The least you could have done was put me up in a decent hotel."

"Where the entire staff, probably half of them Mexican illegals with families living in Vibora-controlled territories, would know you were there and where we'd be putting every guest in the building at risk. Why would we do something as stupid as that?"

"We don't even have a TV in here," he said.

"Look at the bright side." She gestured to the bookcase. "Now's your chance to catch up on Nora Roberts."

Neal Burnside found fresh sheets in the closet, made the bed, and crawled under the covers while Kate remained in the living room, wide awake and standing guard.

Coyotes were howling and owls were hooting in the darkness outside, and Burnside couldn't sleep. The sounds made him think about all those cowboy movies he'd seen where the stupid settlers slept in their wagons and by their campfires, unaware that the howls and hoots were actually communications among the savage Indians, who were closing in on their camp to rape, torture, scalp, and kill them all.

Burnside had an irrational urge to open the bedroom door, run into the living room, and warn Kate that the Indians were about to attack. Okay, he knew that was crazy. He knew there were no Indians out there. But what if the Viboras were out there hooting and howling, getting ready to attack? That wasn't so crazy, right? Burnside gave his head a shake. Of course it was crazy. Why would the Viboras use coyote calls? Besides, nobody but Carl Jessup knew where he was. That was a calming thought. Except whoever Jessup assigned to relieve O'Hare also knew. And whoever that agent might have told, like a wife or girlfriend, and probably while their maid or gardener or pool man was within earshot, who are probably Mexican, and probably illegal, and who probably have a relative, friend, or neighbor with ties to the Viboras. No, no, no, he told himself. FBI agents are trained to be discreet. They wouldn't talk in front of their gardener about a witness they were protecting. Reality check. Who notices the help? When was the last time he'd paid any attention to what he was saying on the phone while Emilia cleaned the house, Enrique cleaned the pool, and mow-blow-and-go Julio did his lawn?

What if there was a Hispanic custodian outside of Jessup's office when he made the call? Or if there was a señorita watering the plants at the U.S. Marshals office when Jessup's call came through?

He knew that the last U.S. Census had revealed that 48 percent of the population of Los Angeles County were Latinos, the majority of them from Mexico, and those were just the people the census takers were able to count. That figure didn't include the roughly 2.6 million illegal immigrants that the Department of Homeland Security estimated were in California, most of them also from Mexico, so the actual percentage of Latinos in Los Angeles County could be much, much, *much* higher. And of those 2.6 million illegal aliens, how many had been smuggled from Mexico into California by someone with connections to the Viboras? And how many were from the vast areas of Mexico under Vibora control? And how many of them, or their relatives back home, were doing business with the Viboras? Whatever that number was, it had to be astronomical. So Burnside came to the horrifying irrational conclusion that more than half the people in Los Angeles could be on the lookout for him.

My God, listen to yourself, he thought. That's ridiculous. Half the population of Los Angeles isn't after you. But he wasn't listening to himself. He was listening to the Vibora assassins outside talking to one another in coyote and owl about attacking the cabin. Burnside gave a sigh of resignation and rolled out of bed. He needed to at least broach the subject of coyote communication with O'Hare. Get the whole insane idea out of his head and into hers so he could get some sleep.

He crossed the small room, cautioning himself not to go off babbling like some drooling moron, but to calmly suggest that she look into the possibility. Not that he actually believed there were Viboras out there, but to simply suggest she keep her ears attuned to the coyote nuances.

He opened his door, and at the same instant a hooded Vibora gunman kicked open the cabin's front door and was immediately shot twice in the chest by O'Hare, who had leapt up from the couch and fired in one smooth motion.

"What?" Burnside said, not able to process what was happening, or determine if it was even real, since he knew it was insane to think the Viboras were there, and yet there was one riddled with bullets on the floor in front of him.

He saw a series of flashes in the darkness outside the open door, simultaneously heard a string of muffled pops, and O'Hare staggered forward, eyes wide in shock and fear. She fell face-first onto the couch, her gun slipping from her lifeless fingers onto the floor, and he saw four bullet holes in her back, oozing blood.

Burnside dove to the floor to retrieve O'Hare's gun. He grabbed the gun and was rolling onto his side to shoot the first Vibora son of a bitch that came through the door when he felt the silencer against his forehead. He looked up into the cold eyes that peered through the slits of the black ski mask worn by the Vibora killer standing over him, and his heart did a painful contraction.

"I don't know where Derek Griffin is," Burnside said, struggling to breathe, dropping the gun. "He doesn't have your money."

A second gunman yanked Burnside to his feet, pulled the lawyer's arms behind his back, bound his wrists together with duct tape, tore a strip off the roll and slapped it over his mouth, and put a black hood over his head. Burnside was pulled outside and forced to walk in his bare feet on the sharp stones and twigs until he came to an abrupt and painful stop when his shins hit what he suspected was the rear bumper of a car. The trunk was opened and he was shoved inside, unable to see or to use his hands to cushion his fall. His ankles were bound with the duct tape and the trunk slammed shut. A moment later the car sped away over the unpaved road, bumping and jostling Burnside so hard against the trunk lid and the floor that it felt like a beating. And as this nightmare was unfolding, there was just one thought he couldn't get out of his head:

I can't believe I was right.

18

Nick, Chet, and Tom drove away from the safe house in a plain-wrap Camry with Willie at the wheel and Burnside in the trunk. Kate had chosen a Camry as their ride because it was the bestselling, most commonly seen car on the road, a staple of rental fleets, and therefore the hardest vehicle to single out and identify, not that there'd been any witnesses to the abduction.

Five minutes earlier, it was Chet who had been the first one through the cabin door, once again getting to play the dead Vibora, and it was Nick who'd held the gun on Burnside. Tom came in last to bind Burnside and put the hood over his head.

After the Camry disappeared down the road, Kate shucked her wet shirt and carefully peeled off the blood pack, which was basically a sheet of interlocking plastic bags that had been filled with red-dyed corn syrup and stuck to her back with heavy-duty bandage tape. On the surface of each blood bag were thin charges with tiny wires attached to them that led to a battery-operated receiver hidden in her pocket. Nick used a remote control to set off the charges, which burst her blood packs and tore holes in her shirt at the same time he fired the blanks from his silenced gun.

Kate pulled a black Hefty trash bag from under the kitchen sink, dropped her soaked shirt and the blood pack into it, collected her gun and flashlight, and then, wearing only her bra and slacks, carried the bundle outside to her car, popped the trunk, and dropped everything inside. She took out the clean T-shirt that she'd stowed earlier in the trunk and pulled it over her head. She opened her gun locker, put the gun loaded with blanks inside, and took out an identical gun, this one loaded with live ammo, and stuck it into her belt-holster.

It wasn't until she was sitting in the front seat of her car, key in hand and ready to go, that she allowed herself a whoop of victory and a smile. It always felt great when an op went as planned, and it didn't matter if it was a legitimate sting or a scam, she realized. Success was sweet. Not that she would share this with Nick. She thought she might be screwed if Nick knew she was enjoying the con.

Burnside was *certain* that he was screwed. He'd been kidnapped by Vibora killers, thrown into the trunk of a car, and taken to God-knows-where to be tortured and killed. It was hard to be more screwed than that, unless you were dead. And the only reason he wasn't dead was the Viboras' belief that he knew where Derek Griffin was and, by extension, where they could get their money back and maybe all the rest of the plunder, too. That was half a billion dollars of leverage.

What Burnside had to figure out was a way to use that leverage to avoid torture, get himself out alive, and, as a bonus for his creativity and cleverness, get some compensation for his pain and suffering. He was a smart man, and a lawyer, he told himself. His lifetime of experience arguing cases and bartering deals had to be useful for the life-or-death situation that he now faced. The key, despite all of the indignities he'd endured, was not to show weakness or fear.

The car stopped, he heard the trunk spring open, and he was jerked out and stood on his feet. His hood was snatched off and one of the masked men cut the tape on his ankles. Burnside wobbled a little before finding his balance. No one was saying anything. He squinted into the darkness and saw that they were parked beside a small private turbo jet that was perched in front of a rusted, dilapidated aircraft hangar in a remote corner of what he guessed was the Van Nuys Airport.

There were no major airlines flying out of Van Nuys. The airport was used for cargo jets and small chartered private and commercial aircraft. It was also a popular location for movie and television productions, which used the hangars as soundstages to house large interior sets and used everything else to re-create military bases or big international airports. It gave Burnside the strong but fleeting sensation that he was in a movie himself.

There were no people in sight besides the two Vibora gunmen. The other hangars nearby were closed and dark. The larger of the two gunmen walked ahead of Burnside into the plane, and the other, slimmer guy walked behind him, prodding him with the barrel of his gun to get moving.

Climbing into the plane with his hands bound behind his back wasn't easy for Burnside, and he banged his head going through the low doorway into the cramped cabin. There were six seats in the plane, three on each side in a row against the bulkhead.

He was shoved into one of the middle seats, and the thin gunman ripped the tape from Burnside's mouth. It felt like a knife cutting across his face and it brought tears to Burnside's eyes. He half expected to see his lips stuck to the tape in the gunman's hand. The tape binding his hands was slashed and bottles of water were passed around. One was dropped into Burnside's lap.

Burnside chugged half a bottle and buckled his seat belt as the plane taxied along the tarmac to the runway. The plane paused for a long moment, the engines revved, and the plane moved forward, gaining speed. It rumbled and shook, and the Vibora sitting across the aisle from Burnside gripped his armrests hard. The plane lifted off, wobbled, bounced down, and lifted off a second time. The second liftoff was like a rocket launching, shoving Burnside back into his seat. He was glad it was dark out so he couldn't see how close they might have come to shaving off the rooftops of the buildings adjacent to the airport.

The plane shook and rumbled some more. It dropped, lifted back up, and dropped again before finally leveling off. Burnside looked out the window at Los Angeles, spotted some landmarks, and realized they were heading south. It was a struggle to keep his eyes open, his brain fogged over, and his last thought before passing out was that he'd been drugged.

Nick unbuckled his seat belt, got up from his seat across from Burnside, and made his way into the cockpit, slipping into the co-pilot's seat beside Willie.

"How's it going?" he asked, taking his hood off.

"Absolutely great," she said. "Sit back and enjoy the flight."

"That's not easy to do when you're flying vertically."

"It's called liftoff for a reason."

"Rockets lift off. Planes take off."

"We're in the air, aren't we?" she said.

They wouldn't be for long because they didn't have far to go. Their destination was the general aviation airport in Thermal, California, so named because the temperature there could be as close to hell as it was possible to get without actually being damned, often making Death Valley feel like the North Pole by comparison.

Thermal was 136 miles southeast of Los Angeles, a two-hour-plus drive by car but only a few minutes travel by plane. The climate and landscape in that corner of the Mojave were very similar to Mexico's Chihuahuan Desert, where the Viboras were waging a bloody war with the Sinaloa Cartel for the control of narco-traffic into the U.S.

Nick glanced at his watch. "How are you feeling about landing the plane?"

"I can't wait. I just hope they have a very long runway," Willie said, and then laughed when she saw the troubled expression on Nick's face. "If you're worried about my piloting skills, you shouldn't have given me a pilot's license."

"It's fake," he said.

"Aren't we all?"

Nick put his ski mask back on and returned to the cabin. Chet was still wearing his mask, too, even though Burnside was out cold. That's because Nick was a firm believer in never slipping out of character in the presence of the mark, no matter what. It kept the crew sharp and prevented them from letting their guard down. He was impressed that Kate seemed to know that instinctively, not even sharing a glance with him back in the cabin, even after Burnside was covered with a hood.

. . .

The first few years of the new millennium had been a boom time in the Coachella Valley. The desert resort communities of Palm Springs, Palm Desert, La Quinta, and Indio had expanded quickly. New homes were sold as fast as they could be built and at well over their asking prices. The demand for vacation properties was so strong that developers scrambled to buy up large tracts of land.

It was only natural that developers turned their eyes to Thermal, despite the fact that the pitiful patch of blazingly hot desert was downwind from the Salton Sea, which was frequently stricken with algae blooms, massive water evaporation, and catastrophic fish die-offs that made the entire area smell like it was under a huge, ferocious fart cloud. Encino Grande was going to be the development that would transform the perception of Thermal, making it a prestigious address for resort living, with its 144 luxury homes built around a shimmering man-made lake and a lush nine-hole golf course.

A grand entrance gate, a stone wall surrounding the property, and three homes were built and landscaped before the economy cratered. One day the developer simply disappeared, leaving behind the homes, an empty lakebed, acres of graded sand, and a dozen foundations in various stages of construction to bake under the scorching sun.

And so it had remained for seven years until Nick Fox came along and, using one of his pseudonyms, rented the property from the bank to use as a location in a low-budget movie about drug smuggling.

Tom Underhill came in with a construction team that worked day and night for three weeks to transform one 6,500-square-foot home into a Vibora drug lord's luxurious but fortified hideaway, with an open-air guard tower and a high, bullet-pocked wall topped with razor wire. The yard at the immediate rear of the house, within the high walls, was landscaped with tropical plants around a swimming pool with a swim-up wet bar. It was an oasis within an otherwise militaristic compound. A zigzag of concrete K-rail barriers was placed inside the gate to prevent attackers from surging into the compound with vehicles. A detached garage was converted into guard quarters, and the pool house was turned into a "prison block" for unwelcome guests. Of course, most of it was fake.

Boyd Capwell watched his mansion take shape and read up on the Vibora cartel, screened Al Pacino in *Scarface* and Ricardo Montalban in *Fantasy Island,* listened to Julio Iglesias CDs, and ate almost exclusively at Taco Bell, which also happened to be the most upscale restaurant in the vicinity of Thermal. He picked out a wardrobe at the stores along El Paseo in Palm Desert, wore the makeup that Chet created for him, and a week before Burnside's abduction, moved into the Encino Grande house and arranged the décor, tended the landscaping, and swam in the pool. And now he stood in his mansion looking out the living room window at the black Suburban driving into the compound, and he knew it was showtime. He was Diego de Boriga, and he would slice Neal Burnside into bite-size pieces if that's what it took to get his money back.

19

Burnside woke up in an eight-by-ten-foot cell. He was on his back, on a thin foam mattress, on a cinder-block shelf. He looked straight up at a large black spider that clung to a web strung across the ceiling and was waiting for some unlucky insect to come along and get stuck. Or maybe, Burnside thought, he's been waiting for me. A shaft of sunlight came through a recessed barred window about the size of an iPad. The light made the stainless steel toilet and sink shine. At least it was clean. The air was heavy and hot, pushed around by fans that Burnside could hear struggling in the corridor outside his cell. He didn't hear any voices or sounds to indicate the presence of any other human beings.

He'd been changed into a T-shirt and loose-fitting sweatpants. The clothes were more comfortable than those he'd worn on the plane, but he was creeped out that someone had stripped him and dressed him. There was a pair of rubber sandals on the floor beside the bed. He stood and slipped his feet into them.

On top of the sink he found a tin cup and an American Airlines toiletry bag, the kind the flight attendants routinely hand out to first-class passengers on long flights. He opened the bag and surveyed the contents: a travel-size toothbrush, toothpaste, mouthwash, a disposable razor, a tube of shaving cream, a comb, a pair of socks, rubber earplugs, and a mask to put over his eyes to block out the light. He figured since there was nothing in the bag that could be used to hijack a plane, it was probably also useless as an escape kit.

He climbed up on the toilet, which had no seat, balanced his feet on both sides of the rim, and got on his tiptoes to peer out of the tiny window. He saw a sun-bleached stone wall four feet from the window. The wall was topped with embedded shards of broken glass and razor wire. He craned his neck and got a glimpse of the clear blue sky above. It wasn't a suite at the Las Ventanas al Paraiso in Cabo, but it could have been a lot worse, he told himself. He could be tied naked to a chair, being beaten with a baseball bat and kept conscious by having buckets of ice water poured over his head. Of course, it could still come to that.

Tom Underhill walked across the yard to the pool house–turned–stockade, wearing camouflage fatigues and carrying an AK-47 loaded with blanks. He'd never acted before, and was terrified to attempt a speaking role, so his performance was simplified: Look mean and bad-ass, like Samuel Jackson. And pretend that Burnside was George Pogue, that sniveling worm of a banker who'd tried to take his house away from him.

Burnside heard footsteps in the hall outside his cell. He stepped down off the toilet and turned to face the cell door, which was iron mesh over iron bars with a slot at the bottom for sliding in a meal tray. The footsteps stopped at Burnside's door, and Burnside looked out at someone he sized up as a guard. The man was wearing fatigues, carrying an assault rifle, and looked like he ate ground glass for breakfast. The guard unlocked the door with a set of keys that were chained to his belt, and motioned Burnside out by swinging his weapon. Burnside stepped out slowly into a narrow corridor with three ceiling fans. There was an open door to the yard at the far end. The guard jabbed him in the back with his rifle to get him moving.

Burnside walked past an empty cell and went outside. What he saw looked like a two-story Spanish Mediterranean mansion built in the middle of a prison yard. The lush landscaping and pool were in stark contrast to the razor wire, the K-rails, and the guard tower. Everything was clean and orderly. Even the brown sand looked as if it was regularly raked.

The guy in camies poked him again with the rifle, herding him toward the house. Burnside looked up at the guard tower that stood outside the wall. He had to squint into the sun, but he could make out two men with rifles up there, both with their backs to him.

Another man in camie fatigues was unloading wooden crates marked EXPLOSIVOS from a black Suburban and carrying them into an armory filled with similarly labeled crates. The man was linebacker big and carried a gun in a shoulder holster. Burnside guessed he could have been one of the two masked men on the plane.

There was a slight breeze, and with it came the stench of rot and decay, like an outhouse on fire. The smell was so strong that Burnside took another glance around, looking for the source, afraid he might spot it.

The living room of the house was open to the patio and the pool. A man sat at a poolside table eating a very thick, very rare steak. There was a glass pitcher of ice-cold sangria, filled with fruit. The pitcher was beaded with condensation. The man wore sunglasses with blue lenses, a pair of dark-denim designer skinny jeans, a Gucci belt, K-Swiss classic high-top sneakers, and an explosively colorful T-shirt covered with sparkles, studs, and roaring lions. He looked like he was auditioning for a part in a Mexican version of *Jersey Shore*.

Burnside stood in front of the table for a long moment, watching the man eat his steak and sip his sangria.

"Welcome to Mexico, Mr. Burnside," the man said, setting down his knife and fork. The steak was so pink it was almost throbbing. "Do you know who I am?"

Burnside shook his head. The man sounded like Ricardo Montalban doing a bad Al Pacino imitation, or vice versa.

"I am Diego de Boriga, one of the founding members of the Vibora cartel. The man behind you is Char, named for his skin, which is black as charcoal, like his soul. He doesn't speak much, but when he does it is with his gun. You will never forget what he says, because you will be dead."

Kate and Nick were upstairs in a soundproof bedroom, sitting side by side in front of a bank of monitors that carried live feeds from cameras located all over the property.

"Omigod," Kate said. "That made absolutely no sense! And 'Char'? Boyd just named Tom after his skin color and his soul? Are you freaking kidding me? Didn't you give Boyd a script?"

"Boyd isn't great at following a script," Nick said.

"You have to talk to him. He can't just go off saying ridiculous things. He's ruining the whole setup. And what's with that accent? I half expected Boyd to say 'Welcome to Fantasy Island.' If I was in Burnside's flip-flops right now, I'd be laughing my ass off."

"You also said Burnside would never be fooled by the mannequins in the guard tower."

"What are you going to do when the sun isn't in his eyes when he's looking at it?"

"The sun will always will be in his eyes whenever we let him into the yard. Remember, *we're* directing the show."

She tapped the onscreen image of Boyd. "Does *he* know that?"

"He's a Vibora?" Burnside asked, tipping his head toward Char.

"Char is a hired gun, and the only man I trust," Diego said. "That is because his only loyalty is to money."

"What happens if someone comes along and offers him more to kill you than what you're paying him for his protection?"

"Then I am dead," Diego said.

Burnside looked over his shoulder at Char. "How much are you making?"

Char didn't answer.

Diego laughed. "Are you going to make him a better offer?"

"I might."

"Even if you could, and Char accepted, and assuming he could kill all the other men patrolling this compound, you are in the middle of the Chihuahuan Desert. A man who killed a Vibora leader would not get very far." Diego stood up and ambled into the living room. Burnside followed, shadowed closely by Char. "Have you noticed that delicate scent in the air, carried in the morning breeze?"

Delicate? Burnside thought. No amount of flowers and tropical landscaping could mask the stink of rot, which he'd first noticed walking over from the stockade. "It's awful."

Diego took a deep breath and let it out slowly. "I find the fragrance invigorating."

"What is the smell coming from?"

Diego strolled to an oil painting over the mantelpiece that depicted a large flower in bloom, its single-stem inflorescence wrapped in an enormous, flowing white–and–lime green petal that was a deep, rich purple on its furrowed inner folds.

"This is the *Amorphophallus titanium,* found naturally only in the rain forest of Sumatra. It blooms for only two days at a time, and rarely in its forty-year lifespan. When it blooms, it's a gloriously beautiful sight, as you can see, but the fragrance it emits, likened to that of a herd of decomposing elephants in a swamp of excrement, has earned it the nickname 'the corpse flower.' "

"That's what I'm smelling? A corpse flower?"

"No, this scent comes from the mass grave about a hundred yards away from here, midway between this compound and the village. That is the smell of people who've dared oppose me. That, Mr. Burnside, is the scent of power. My corpse flower. And it is *always* in bloom."

Kate made a gagging gesture at the screen, where Boyd was staring directly into the hidden camera. "I didn't think it could get any worse, but Boyd just managed to take his performance to a whole new level of overacting. Is there actually a corpse flower? Who would believe something like that?"

"That man is a natural!" Nick leaned back in his chair, his hands behind his head, a smile on his face. "And that was sheer brilliance. Boyd took the reeking Salton Sea and used it as a prop. Look at Burnside. He's gone pale."

"Look at Tom," Kate said. "He's choking back laughter."

That was true. Luckily, Burnside's back was to him.

"Tom will control himself," Nick said. It was more of a strongly expressed hope than a fact.

"It's not Tom I'm worried about," Kate said. "Boyd should stop hamming it up for the camera and start squeezing Burnside for information."

"He's already begun," Nick said. "It's subtle."

"Subtle? He just said that he fills mass graves with his enemies and that he enjoys the fragrance of their rot."

"That was setting the stage, creating an environment of terror. Now he'll make it personal."

Diego motioned to Burnside to take a seat on one of the plush couches, and Diego sat on a facing couch. Char remained standing.

"All of the surviving inhabitants of the nearest village, recently rechristened 'Boriga,' work in some aspect of my business. I pay them very well. But they are a simple people. They don't know how to handle money. So they've entrusted their savings to me to protect and to invest. I take the responsibility very seriously. I invested their money and my own with Derek Griffin, which brings us to why you are here."

"I had nothing to do with Mr. Griffin's business."

"You merely tipped him off to his impending arrest and helped him escape with five hundred million dollars."

Burnside leaned back on the couch and crossed his legs, trying to project the image that he was a man at ease, not someone whose chest felt like it was being crushed in a vise. He hoped he wasn't having a heart attack.

"You're mistaken," Burnside said. "I had nothing to do with his disappearance. I don't have any idea where to find him or the money he invested for his clients."

"That's a shame," Diego sighed wearily. "I apologize for inconveniencing you for nothing. Char, take him outside and execute him."

Char took a step forward. Burnside sat up straight and held his palms out in a halting gesture. "Wait, wait, wait. You don't have to kill me."

"You expect me to fly you home?"

"I can be an asset to you," Burnside said.

"I don't see how."

"I could be your legal counsel in Los Angeles."

"Do I strike you as someone who gives a damn about laws? I lost two men bringing you here. I must now support their families. At least I will have the satisfaction of ridding the world of another lawyer. Put him up against the wall, Char, and be sure to hose off the mess right away."

Char took another step forward.

"Wait," Burnside said again, more emphatically this time. "The only reason I am alive right now is because you think I have information that you want. Assuming I do, if I were to reveal what I know then there would be nothing stopping you from killing me."

"There is nothing stopping me now."

"What assurance do I have that you'll let me live if I tell you what you want to know?"

"None at all."

"Okay, then fuck you and your money." Burnside suddenly felt the pressure in his chest ease and he waved Char over. "C'mon, get your ass over here and shoot me."

"That's it, game over," Kate said.

Nick slid a sideways look at her. "I have to say, conning people was a lot more fun before I had to listen to your running commentary. Have some faith."

"Boyd overplayed his hand and Burnside nailed him. There's no coming back from this."

"You have a lot to learn about swindles. Boyd is giving Burnside a little slack, that's all. Burnside doesn't want to die. He knows he's going to have to put himself entirely at Boyd's mercy and is looking for a way to do it that salvages some shred of his dignity, even if it's an illusion. Boyd just gave it to him. It's a shrewd move."

"You're giving Boyd too much credit. He's an actor, not a con man."

"All actors are con men. They get you to believe they are somebody they aren't and to suspend your disbelief about everything else."

Diego shook his head at Char, who stayed put.

Good sign, Burnside thought. As long as they were still talking, and he wasn't getting shot or tortured, he was making progress.

"Do not delude yourself, Mr. Burnside. You will talk, but since you have no loved ones I can torture and kill in front of your eyes, it just comes down to how much agony you can stand and the number of body parts you are willing to sacrifice before you do."

"If I am going to die either way, why would I want to give you the satisfaction of getting your money?"

"To enjoy the sweet release that only death can bring from your unbearable agony."

"You want to know what will get me through the agony? The certainty that once the good people of Boriga find out that you've lost all of their money, that the all-powerful Oz got shaken down like an old lady, and that all of their misery, mourning, and ass-kissing was for nothing, they won't care if they live or die anymore, and they will storm this place and rip you to shreds. And when Char over here sees that enraged horde coming, he'll switch sides and not look back. He'll cut off your head, stick it on a spike, and wave it around as his flag of surrender in the desperate hope that it will save his life. So bring it on, Diego, I'm ready to die. Are you?"

"We're done," Kate said.

"You keep saying that," Nick said. "It's almost like you want it to be true."

"In case you weren't listening, that was his closing statement to the jury, and it sounded pretty persuasive to me."

"Has anyone ever told you that you're a very pessimistic person?"

"Face it, Boyd was overmatched. There's a big difference between being convincing as Willy Loman in an all-you-can-eat-buffet performance of *Death of a Salesman* and outmaneuvering a top-notch criminal attorney."

"The only difference is that we don't have a buffet," Nick said. "I wish we did. I could go for some fried chicken."

Burnside leaned back on the couch again and looked Diego in the eye. But Diego didn't seem thrown in the least. If anything, he seemed amused.

"I like you, Mr. Burnside. You have *cojones,* at least for the time being. I will make you a deal. You will tell me where Derek Griffin is and I will send some people to get him. During that time, you will remain as my guest. If you have told me the truth, you will live. If you have deceived me, then I will cut off your left arm and beat you with it until you tell me the truth. If those terms are not acceptable to you, then I will execute you now."

Burnside considered his options. Since there were none, it made his deliberations easy.

"Derek Griffin is in Indonesia, living on Dajmaboutu, his private island in the Flores Sea."

"Why Indonesia?"

"Because they have seventeen thousand islands, a notoriously corrupt government that's easily bribed, and no extradition treaty with the United States."

"So how are we supposed to find Dajmaboutu?"

"I'll give you the exact longitude and latitude. As a bonus, you can have your boys bring you back an actual corpse flower while they're in the neighborhood."

20

Tom led Burnside back to his cell and gave him a tray of beans and tortillas, a glass of sangria, and a book of crossword puzzles. He returned to the house and joined Boyd, Chet, Nick, and Kate in the kitchen. They were all standing around the center island drinking sangria.

Boyd was ebullient, pacing around, still jacked up from his performance. "That was one of the best acting experiences of my career."

"You were terrific, Boyd," Nick said. "Utterly convincing."

"You know why? Because I was given free rein to make the character my own, to fully inhabit him in every way. Thank you for that. And I must say, Neal Burnside was a joy to work with. I've never had that kind of freewheeling give-and-take with an actor before."

"Maybe that's because Burnside wasn't acting," Kate said.

"Yes, he was," Boyd said. "He was acting like he wasn't scared.

My favorite part was the corpse flower bit. I worked on that soliloquy for a week, hoping I could find an opportunity to slip it in."

"I almost messed my pants when you told him about the corpse flower," Tom said. "How do you think of stuff like that? And man you've got to have a lot of guts to take it for a test drive."

"I thought it made everything more visceral and, therefore, more memorable," Boyd said. "Now every time Neal Burnside smells that stench, or sees that painting, it will send a tremor of fear through him that only reinforces my character and the illusion of this set."

"Very true," Nick said.

"I wish I could have heard it," Chet said.

"You can watch the footage," Boyd said. "I'm eager to see it myself."

"What footage?" Kate asked.

"The playback from all of the cameras," Boyd said. "No need to edit it together. We can pick my best angles from each one as we go along. I was careful to hit all of my marks."

"You had marks?" Kate asked.

"I studied where each camera was placed, then I hid little markers that only I'd recognize to show me where I should sit or stand to guarantee that I would be in focus, and showing my best angle, wherever I happened to be in the house or outside. Something I picked up from my work in three-camera sitcoms."

"You were on a sitcom?" Chet asked.

"A little show called *Friends,*" Boyd said.

"I loved that show," Tom said, "but I don't remember you being in it. What part did you play?"

"I was the barista who served the friends coffee for a few episodes. But I was let go over creative differences."

"What were they?" Chet asked.

"I thought my character should have a name," Boyd said, "and that he should have a few lines. And that Matt LeBlanc shouldn't block my face from the camera with his enormous head whenever I set down their coffees."

"We didn't record it," Kate said.

Boyd looked at her in disbelief. "Are you saying my performance of a lifetime is lost?"

"It was never going to be kept. We can't leave any evidence of what has happened here," she said. "Don't forget, we kidnapped Burnside and are holding him prisoner. That's a felony."

"But Burnside is a crook," Tom said. "He helped Griffin escape with all of that stolen money."

"That's true," Kate said. "What we're doing is for a good cause. But it's still a crime, and the last thing we want is a recording of it. The reason we have the cameras and microphones is for surveillance and security, not posterity."

Boyd took a seat on a bar stool, his shoulders slumped, his head hung low. "No one will ever know what occurred here today."

Nick took a seat beside Boyd. "This was like your stage work. Your searing performance as Stanley in *A Streetcar Named Desire* at the Starlight Lanes and Lounge wasn't filmed, either, but that didn't make it any less meaningful."

"The difference is that on stage I have an audience," Boyd said. "They remember my performance and it lives on in everyone they tell about it. Who will tell the tale of Diego de Boriga's corpse flower?"

"This performance lives on, too, not in a mere retelling but in the stunning revelations that your performance evoked and the life-changing events that will follow for so many people as a result," Nick said. "In many ways, this performance will have a more lasting and indelible impact than any you've ever given before."

"I hadn't thought of it that way," Boyd said.

Nick's good, Kate thought. Full of crap, but he sells it so well. And he looks amazing in those jeans.

"And it's not over yet," Nick said. "You've got to stay in character until we come back with Derek Griffin."

"You all do," Kate said. "But in small doses. You need to interact as little as possible with Burnside from now on."

"She's right," Nick said. "The more you say, the more opportunity you have to slip up. The same goes for this set. We have to limit Burnside's exposure to it, what he sees, how much of it he sees, and how long he sees it. We want him to get only the big picture, not the telling details. He shouldn't be allowed out of his cell for more than a few minutes each day, and even then his movements on the property must be very limited and constantly supervised."

"I'll switch out the mannequins up in the tower," Chet said. "And stand watch up there a few times myself. I've got some great sound effects lined up for Burnside, too, to hear while he's in that cell. Trust me, he'll believe this place is crawling with Viboras."

"That's the idea," Nick said. "It's crucial you maintain the illusion while we're away."

"How long is that going to be?" Tom asked.

Kate looked at Nick. It was a very good question.

Nick shrugged. "Don't know."

Kate left the house and drove the few miles to Indio, where she and Willie had rooms at the Fantasy Springs Resort Casino. Willie had spent her night at the twenty-four-hour bowling alley and her day lazing around the pool, fending off advances from old men eager to put their Viagra prescriptions to use.

Kate stopped by the pool to check on Willie and to let her know that Burnside had spilled that Griffin was in Indonesia, so they might be heading there soon, but she couldn't tell her what they'd actually be doing once they arrived.

"Cool," Willie said with casual acceptance, as if they were talking about nothing more unusual or uncertain than going to a movie.

"Really?" Kate asked.

Willie was sprawled on a chaise, looking to beef up her tan. She opened a single eye and squinted at Kate. "It's an exotic place on the other side of the world. What's not to like about it?"

"The possibility that you might not come back."

"Sweetie, it's all part of The Big Adventure."

Kate thought that was a terrific attitude. She just hoped The Big Adventure didn't include a cell in Sukun Women's Prison in Malang.

"Okey-dokey," Kate said. "Stick close to the hotel in case we have to move."

"I'm in hog heaven here," Willie said. "There's lots of cold shrimp, piña coladas, and twenty-four-hour bowling. What more could a girl want?"

Kate headed up to her room, wondering as she rode the elevator to the tenth floor what their next move would be now that they knew where Griffin was hiding. If it was up to her, Kate would drop a strike team of commandos onto the island and remove Griffin by force. She doubted that Bolton would authorize an operation like that, since it would require air and sea support and could attract the attention of the Indonesian military. To capture an Al Qaeda terrorist the U.S. government might be willing to go along with an armed incursion into a sovereign state and risk the political fallout if it went wrong. She didn't think they'd do it for some Wall Street embezzler, not even one who'd fled with half a billion dollars. Robert Vesco had proved that back in the 1970s when he ran off to Costa Rica with $200 million he'd plundered from his investment firm. He continued to move between countries without U.S. extradition treaties for decades before finally dying in Cuba, where he'd been imprisoned for drug smuggling.

Kate let herself into her room, called Jessup, and told him everything, including the longitude and latitude of Dajmaboutu, a twelve-acre speck of an island in the middle of Indonesian waters, half a world away.

"Well, it could be worse," Jessup said. "He could be in North Korea, Iran, or Myanmar. Indonesia is unique, it's an archipelago of thousands of islands scattered over seven hundred fifty thousand square miles of open sea, where the rule of law is often either nonexistent or impossible to enforce. That's undoubtedly why Griffin chose to hide there, but it also works in our favor. Plenty of ways in and out without crossing physical borders."

That was true. And because Griffin was on a tiny remote island, they stood a chance of pulling off whatever they were going to do without attracting the attention of the Indonesian military or the police. But they still had to go into the heart of Southeast Asia and navigate a maze of islands in foreign waters that were notorious for being rampant with vicious, well-armed pirates.

"How are our relations with Indonesia these days?" she asked.

"Rocky enough that if you get caught, there will be a Katrina-size shit storm that could set foreign policy back decades if anybody can prove you weren't rogue. I'll have to run this all past Bolton, but I'm sure he anticipated an endgame like this, and that he is going to tell you to go grab Griffin and haul his ass back here, or at least into international waters. But if anything goes wrong, don't expect your country to haul your butt out of the fire."

"That's what I figured."

"How are you going to pull it off?"

"It's only been a couple of hours since we discovered where Griffin is. We might need another twenty minutes or so to come up with a plan."

"You've done great so far. If either Bolton or I knew what you were doing, which we don't, we'd be impressed."

"Thanks," she said. "How much heat have we got on us?"

"The LAPD is investigating Burnside's disappearance, of course, but they've got nothing at all to go on. We haven't been much help to them, either, the poor souls."

"What's the latest on the manhunt for Nick?"

"Ryerson is chasing a lead from Interpol that Fox may have impersonated some Italian count to fly out of Europe and into St. Louis, where the trail goes cold. I told him that was ridiculous. Why would he come back here? And why St. Louis? What's Fox plotting to do, steal the Arch?"

"It wouldn't surprise me," Kate said, and disconnected.

She set the alarm clock on the nightstand to ring in forty-five minutes, pulled the comforter off the bed, slipped her gun under one of the pillows, and went to sleep on top of the blankets. When the alarm woke her after what felt like three seconds, she smashed it with her fist until it was silent and cracked, and she went back to sleep.

The next time Kate came awake it wasn't because of the alarm.

It was because of an uneasy feeling intruding on her sleep, dragging her into consciousness. She lay perfectly still, eyes closed, all other senses alert. She heard the soft rustle of clothing and knew she wasn't alone. She stretched and slipped her hand under her pillow, found her Glock, and bolted upright, aiming at a shadow at the foot of the bed.

"How sweet," Nick said, gesturing to the Glock. "Just like old times."

He was in a chair facing the bed, eating a Toblerone. A bottle of white wine and two glasses were on the table beside him.

"You're lucky I didn't shoot you. How did you get in here?"

"To your knowledge, how many times have I visited the Louvre after it was closed?"

"Three," she said.

"It's seven, actually." He unscrewed the top off the bottle of wine and filled two glasses. "With that in mind, do you really think your hotel room door was a challenge for me?"

Smug bastard. She should have shot him. But it was a nonsmoking room, and they charged a $275 cleaning fee for cigarette smoke and ashes, so she figured that their price for scrubbing away blood and brain matter was probably astronomical.

"You could have knocked," she said.

Nick held a glass of wine out to her. "I didn't want to wake you."

She slid down to the end of the bed and took the glass from him. "How did you know I was sleeping?"

"Anyone walking by your room would have known. You were snoring like a hippo giving birth."

"I don't snore," she said, and drank half the glass of wine. "You broke in to raid my minibar, like always, and didn't expect to find me here."

"I'll say that's what happened if it will make you feel better."

"If that's not it, then what *are* you doing here?"

"I thought you'd like to know how we're getting Derek Griffin." His gaze dropped to her shirt. "Is that cocktail sauce?"

Kate looked down and sighed. "Willie was at poolside and I snitched a shrimp off her platter."

Why me? she thought. Why doesn't *he* ever have food stains on his shirt?

21

"You've figured out the con already?" Kate asked Nick.

"Yep. The honey trap. It works in any situation where a man is vulnerable to the charms of a beautiful woman. And it helps if he has an unfulfilled desire for sex."

Kate foraged in the minibar, came up with a Snickers, and bit off a chunk. "So basically any man on earth with a heartbeat in any situation at all."

"Pretty much," he said. "You're going to be a rich, bored, man-hungry heiress cruising the Flores Sea in a multimillion-dollar yacht with a two-person crew."

Kate's mouth dropped open and some candy fell out. "No! No way. Not gonna happen. I am *not* going to be the honey in the trap."

Her short hair was a wreck, overgrown for a pixie cut, not long enough for anything else. She had perpetual food stains. She didn't own an iron and had no interest in buying one. And it didn't matter anyway because her clothes were all wash-and-wear and chosen for their ability to hide a gun. There were times when in all honesty she did feel a little man-hungry, but she had no confidence that, even on her best day, could she pull off the honey trap.

"Willie can be the honey trap," Kate said. "She's good at it."

"She's going to captain the yacht," Nick said.

"How is she going to do that?"

"She's had boating experience."

"Little pleasure craft. This is a freaking expensive boat."

"The boat is all computerized. She'll pick it up in no time. We're talking about a woman who once took a freight train for a joyride. And the real problem with her being the honey is her age. She's too old. Griffin will be seeing her in daylight. Do you want to hear the rest of the con or not?"

"Not! I'm not doing this."

"Of course you'll do it. You're a team player. We'll lease a yacht out of Benoa Harbor in Bali. The yacht will run into engine trouble and end up stuck in the waters off Griffin's island. We'll hang out on the island while the yacht is being repaired. You'll entice Griffin to the point of insanity while I nose around and see if I can figure out where the money is."

"He's not going to have the half billion dollars in cash in his sock drawer or even in a safe. You won't find it on the island," she said. "At most, he might have five hundred million rupiah stashed in a hollow coconut somewhere."

Nick nodded. "The money is in a bank account. The key is to find out where that bank is, and Griffin's password so we can access his account and empty it. Once we've done that, or at least have a line on the information, you lure him onto the boat, we overpower him, and we take him on a ride into international waters, where we leave him floating in a dinghy for the U.S. Navy to apprehend."

"It doesn't seem very well thought out."

"Of course it's not, it's only the broad strokes. I'll fill in the blanks as I go along."

Kate put her glass and the Snickers wrapper on the table. "I have a better idea. We use the yacht and a cruise as our cover. We anchor near Griffin's island in darkness, then I go ashore, grab him, and bring him back to the boat."

"He'll have protection."

"I'm pretty tough."

"We're not."

"You and Willie will stay on the boat. I don't need you."

"You might, and while I can handle myself, I'm much faster with my mouth than with my fists."

"No one is asking you to kick ass. That's my department. I've done this kind of thing before."

"If what Bolton wanted was a military strike force, he wouldn't have put the two of us together and funded this operation. He knows as well as I do that what this situation requires is finesse," Nick said. "If Griffin comes to the boat willingly, and *then* you put a gun to his head, nobody gets hurt, and no alarms are raised."

"Okay, fine. Have it your way, but Willie needs to be the honey trap. Some men like mature women. And she's got bigger boobs than I do."

"True, but that's not the way it's going down."

She did an eye roll that was so massive it almost gave her a headache. "I was in the U.S. Navy. In case you have forgotten, that's the branch of our military that operates on the water, so I know a thing or two about operating boats and navigating the high seas. Besides, you said these yachts practically pilot themselves."

"They do if you already have a natural affinity for piloting vehicles. That's not your super power. It's Willie's."

Kate flopped back onto the bed and squeezed her eyes shut. "I don't want to be a honey trap. I hate that stuff."

"All you have to do is be smart, sexy, and seductive and make Griffin want you enough to get on a boat with you for a little erotic cruise. How hard could that be?"

"I'd rather punch him in his face."

"And you wonder why you're single."

"I don't wonder," she said. "It's a conscious choice. With the job I have, I don't have time to commit to a steady relationship, but that doesn't mean I'm a nun."

"You play around?"

"Define 'play around.'"

Nick grinned at her. "If you have to define it, you don't do it."

"I've been busy. Besides, what sort of person do you think I am? And if you think I'm going to sleep with Derek Griffin, you're wrong."

"I'm not asking you to. I'm asking you to make Griffin *believe* that you will if he gets on the boat with you."

"It's not that easy," she said.

"Sure it is. Just show some boob and thigh, maintain eye contact too long, lick your lips, invade his personal space, basically do all the things you usually do when you want to distract and manipulate a man."

"I don't do those things!"

Nick gave her the thousand-watt smile and rose from his seat.

"I have total confidence in you. Meet me in the lobby at nine A.M. sharp. We need to go shopping."

"What are we shopping for?"

"Sexy clothes that will make you irresistible to Derek Griffin."

"No problem," she said. "Is there a Kohl's or Walmart around here?"

"We're going to aim a little higher than that."

"Where are we shopping?"

"Where a spoiled, rich heiress would," Nick said.

"Spoiled, rich heiresses aren't on FBI expense accounts."

"Neither are you," he said.

El Paseo was the Rodeo Drive of Palm Desert. It was a wide, palm-lined street of swanky shops, galleries, restaurants, and lush flower beds improbably situated on a patch of bone-dry desert that General George Patton had used to prepare his troops for battle in the Sahara. But now, instead of tanks and jeeps rumbling across the parched earth, battalions of sun seekers in Mercedes-Benzes and Jaguars cruised for prime parking spots.

The shopping experience on El Paseo was about the same as Rodeo Drive when it came to the stores with their ultraexpensive brands. The only difference here was the fleet of yellow seven-seat courtesy carts that went up and down the street giving free rides to retirees too frail or too burdened with shopping bags to manage the one-mile stretch of glitz on their own.

Nick and Kate had chosen to forsake the ride and walk, and Kate was lagging behind.

"Could you pick up the pace?" Nick said to Kate. "We just got lapped by someone dragging an oxygen tank."

"I hate shopping for clothes," Kate said. "I liked when I was in the military and all I needed was camouflage gear."

"Shopping can be fun. Especially when it's for a con. It's the first step in creating a character. Isn't there anything you enjoy buying? Lingerie? Shoes? Jewelry?"

"Shoes are okay. I don't have to take my clothes off to try them on."

"You don't like to take your clothes off?"

"It's the lighting in the dressing rooms. It makes you look fat and anemic. And pulling clothes on and off wrecks my hair."

Nick put his hand on her head and ruffled her hair. "Like this?"

Kate jumped away. "Stop it! I have enough hair problems without you making it worse."

"Maybe if you ran a brush through it once in a while."

"Maybe if you'd keep your hands off it!"

Nick grinned and hugged her into him. "Are we a team, or what? Stick with me and I'll get you to enjoy taking your clothes off."

"You're flirting with me."

"Stating a fact," Nick said.

First stop was a boutique with a French name and staffed by extremely thin young women with slicked-back hair and lots of eye shadow. Nick picked out a Michael Kors silk racerback tank top from the first display table he saw and handed it to Kate.

"You would be a knockout in this," he said.

She held the tank out in front of her for inspection. Simple, stylish, and practical. Perfect for a relaxing lunch, a brisk walk on the beach, or hand-to-hand combat.

"I like it," she said, "but it's four hundred seventy-five dollars. I can get a tank top for twenty-five dollars at T.J. Maxx."

"It's not the same."

"Yeah, one is reasonably priced and the other is insane."

Nick took three of the tank tops from the table and handed them to the salesgirl, who was lucky she didn't tip over, since the combined weight of the garments was probably greater than her own. "We'll take these."

"No, we won't," Kate said.

"You need those clothes."

"Fine, but we'll get them at T.J. Maxx."

Nick pulled her aside out of earshot of the salesgirl. "No, we won't. You need designer clothes, shoes, and accessories to instantly sell your cover to anyone who lays eyes on you. If you stroll off the plane in Bali wearing three grand worth of clothes and dragging a Louis Vuitton bag behind you like a gunnysack in a country where the average monthly wage is less than fifty dollars, you will do that."

"This is so totally wrong," Kate said.

"Obviously you opted out of the honey trap class when you were in SEAL boot camp."

"It conflicted with the one on nose breaking and eye gouging."

Nick added a $900 red silk sarong dress and an $800 cashmere T-shirt and handed the salesgirl his credit card. "We'll take all these."

From there they went to a store that featured clothes by Hervé Léger, a label Nick chose for Kate because their fashions would perfectly accentuate her toned body. And because the store served their customers Dom Pérignon champagne in Baccarat crystal flutes.

Kate liked the champagne, but she was skeptical about the clothes.

"Try this on," Nick said, selecting a royal blue bandage dress.

"I don't think so," Kate said. "I can't see myself in this."

"Just try it."

Kate belted back some champagne and marched off to the dressing room. She shimmied into the sleeveless, skintight dress, with its plunging halterneck and a zipper that followed the contours of her back. She tugged at the bottom of the dress but it instantly rolled back up to midthigh. Jeez Louise, she thought, how was she ever going to sit in this? For that matter, how was she going to breathe? She looked down at her cleavage and wondered where it had all come from. She'd always thought she had okay but not spectacularly large breasts. The bandage dress had everything squished up and looking like there wasn't enough bandage to go around, as if her breasts had grown in the last fifteen minutes.

"I can't wear this," she said from inside the dressing room. "It's too small."

"Let's see," Nick said. "Come on out."

"Get me a bigger size. A *lot* bigger."

Nick opened the door and looked in at Kate. "Whoa," he said on a gush of air. His pupils dilated to the point where his brown eyes were almost totally black, and Kate decided the dress must look better than she'd first thought.

"Well?" she asked.

"I think I'm in love," Nick said. "But then my brain isn't completely engaged right now. That's not where the blood is flowing."

"Too much information," Kate said. "It would have been enough to tell me I look okay."

"Honey, you look a lot better than okay."

"You don't think it's a little slutty?"

"Not at these prices," Nick said.

By the time they reached the Louis Vuitton store and she paid more for a single Pégase suitcase than she'd spent on her first car, Kate was sweating and popping Rolaids like they were Life Savers. Their last stop was Neiman Marcus, where they picked up sunglasses and other accessories.

"How many bikinis do you have?" Nick asked.

"None."

He grinned. "You swim nude?"

"I do my swimming in the ocean, in a wet suit," she said. "So I don't need a bikini."

"You're going to need one in Bali," he said.

"I can't spend any more money. I'm having an anxiety attack. I can't feel my fingertips."

"Fine," he said. "Leave it to me."

"You don't know my measurements."

"Trust me," he said.

"That's a tough one."

They drove back to the Fantasy Springs Resort Casino and Nick walked Kate and her bags to her room.

"I'm going to check us out," he said. "I'll see you and Willie at Ngurah Rai airport in Denpasar, Bali, in three days. Your passport, prepared by the finest forger in the United States, will be waiting for you at the front desk in the morning, along with one for Willie. Be sure to travel first-class. You need to look the part from the moment you step on the plane. And I need you to wire two hundred thousand dollars to my account at DBS Bank in Singapore."

"Why Singapore?"

"That's where I'm heading. I'm on a flight out of LAX this evening so I can lay the groundwork for the con in advance of your arrival. I've written down the bank account information and the phone number where you can reach me once you've made your travel arrangements."

He took a folded piece of paper out of his pocket and was about to hand it to her when she slammed him back hard against the wall, pinning him there with the palm of her hand flat against his chest.

"You expect me to give you two hundred grand and let you jet off alone to Southeast Asia?" Kate asked him, more accusation than question. "You aren't thinking about going after Griffin and the half a billion dollars yourself, are you?"

"Never crossed my mind."

They were so close that their lips were practically touching, and she could feel his heart beating under her hand. She'd sort of hoped his heart would be racing, but his heart was steady. *Her* heart was the only one racing. *Dammit.*

She saw his eyes darken just as they had in the dressing room. He leaned in to her ever so slightly, and a hot rush of panic flashed through her. The panic was followed by something she feared was desire. Holy Toledo, she thought, he's going to kiss me.

"See you in Denpasar," Nick said, his lips lightly brushing hers when he spoke.

"Mmm," Kate murmured, ready for the kiss. "Denpasar."

Nick stepped away, smiled at her, and messed up her hair.

"Wear something sexy," he said, and then he turned on his heel and sauntered off down the hall.

Kate snapped her mouth shut, and narrowed her eyes. The hideous man had conned her into thinking he was going to kiss her! That was so typical of him, so sneaky, so *horrible.* She looked around for something to throw at him. Finding nothing she kicked a shopping bag.

"I hate when you mess up my hair!" she yelled after him, but he'd already disappeared into the elevator.

22

On her way to Encino Grande later that day, she called her father and invited him to the Fantasy Springs Resort Casino for breakfast the next morning.

"Sure," he said. "I could play some blackjack and break in my AARP discount card at the outlet stores in Cabazon."

Kate had an easy time seeing her father at the blackjack table. Seeing him using an AARP discount card at the Cabazon outlets was a struggle. She disconnected from him, and minutes later she rolled into the compound at Encino Grande. Boyd was floating on a raft in the pool, and Chet was returning to the house after serving Burnside his dinner tray in his cell. Tom had already gone back home to be with his family for the night but would be returning early in the morning to relieve Chet.

Boyd abandoned his raft and joined Kate and Chet in the kitchen. Kate made herself a bologna sandwich, and Chet tore open a bag of chips.

"It looks like Nick, Willie, and I are going to be gone for at least two weeks," Kate said.

Chet stopped eating for a beat. "That's longer than I expected. You really think we can pull off this charade for that long?"

"I did 212 performances of *Love Letters* on the dinner theater circuit with a different woefully untalented local actress every night. I can handle two weeks of this," Boyd said. "Of course it took a lot of alcohol to get me through *Love Letters*."

"I'm arranging for a senior operative to stop by from time to time," Kate said. "His name is Jake and he's a pro. Do as he says. And if anything goes wrong, and he's not around, call him at this number."

She passed Boyd a piece of paper with Jake's cell phone number on it.

"What happens in two weeks?" Chet asked.

"If it's not practical for Griffin to get picked up at sea, we might have to bring him back here for act three," Kate said.

"I wish I could be there for act two," Boyd said. "It's poor storytelling to have the central character off the stage for so long."

"I thought Derek Griffin was the star of this show," Chet said.

"I'm the character that ties together all of the plotlines," Boyd said. "I'm like Hannibal Lecter in *The Silence of the Lambs,* only without all of Anthony Hopkins's outrageous overacting. Remember how the movie dragged when his character wasn't around?"

"Not for me. I loved Jodie Foster," Chet said. "There was something really sexy about her as that FBI agent."

"Clarice Starling," Kate said.

"Yeah. Even though she was all buttoned up and tightly wound, there's something hot about a take-charge woman with a gun and a badge."

Kate perked up at that. She had a gun and a badge and she was take-charge.

The faux stack-stone décor of the Fantasy Springs Resort Casino was the same as the lobby of the Ventura retirement home that Kate had visited with the MPAA investigator weeks ago. There was also a similarity in the clientele. When Kate stepped out of the elevator at 10 A.M., there were already dozens of seniors ramming money into the slots, one hand poised on the big red button, ready to hit it as soon as the cherries stopped spinning.

She picked up the passport envelope Nick had left her at the desk and went to the coffee shop. Her dad was in a booth with a stack of hotcakes, two eggs, four strips of bacon, rye bread toast, and a cup of coffee in front of him. He smiled when he saw her.

"You look great," he said.

She sat down across from him. "I do?"

"Like you're about to leap out of a plane over Greece."

"There's a look for that?"

"It's called happiness, Kate. You are in your element."

"That's funny, because I sure don't feel like it." Kate waved over a waitress and ordered the same breakfast as her father's. "Thank you for coming all this way on such short notice."

"Are you kidding? They're having a seniors slot tournament this afternoon and Engelbert Humperdinck is playing here tonight. I've always admired that man."

"Why?"

"It takes balls and an iron will to stick with a name like that and become a success."

"That's not his real name," Kate said. "It's Tommy Dorsey or something like that."

"There was a big-band leader named Tommy Dorsey."

"Now you know why he changed it to Humperdinck."

"Well, it still takes guts. He could have changed it to Bobby Darin."

"There already was a singer named Bobby Darin."

"Yeah, but *his* real name was Walden Cassotto. See my point?"

"Not really," Kate said.

"How's the op going?" Jake asked.

She told him everything, and the telling took them through breakfast and two more cups of coffee. When she was done, he stared at her over the rim of his coffee mug.

"You left a makeup artist, a playhouse builder, and an actor in charge of holding a prisoner?"

"That's why I called you. They could use some backup."

"I'll stick around until you return, and I'll bring in another man. You remember my buddy José Rodarte? We did a lot of missions together. He's a big, mean Mexican."

"No, he's not. He's absolutely lovable. That's why he played Santa Claus for the kids on the base every Christmas. Come to think of it, didn't he just have a hip replacement?"

"That's what makes him so mean. He told me it feels like they gave the hip serrated edges, heated it up until it was white hot, and then shoved it into place through his ass."

"That's too vivid," Kate said, glad that she'd already eaten before she had that image in her head.

"José lives in Palm Springs now with his wife, who plays mahjong with her friends every day in their house. It's worse than being in a Turkish prison. He'll appreciate the excuse to get out of there."

"If this goes wrong, Dad, you'll both be accomplices in the commission of a federal crime."

He waved off her concern. He did that a lot lately.

"José and I both took an oath to serve God and country and I think this qualifies, even if some judge might disagree," he said. "When are you heading to Bali?"

"Tomorrow morning," she said.

"I was there when we propped up Suharto in '66 and again thirty-two years later when we brought him down. Spent some time in East Timor, too. More bullets in the air than mosquitos."

"That was a while ago. Indonesia has calmed down since then. It's a tourist destination now, a big honeymoon spot."

"It may look like a tropical paradise with its white sand beaches, swaying palm trees, azure waters, and colorful fishies, but it's a mirage. It's like putting a flower bed on a minefield."

"I can think of worse places to be. You haven't seen Thermal yet and smelled the Salton Sea."

"You're going into a country made up of hundreds of different cultures speaking hundreds of different languages spread out over thousands of islands that are consistently ravaged by malaria, dengue fever, volcanic eruptions, earthquakes, tsunamis, foreign invasion, ethnic warfare, rampant corruption, and extreme poverty. And that's just in the last hundred years and on a good day. Don't be fooled by all the pink Aussies on the beach sipping cocktails served by beautiful Indonesian women with big smiles. It's a dangerous place. So I'll have a little care package waiting for you at Benoa Harbor when you get there."

She smiled at her father. "A basket of fruit, bottled water, suntan lotion, and insect repellent?"

"Something like that," he said. "Who should I send the fruit to?"

Kate opened the envelope she'd picked up at the desk and pulled out her passport. "This is so *not* funny," she said.

Jake raised his eyebrows. "Bad passport photo?"

"Nick Fox has an annoying sense of humor. Send the fruit to Eunice Huffnagle."

Jake gave a bark of laughter. "That's a hideous name."

"It's the least of my problems."

Kate gave him directions to Encino Grande and went looking for Willie. She found her still at poolside reading *Chapman Piloting & Seamanship*.

"I see you're cramming," Kate said.

"Compared to flying an airplane, piloting a yacht is like riding a skateboard. When are we leaving?"

"We're checking out of here today, spending the night in the Sheraton at LAX, and flying out tomorrow morning."

"Great, what will I be flying?"

"An economy-class passenger seat," Kate said.

While Kate and Willie were packing up and checking out of Fantasy Springs, Nick Fox was sipping champagne high above the Pacific Ocean, sitting up on his full-size bed in his first-class compartment on a Singapore Airlines Airbus A380. His cubicle was private and wood-paneled, with a 23-inch flat-screen television, wireless Internet connectivity for his MacBook, a personal refrigerator, and a separate dining table, where his snack of lobster salad, caviar, fresh bread, and an assortment of fruit and cheese was laid out for his dining pleasure on a set of fine china.

He sipped his champagne and thought about the FBI. This plane trip, the entire covert op, were being paid for by a secret FBI slush fund filled with money taken from crooks. Nick wondered how long the agency had been skimming from confiscated cash. What else were they doing with it? And more to the point, how much money had they stolen? And where was it stashed? The money certainly wasn't on any accounting ledgers that the Justice Department or Congress could see, and if it went missing the feds couldn't really go after anyone for stealing what they shouldn't have had in the first place. The FBI was running a huge con. He thought it was very cool. And he thought it would be even cooler if he could scam them out of the money.

23

Kate and Willie left Indio around noon for the two-hour-plus drive to the Sheraton at LAX, where Kate had booked two rooms for the night on a "fly package." They rolled into the Sheraton, dumped their suitcases in their rooms, and hustled across the street to Denny's.

Kate had a grilled cheese with bacon, fries, and a chocolate shake, and Willie put away a Macho Nacho Burger with a banana split chaser, for a combined calorie count that was reaching five figures.

"So what's the deal with you and Foxy?" Willie wanted to know, scraping up the last of her ice cream.

"There's no deal. We work together."

"If it was me there'd be a deal. The guy is hot. He could talk a girl out of her panties before she even knew what was happening. And have you noticed how his eyes sparkle when he smiles? How does he do that?"

The sparkling eyes were good, Kate thought, but they were chump change compared to the way his eyes had gotten dark when he looked at her in the bandage dress.

A couple hours later, Kate was in her hotel room, trying to push thoughts of Nick Fox and his dark eyes out of her head, when he called.

"Just checking in," he said. "How's it going?"

"It would be going a lot better if you'd grow up. 'Huffnagle'? Are you kidding me? Was it really necessary to put 'Huffnagle' on my passport?"

"I'm a sentimental kind of guy. Eunice Huffnagle will always have a special place in my heart."

"Where are you?"

"Singapore. The Raffles hotel, to be exact, on my veranda, having a red prawn Niçoise salad with Mediterranean sardines."

"What are you doing in Singapore?"

"Establishing our covers, and making the arrangements for your arrival in Bali. The truth is, I'm enjoying my layover. I couldn't come all of this way without spending at least one night at Raffles."

"Why's that?"

"It's colonial elegance from another, more adventurous time. The hotel was built in 1887 as a bastion of British elegance and nobility in an exotic land. From my veranda I can almost see Somerset Maugham, the writer and spy, sitting in a rattan chair under a frangipani tree in the Palm Court garden, writing one of his stories in longhand. Or I can go to the hotel bar for a Singapore sling and sit under the vintage wicker-blade ceiling fans that were churning the humid air on that day in 1902 when the last surviving wild tiger, perhaps lonely and looking for a cocktail, strolled inside and was shot dead. You'd love it here."

"Maybe someday," Kate said, not completely convinced she'd love Raffles what with the poor last tiger getting shot when all he wanted was a cocktail.

"When do you arrive in Bali?" he asked her.

"Willie and I will leave L.A. in the morning on a Cathay Pacific flight to Hong Kong. We'll switch planes for the second leg of the trip, arriving in Bali at midday."

"Perfect," he said. "Sam, your loyal butler and chef, will be there to greet you. Make sure you look the part."

That had Kate smiling. She knew he'd eventually assume the persona of the *Cheers* womanizing bartender Sam Malone.

"I'd *better* look the part after what we spent on clothes," Kate said.

"What are you wearing now?"

It was a playful, provocative question and she was tempted to tell him "Nothing at all," but big brave Special Agent O'Hare chickened out. "A bathrobe and pink fluffy slippers," she said.

"Victoria's Secret?"

"Costco."

"And your gun?"

"Loaded."

"Leave everything but the slippers at home," he said.

"I can wear pink fluffy slippers and still be a honey trap?"

"Sure," he said. "If that's all you're wearing."

"This trip to Hong Kong is a first for me," Willie said to Kate as they left the Sheraton. "My Big Adventure never took me out of the country before. I never had money to fly legally. What do people do on a big airplane trip?"

"It's simple," Kate told her. "All you have to do is sit in your chair, look out the window, watch a movie, read a magazine, listen to some music, eat some food, or sleep through the whole trip."

Kate, on the other hand, was used to long international flights, mostly buckled into a hard bench seat mounted along the windowless interior bulkhead of a Lockheed C-130 military transport plane. An armrest would have been a frill. She'd also flown plenty of times, all across the country, in economy class on commercial airliners and sometimes in stripped-down government jets. This was the first time she was going to fly in a featherweight cashmere tank top, skinny pants, and leather flip-flops, and carry a genuine designer handbag. And it was the first time she was going to fly first-class with the promise of a cocktail and hot, salted nuts being offered before takeoff. She thought this was pretty darn exciting because nobody had ever offered her hot nuts before. At least none that came in a dish.

Hours later, after flying halfway around the world, Willie clomped through the Hong Kong airport in her five-inch wedges. She had her arm looped through Kate's, and she was gesturing with her free hand.

"This is just like being on *The Amazing Race*," Willie said. "I could practically hear the theme song playing. I feel like I should be running through the terminal."

"Not necessary," Kate said. "Our next gate isn't that far away. We have plenty of time."

"Yeah, but it would be fun to run. They run through terminals on *The Amazing Race* all the time."

"That's because they're late."

"No, it's because it's television, and it's fun. What do you do for fun, anyway? I never see you having any fun. You didn't lie out at the pool or go bowling or anything."

"I was working."

"Honey, from what I can see you're always working. I understand what it's like to love your job because nothing gets me off like driving a big-ass Caterpillar excavator. I drove a C15 once and I gotta tell you my panties were wet. But a girl needs to have some variety to her fun. What do you do for fun besides shoot blanks at people?"

Kate searched her memory bank for fun. "Sometimes I drink beer with my dad," Kate said.

Willie nodded. "That's a start. I had fun on the plane from L.A. I watched movies, and played videogames, and I sat next to a guy who knew how to fly a Boeing 777-300. What did you do in first class?"

"I had hot nuts."

"No shit."

"Yep. Hot, salty nuts," Kate said. "Just like it said on the airline website."

"Damn, there's not much better than hot, salty nuts."

"They were fun," Kate said, not sure they were talking about the same kind of hot nuts.

"Freakin' A," Willie said. "And now look at us. We're in China. I read that two islands had to be completely flattened to build the airport. The main terminal alone is three quarters of a mile of vaulted glass and has virtually all the same stores that are on Rodeo Drive. And they have a Popeyes Chicken here!"

The five-hour connecting flight to Denpasar cut southwest over the Strait of Malacca and the Java Sea, flying over countless islands and coral reefs. The plane began its descent over Bali, and an archipelago of puffy clouds blunted some of the sunlight and cast blotches of shadow over Ngurah Rai International Airport. Much like my life, Kate thought. Her life had turned exotic, filled with new experiences, shadowed by a cloudy future. Truth is, her new assignment was scary. She'd always felt safe under the protective blanket of the FBI, and now she was operating without the blanket. And she was partnered with a man who was exciting and smart, but who she didn't completely trust.

Kate deplaned with the other first-class passengers, visited the visa counter, and bought her 238,500 rupiah tourist visa, which was $25 American. She got her forged passport stamped at the immigration desk and made her way to baggage claim. She knew she was actually in Bali, but she couldn't shake the feeling that the Balinese architectural elements in the airport were fake. The terminal reminded her of an old International House of Pancakes in Northridge that someone had tried to transform into a Chinese restaurant by carving a five-clawed dragon into the front door and adding curvy points to every corner of the roof. That still didn't stop people from coming in and asking for a stack of buttermilk pancakes.

Willie clomped over just as the bags began to tumble down the chute and onto the carousel. They found their bags and dragged them to customs, handed the stone-faced Indonesian officers their declaration forms, and walked out into the arrivals lobby. The room was crowded with Javanese taxi drivers clamoring for fares, and bewildered tourists looking for transportation. In all this congested mix of sweaty humanity, Kate had no problem finding Nick. Nick Fox stood out in his fitted white polo shirt with a corporate logo on the chest. The logo was a blue planet with a streak of lighting across it that carried the words ***HUFFNAGLE GLOBAL*** in a bold, italic action font that suggested urgency and determination. He had a broad hospitality smile on his face, the kind the best hotel clerks, concierges, and flight attendants work years to achieve, one that convincingly proclaims: *My life was meaningless until I had this wondrous opportunity to lay my eyes upon you and cater to your every need.*

He rushed to take Kate's bags. "*Selamat siang.* Welcome to Bali, Ms. Huffnagle. I hope you had a pleasant flight."

Kate and Willie followed Nick outside into the hot, humid afternoon, where a sparkling but not very recent Mercedes, provided by the Benoa Bali Regal Resort Hotel, was waiting for them at the curb, a uniformed driver at the wheel. Kate slipped into the backseat, Willie got in beside her, and Nick took the front passenger seat. The streets were narrow, crowded with taxis, motorcycles, bikes, and mopeds, and lined with palm trees and whitewashed buildings covered with signs vying for the attention of rich tourists. The Mercedes turned a corner onto a street packed with outdoor restaurants where diners sat cross-legged at tables eating rice with their hands. The air was thick with the smell of spices carried in the steam from hundreds of sizzling pots.

Up and down the sidewalks, and crouched between parked motorcycles at the curbs, were roving vendors carrying their kitchens either on rolling carts or balanced on sticks across their shoulders. Each stick had a sling with a wok on one side and a bundle of ingredients on the other, and dishes were prepared on the spot wherever vendors found a hungry paying customer. The vendors were so close to the car that Kate was tempted to reach out the window and snatch a bowl from one of them.

24

The Benoa Bali Regal was a five-star resort built on the pristine golden sands of the Tanjung Benoa peninsula. Once home to ramshackle fishing villages, the peninsula was now a prime tourist destination with high-end hotels taking advantage of the swaying palms, sugary beaches, bright blue seas, and breathtaking vistas.

Nick saw the luxurious resorts of Southern Bali as a successfully executed multibillion-dollar con. The travel industry had convinced people to fly tens of thousands of miles to stay at Bali-themed resorts rather than experience the authentic villages, rice paddies, temples, and tropical forests of Bali itself. The real Bali, even more beautiful than the re-creation, was a few miles farther north. Fortunately the con worked for everyone's good, ensuring that the real Bali didn't get overrun with hordes of tourists demanding flush toilets, while the resort Bali brought money into the economy and provided the tourists with a porcelain paradise featuring overhead rain showers and the latest in Japanese toilet technology.

Kate followed Nick through the resort lobby to their private three-bedroom beachfront villa, with its coconut wood paneling, open-air living room, and personal lap pool in a tropical garden. She stood at the edge of the pool and had to admit to herself that a life of crime had some advantages. This beat the heck out of her one-bedroom apartment over Al's Pizza Pit on Ventura.

Nick tipped the bellman and joined her. "What do you think?"

"Nice."

"It has a spa pool that has three different kinds of jets and soft lighting at night. Perfect for getting into the mood."

"What mood would that be?" she asked him.

He was so close she could feel his body heat, and his breath whispered against her neck. "A romantic mood."

Her heart skipped a couple beats.

"So let me know if you want me to turn the jets on," Nick said.

"Yep. Sure will," Kate said. "Thanks for the offer."

Jeez Louise, the man was diabolical, Kate thought. Wasn't it enough he was tempting her with a lap pool and a designer handbag? Now he was torturing her with the spa and possibly his body next to hers, pressed against the three different kinds of jets.

"I'm going to unpack now," she said, anxious to put distance between them. "Maybe I'll investigate the beach and go swimming."

"Need help unpacking?" he asked.

"Nope. I'm good."

"Maybe you need help getting into your bathing suit."

"No!" She narrowed her eyes at him. "You're baiting me."

"Maybe," he said. "Maybe not."

Kate stalked off to the master bedroom suite and unpacked her bikinis. Up to this point she hadn't given them much thought, but she now saw the error in foisting the bikini buying off on Nick. The tissue paper the bikinis were wrapped in was more substantial than the bikinis.

Kate did a trial run on a little white number that had a halter-neck and ties at the hip. She stood in front of the mirror, looked at herself from the back, and grimaced at the amount of cheek hanging out. She checked herself from the front and didn't see anything specifically private in full view, although there were hints of lady parts here and there. She bent at the waist and nothing fell out of the top. She blew out a sigh and grabbed a towel. She was willing to go the extra mile for her job, but criminy, this was about the scariest thing she'd done so far.

Nick missed Kate's grand exit because he was explaining to Willie why she needed to wear khaki shorts and the white shirt with the Huffnagle Global logo.

"I paid good money for my breasts," Willie said, "and you want me to stuff them into one of these boring shirts?"

"This isn't any ol' shirt," Nick said. "The shirts in your closet are one hundred percent Egyptian cotton and are made by Chiang Yick Ching, Singapore's oldest custom shirt maker, who's been making meticulously cut, finely stitched clothes for me for years."

"Sweetie pie, you can paint a cow red, but it ain't never gonna be a tomato. This is not a shirt that says *Come look at me 'cause I've got nipples*."

"You're supposed to be the captain of a multimillion-dollar yacht. You're not selling nipples."

"I never said I was selling them. I just like when people notice. It's like you and all those white teeth. Caps, right?"

"Nope," he said. "They're mine. I brush twice a day."

"How about if I wear the stupid khaki shorts but I trade the shirt in for a white tank top?"

"Done," Nick said.

Willie grabbed him and kissed him. "Perfect! This is going to be great. I can't wait to see my yacht. This is like one of the happiest days of my life. I'm renaming The Big Adventure. I'm calling it The *Really* Big Adventure."

"Good to know you're happy," Nick said.

Willie looked him up and down. "You want to make me even happier?"

"Maybe not that happy," Nick said, "but I appreciate the thought."

Kate was out in the ocean in her bikini and Willie was off exploring in her shorts and tank top when their personal chef arrived to begin preparing their dinner. Nick went over the menu with the chef, then walked out to the thatch-roof cabana on their private deck. He was standing there, enjoying the tropical air and the view, when Kate emerged from the azure water, her oiled skin glistening in the sun.

Nick thought she looked straight out of a James Bond movie. The only thing missing from the picture was a knife in a sheath clipped to a dive belt. And this annoying, amusing, amazing, beautiful, mostly naked woman was off-limits to him. How crappy was that? He was fairly certain if he put his mind to it he could get into her bed tonight. He was 100 percent certain she'd hunt him down in the morning and he'd be roadkill. And if he actually survived to continue with the partnership, she'd make his life a living hell.

Kate approached him, and he offered her a towel. "The chef is in the kitchen, *Ms. Huffnagle*."

"Thank you, Sam," she said, ignoring the towel and strolling past him to a chaise, making the most of her role as Eunice Huffnagle. "I'll take a drink now, something cold and fruity, with plenty of alcohol. Something to take the salt off my lips."

"Of course," Nick said.

He looked down at her stretched out on the chaise, eyes closed against the sun, and he thought it might be worth getting kicked down the road and smacked with a tire iron for a night of killer sex with her.

"Anything else?" he asked. "A massage, perhaps?"

"Does the hotel have a masseuse available at this hour?"

"No, but I'm here, and I'd be glad to help you work out any kinks you might have. Any kinks at all."

"I'll let the drink do that. Hurry along, Sam. I can feel my lips chapping with each passing moment."

"Yes ma'am," Nick said. "Wouldn't want your lips to chap."

"Do I detect a hint of attitude?" she asked him.

"Not from me," Nick said. "I'm your faithful manservant. I'm here to fulfill your every desire."

Nick, Kate, and Willie sat barefoot and cross-legged on mats at a low table that faced a fire pit circled with lava rocks. Beyond the fire pit was the beach, and beyond the beach moonbeams surfed the gentle waves. Behind the fire pit was the three-bedroom villa and the personal chef slaving away in the outdoor kitchen creating a multicourse meal of Indonesian dishes. One of the dishes was vegetables in peanut sauce. There was also pork boiled in vinegar and pig's blood, and nasi campur, which was steamed rice and vegetables mixed with fried nuts, grilled tuna, coconut milk, fried tofu, curried chicken, assorted herbs and spices, and shredded coconut. All the foods were served with a generous side of sambal, a chili pepper sauce that was the Indonesian equivalent of ketchup and used liberally on everything.

"You eat with your fingers," Nick said, pinching chunks of fish, meat, and vegetables between bits of sticky rice.

Easy for him and Willie, Kate thought. They were dressed in wash-and-wear Huffnagle Global uniforms, while she was trying not to slop food on her megabucks halter and shorts. Being a rich bitch wasn't as simple as one might think.

When they were done with the meal and the chef left, Nick spread maps and navigational charts out on the large dining room table.

"We're leaving at nine A.M. for Benoa Harbor," Nick said. "The yacht I rented will be fueled, stocked, and ready to go. Griffin's island, Dajmaboutu, is about four hundred miles away in the Flores Sea. It's between a stretch of large islands known as the West Nusa Tenggara and South Sulawesi. We're going to travel through the heavily trafficked Lombok Strait and then west into the open sea, where we'll sail a weaving course through the islands, islets, and atolls until we reach Dajmaboutu. The yacht is equipped with state-of-the-art GPS, radar, and autopilot. And if we don't want to dock by the seat of our pants it has a computer-controlled docking system that takes over the engines, steering, and the thrusters at the bow and stern to take all the risk out of fitting into a tight spot."

Kate studied the charts. "To bring Griffin into international waters, we'll have to head back the way we came, through the Lombok Strait, then southwest into the Indian Ocean, where a U.S. Navy vessel can pick him up. That's roughly another six hundred miles."

"No problem," Nick said. "I chose a fifty-five-foot Phelan SevenSeas 550LR, which I got at the bargain price of ten thousand dollars a day because Eunice Huffnagle insisted on using her own crew."

He dropped the owner's manual onto the table and turned to a photo of the Phelan under power. It was a beautiful vessel, with a blue hull and white deck, and windows on the main cabin that looked like wraparound sunglasses. Its most distinctive feature was its flybridge, which cantilevered over the aft deck and had standing fins on either side that evoked a 1959 Cadillac.

"It's a trawler that's going to lumber along like an elephant," Kate said. "We'll be lucky to get eighteen knots out of it."

"You're approaching this like a military op," Nick said. "You want a quick entry and exit. But that's not what we're doing."

"We're kidnapping a guy and taking him out of the country," Kate said. "We don't want to linger around working on our tans. We need to get the heck out."

"That's the wrong attitude. What we're doing is more like a heist, only with a person instead of an object. A successful heist is one that nobody notices until it's over and the thieves are long gone. But I understand your concerns. I have them, too, which is why I picked this particular yacht. The Phelan SevenSeas 550LR is no ordinary trawler. It can reach a top speed of twenty-two knots and cruise at sixteen. It can plane and plow," Nick said. It was a phrase he stole from the brochure that he understood the gist of, if not the actual meaning.

"We'll see," Kate said. "I'd still rather punch him in the face and spirit him away in a jetboat."

"And I'd rather be driving the jetboat, but I'll settle for this," Willie said, gathering together the literature on the yacht. "I'm going back to my room and study up on this boat so we don't end up like the *Titanic*."

25

Benoa Harbor had a seedy, industrial feel despite the presence of dozens of sleek yachts stuck in between all of the fishing trawlers, longboats, rusted tankers, thatch-roofed houseboats, ferries, motorboats, huge cruise ships, and the colorful two-masted Bugis schooners with their long, curved bows that resembled a leprechaun's shoes. Fruit vendors in longboats puttered among the tightly packed boats, selling bananas and oranges to people who reached out of open portholes or leaned perilously over their boat decks to pay for their purchases.

There were two Javanese men sitting on a wooden crate, about the size of a bag of golf clubs, on the dock beside the gleaming new Phelan SevenSeas 550LR when Kate, Nick, and Willie arrived. Kate approached the men, and looked down at the crate. As expected, it was the bon voyage gift from her dad.

"You can put that in the master stateroom," she said to the men, gesturing to the boat.

Nick repeated her orders in rough Indonesian and the two men lugged the crate up the gangway onto the yacht. Willie followed them on board, tossed her bag into her cabin, and climbed up the stairs to the secondary helm atop the flybridge.

"Play the role," Nick whispered to Kate. "People are watching."

Kate's only point of reference to Eunice Huffnagle was Goldie Hawn in the movie *Overboard,* so she channeled Goldie and did some improvising. She walked up and down the dock in her strappy gold high-heeled sandals, expensive little black halter top, and skinny white linen slacks that sat low on her hips. She walked and frowned and pouted as she examined the yacht, aware of the attention she was getting from the Indonesians aboard the nearby fishing boats and even some of the tourists lined up for the ferry.

"It's so tiny," she said. "It doesn't even have a helipad."

"I'm sorry, Ms. Huffnagle," Nick said. "It's the best we could do on short notice."

"I'd hate to see your worst." She shook her head and got on board, Nick following after her.

The two Javanese men emerged from the master cabin and stood waiting for payment.

"Give them fifty thousand rupiah for their troubles," Kate said to Nick, "and let's get out of this dreary place."

Kate had seen *Overboard* a couple years ago and couldn't totally remember it all, but she was pretty sure Goldie would be proud of her performance.

"Yes, right away, ma'am," Nick said.

Kate marched past the men into the cabin. The floors were bleached oak, the leather settees were tan, and there was decape oak cabinetry throughout. The pinpoint halogen lighting, silver accents and hardware, and the curvy lines of every counter and design element gave the entire salon a smooth, contemporary style that evoked forward motion.

Two steps up, and on the port side, was a chef's galley with top-of-the-line stainless steel appliances, German fixtures, and granite countertops. On the starboard side was an impressive lower helm station that continued the curvy theme, presenting the array of screens, keypads, joysticks, and controls in an elegant dashboard arrangement of leather, oak, and brushed aluminum that was Bentley elegance married to Apple sleek.

Kate was dying to take the helm, but she knew she wouldn't be able to pry it out of Willie's hands without punching her unconscious first. And probably Goldie wouldn't take the helm anyway. Have patience, she thought. The journey to Griffin's island would take about twenty-four hours, if they kept at constant cruising speed. So she could take a shift at the helm once they were out in open sea.

She went down the curving staircase to the lower deck, where there were three staterooms and two heads. The master stateroom, by far the largest and most comfortable, was amidships, where the hull was widest and deepest, and was filled with natural light from two large windows port and starboard. There was a queen-size berth that had plenty of room on either side of it, even with the crate on the floor. There was a roomy C-shaped settee and collapsible dinette under the starboard window, a thirty-two-inch flat-screen television in front of the bed, a port-side cabinet with a minibar and safe, a full-height closet, and a private head with a full-size shower.

Nick followed her into the master stateroom. "Who sent you the crate?"

"I did. I couldn't pack everything I needed into my bag."

"Like what?"

"Handcuffs," she said.

"I like it," Nick said. He gave her a salute, and left.

Kate changed into her bikini because it seemed like something Goldie would do, and while she was putting on suntan lotion the yacht started with a lurch that nearly knocked her to the floor. Willie getting the feel of the controls, she thought. Kate hoped that Willie was a fast learner. She grabbed a hat and sunglasses and went topside.

The ride out of the harbor and into the busy Lombok Strait was uneventful. Willie was at the helm on the flybridge, steering the boat through the gauntlet of ferries, tankers, longboats, and pleasure craft. A rusting wreck in the center of the bay bore testament to the dangers of navigating in and out of the harbor.

They reached open water and Willie rammed the throttle to full speed, anxious to see what the yacht could do. Kate braced herself when the boat lifted and jolted forward. She turned to look at Willie, and Willie gave her two thumbs up. Willie slowed down to cruising speed after a few minutes, and Kate made her way to the stern and climbed the stairs to the flybridge.

Nick was barbecuing shrimp and chicken on the built-in grill that sat beside a fully stocked minibar and a sink, all within serving reach of the aft dinette area. Willie stood at the starboard-side pilot station, looking ahead to the cluster of islands on the horizon, the wind whipping her hair into a frenzy of overprocessed yellow snarls, her barely contained nipples saluting the bow.

The communications and radar array were located at the top of the mast, and toward the bottom was an outdoor shower. Kate bypassed the shower and went to Willie.

"How is it going?" Kate asked.

"It would be going better if I had a cold beer," Willie said. "Other than that it's fantastic."

Nick brought Willie a plate of rice, chicken, and shrimp. "I can take the helm if you'd like a break."

"No way. I never want a break. I could drive this mother forever. This thing's better than a Zamboni."

"Yeah, and we don't have to freeze the water," Nick said, moving Kate away from the pilot station and toward the dinette, where he had their lunch set out.

"I didn't know cooking was among your talents," Kate said, sliding onto the C-shaped settee, spearing a grilled shrimp with her fork.

"I have a lot of talents you don't know about."

Kate paused with the shrimp halfway to her mouth. "Such as?"

"I'm a good chess player."

No surprise there, she thought. "And?"

"I can iron a shirt, but I'd rather not. I can play the piano halfway okay. I can touch my nose with my tongue."

Kate lost her grip on her fork, and the fork clattered onto her plate.

Nick smiled. "I knew you'd like that last one."

After lunch, Kate went to her stateroom, opened the crate, and sorted through the care package from her dad, amused by his thoughtfulness and impressed by his resources. He'd clearly amassed a huge network of contacts and plenty of favors during his years of covert military service. And it was paying off for her now. She locked a few items in the safe, then slipped her filmy red sarong over her bikini and went abovedeck, where Willie was now piloting the yacht from the helm console in the cabin.

"What's our ETA?" Kate asked.

"At this speed, we should arrive at Dajmaboutu by early morning."

Nick was at the table, reviewing the charts. "Or we could anchor off any of a dozen islands along the way for the night, get an early start tomorrow, and show up midafternoon."

"We aren't on vacation," Kate said. "We have a mission to complete."

"Hard to remember the mission with you in that red silk thing," Nick said.

Kate flapped her arms. "I don't have anything else! We only bought mantrap clothes." She looked down at herself. "Actually it's really comfy. It lets a lot of air in."

"So?" Willie asked. "What's the plan?"

"We're pushing on," Kate said. "We'll pilot in shifts. I'll take the next one."

Kate chose to do her time on the flybridge station, where she could feel the night air and see the stars. It was nice to have the GPS, but she felt more secure having the solar system up there as backup and her father's trusty sextant, which he'd kindly included in his care package. Nick left her alone, only intruding on her solitude to bring her sandwiches and coffee. Shortly after midnight, he tapped her shoulder and told her it was time for her to hand over the helm to him.

"Do you know how to pilot a yacht?" she asked.

"No, I don't, but I thought it would be fun to try it in pitch-darkness in the middle of the Flores Sea," Nick said, smiling. "They light up the islands, right?"

"You're such a smart-ass."

"I know, but I'm a charming smart-ass."

This was true, Kate thought. He was a charming smart-ass.

Kate awoke after dawn, jolted out of sleep by a sudden surge in the yacht's speed. She got out of bed and nearly lost her footing when the yacht banked sharply to one side and then the other. She opened her door and saw Nick coming out of the other stateroom.

"What's going on?" Kate asked.

"I don't know," Nick said. "Willie took over for me an hour ago."

They rushed up the stairs to the flybridge, where Willie had the boat at top speed passing what appeared to be a small, uninhabited islet with a jagged shore and a thick forest of trees. Two old, beaten-down speedboats were about fifty yards behind them and closing fast. Kate guessed there were half a dozen men in each boat.

"They came out of nowhere as I was passing that little island," Willie said. "I saw guns, and I hit full throttle."

"Guns? What kind of guns?"

"The kind with bullets," Willie said. "I've been swerving side to side to create a bigger wake, but they're still gaining."

Kate grabbed binoculars from a shelf beneath the console and took a closer look. The boats were full of men carrying grappling hooks and automatic weapons. Kate lowered her binoculars as one of the speedboats surged forward and closed in on their starboard side.

"They're pirates. We aren't going to be able to outrun them. They're twice as fast," Kate said.

Willie looked over at her. "Are you suggesting we give up?"

"No. Keep doing what you're doing."

"No problem," Willie said. "This is the kind of cruising I'm used to."

Kate and Nick ran aft to the stairs and were on their way down when the speedboat opened fire. Kate hit the stern deck hard, taking Nick down with her. Bullets raked the port side, shattering windows and punching holes in the cabin.

It was a warning, but Willie took it as a challenge. She veered hard toward the pirates, like she was playing bumper boats at the county fair, and they steered away to avoid a collision.

"She's good," Kate said, getting to her feet.

"Yeah, but it's pointless," Nick said. "We'll have to stop, and when we do, just play the frightened heiress. I'll do the talking."

Willie swerved back around and headed straight at the boat that had been following them. The other pilot easily steered clear, but not before opening a volley of shots at the flybridge as he passed. Everyone hit the deck as bullets tore up the dinette and shattered the minibar, spilling drinks on the floor, a tiny waterfall of alcohol splashing down the stairs to the stern.

"That was another warning," Nick said. "The next time they shoot, they could kill one of us."

"Good thing we didn't get a faster boat," Kate said. "Do what you have to do. I'm screaming in terror and going below."

"Make a show of it," he said.

Kate screamed, waved her arms in the air for good measure, and ran below.

Nick yelled to Willie, "Stop the boat!"

"Are you kidding?" Willie yelled back. "They'll be all over us."

"Just do it," Nick said.

He took a white towel from a cabinet at the stern and waved it above his head as a flag of surrender. The speedboats were behind them now, almost side by side. One boat hung back while the other one approached. Nick could see two men stepping forward with their grappling hooks to secure the yacht.

They were about ten yards away, coming up the starboard side, when the men suddenly dove off their boat. Nick looked over his shoulder and saw Kate standing behind him with a rocket-propelled grenade launcher resting on her shoulder. It may have been the sexiest thing he'd ever seen.

"Get down," she said calmly to him, and fired.

The grenade streaked across the water and smacked into the abandoned speedboat, igniting the fuel on board and setting off a massive white-hot blast of flame, smoke, and shards of fiberglass.

Willie didn't wait to be told to punch it. She used the distraction, and the cloud of smoke, to hit full throttle. Kate stood her ground, staring into the cloud of black smoke as the other speedboat circled back to pick up the men splashing in the water.

Nick got to his feet, grinning. "*That's* what you had delivered? A rocket-propelled grenade launcher?"

"No girl should ever leave home without one," Kate said, and tossed it onto the settee as if it was her purse.

26

The three of them regrouped in the cabin with Willie at the helm, while Kate used a rolled-up navigational chart to wipe glass fragments off the dinette table.

"I want to see how close we are to Griffin's island," Kate said, smoothing the chart out in front of her. "We need to get out of the open sea and into a protected cove. Those two speedboats weren't out here alone. There's a mother ship out there somewhere."

"And we can't call anybody for help," Willie said. "They shot off the top of our mast, taking out our nav and communications array."

"We don't need them," Nick said. "We're in terrific shape."

Kate hated to be the one to ask the question, but she knew someone had to do it. "How do you figure that?" she said.

"Look around," Nick said, and swept his arm in front of him, gesturing to the shattered windows, the bullet-pocked couches, and the chunks of scorched fiberglass that littered the stern. "The pirates were a godsend. Now Griffin won't question why Eunice is seeking shelter on his island. It will be obvious. She's terrified, in desperate need of comfort and security, after being attacked by a horde of bloodthirsty pirates. If I had their address, I'd send them a fruit basket. They did us a huge favor."

"It might have turned out differently if I didn't have that grenade launcher," Kate said.

"But you did," Nick said. "Because that is who you are. Sometimes when a plan is right, everything else, all the things you can't control, falls into place just the way it should. I've got a good feeling about this."

"You're the only person I know who'd consider nearly being hijacked by pirates as a positive sign," Kate said, and tapped a location on the map. "We're only thirty or forty minutes from Griffin's island. If our luck holds, we can make it there before the mother ship comes looking for us."

"And if it doesn't," Nick said, "what else have you got in that crate?"

"The usual touristy things."

"Like what?"

"Handcuffs."

"Kinky," he said.

"A Glock," she said.

"Naturally."

"A garrote."

"Always handy."

"Night-vision goggles, a switchblade, a Kevlar vest, plenty of ammo, and a spare rocket-propelled grenade launcher."

"The bare necessities," Nick said.

"My God." Willie looked back at Kate. "What kind of vacations do you take?"

"Ones like this," Kate said.

A few years ago, Derek Griffin realized that it would soon be impossible to hide the monumental extent of his fraud from his clients or the SEC. So rather than wait to get caught, he began quietly arranging his inevitable flight from justice. With Neal Burnside's help, Griffin bribed Indonesian government officials to allow him to lease a beautiful tropical island for fifty years from a destitute tribe that had dwindled in number to just a few dozen people. He paid most of the tribe to leave the island in favor of condos in Sulawesi, but he kept a few of them around to take care of him and fulfill his halfhearted promise to maintain their ancient burial grounds.

Under the guise of developing the island as a resort, a requirement of the lease, he'd mowed down most of the tribe's village and built a luxurious compound that architecturally mimicked the traditional Tongkonan style, which featured sharply curved bamboo roofs that looked like the top of Batman's head.

Griffin prominently displayed a stack of fifty water buffalo horns, a symbol of wealth and status in the Torajan culture, on the front of his house to let everyone know he was loaded. It was the Torajan equivalent of parking a Ferrari in the driveway. So the horns were a must, as was having a herd of living water buffalo around, just to remind everyone who was boss and inspire the requisite envy. It was like parading around Beverly Hills with a twenty-two-year-old trophy wife, or top model girlfriend, or both.

He'd been well into the process of quietly moving his most

prized possessions from Los Angeles to the island, including his library of first editions and his collection of modern art, when Neal Burnside alerted him that his arrest was imminent. Griffin fled within the hour, and now here he was, halfway around the world, the king of his own tropical island, half a billion dollars tucked away in a secret bank account.

Unfortunately Burnside's paradise was missing a key ingredient. There were no women on the island, except his chef's wife and the plain-looking tribeswomen who tended to his home and grounds, and they didn't count. This sad state of affairs was very much on Griffin's mind that morning as he sat on his veranda, eating his rice flour pancakes embellished with fruit, brown sugar, and coconut milk. He gazed out at the carved jackwood effigies of the dead that stared wide-eyed at him from their hand-chiseled alcoves in the mountain beside his house, and he felt his manly urges percolating. So much so that even the tribeswomen, who tended his fields in their caftans and straw hats, their lips scarlet with betel nut stain and their faces white with rice powder, were beginning to look desirable to him.

That's when Dumah, his property manager and head of security, came lumbering out onto the deck. He was a fierce-looking Torajan, part of a tribe that, in the not too distant past, were known as headhunters and slavers.

"There's a yacht dropping anchor in the cove," Dumah said, and offered his boss a pair of high-powered binoculars.

Griffin looked out at the cove. The yacht was new and nicely designed, but it had been strafed with bullets and the mast was missing its antennas. Some dumb, rich tourists who'd run into trouble, he thought. He was about to tell Dumah to send them away when he spotted the woman on the flybridge. She had drastically bleached blond hair pulled up into a frizzed-out ponytail, a set of fun bags that could knock your eye out, and it looked like her ass was okay too. She was sort of wearing a crew uniform. He felt a stirring of desire, but not strong enough to risk letting whoever was on that yacht come onto his island.

Griffin was ready to tell Dumah to give them the heave-ho when Kate walked into his line of vision, and it was like someone had just jolted him with defibrillator paddles. His heart nearly exploded out of his chiseled chest. She was wearing a thin red silk dress that was translucent in the bright sunlight, showing Griffin everything he'd been yearning for and more. And this creature of erotic delight had just been delivered to his door like a Domino's pizza. He lowered his binoculars, licked the brown sugar from his lips, and thanked God for answering his unspoken prayers.

"These people are in trouble," Griffin said. "We're going to help them."

Nick released the motorized dinghy that was attached to the stern and helped Kate and Willie get on board. Once they were settled, he fired up the outboard and steered them toward the beach. He could see some natives gathering on the white sand in their hand-woven straw hats and bootleg Ralph Lauren shirts. At least he hoped for Ralph's sake the shirts were bootleg, because the oversize and misproportioned insignia looked like a monkey on a camel.

Kate saw Griffin drive up in a golf cart, and watched him step out from behind the wheel. He was wearing a white short-sleeved shirt and white shorts. He was deeply tanned, with a sprinkling of premature gray in his hair, and his body was muscled in the way that men get muscled from working out in a prison yard, lifting weights and running along the fenced perimeter day after day because it's all there is to do. Griffin's prison was his tropical island.

"Go get him, tiger," Nick said to Kate. "Turn his world upside down."

"I'm not sure I can do that," Kate said.

"You did it to me," Nick said. "And you can do it to him."

As the boat neared shore, Kate tried out some of Boyd's Method acting, imagining herself in the afterglow of sex, parts of her still swollen and pulsing, her heart still beating fast, her skin flushed.

"Are you okay?" Nick asked. "You sound like you're hyperventilating. Do you need a paper bag?"

"I'm fine," Kate said. "Got a little heartburn from your cooking."

Okay, she thought, maybe I should dial back on the Method stuff.

Griffin saw the hot bitch in the red dress studying his body, and he saw the smile it brought to her face. Nice, he thought. This was starting out very well and they hadn't even met yet. He gestured to his men to help bring the dinghy ashore. Three of the tribesmen sloshed out into the water and pulled the boat up onto the beach.

Dumah stepped up beside Griffin. "I don't like this. We have no idea who they are."

"She's a wealthy young woman who decided to take a cruise in pirate-infested waters on an expensive yacht with a flag on the mast that said 'Come and get it.' "

"And yet here they are," Dumah said. "How did they escape?"

"I'm sure there's a good explanation," Griffin said. "You keep an eye on her crew. I'll watch her."

Griffin stepped into the warm, shallow water and offered his hand to the woman as she climbed out of the boat.

"Oh, thank God," she said. "A friendly face. For a minute there, I was afraid we were trading one bad situation for another. What if we'd come ashore on an island occupied by pirates?"

"Fortunately, that's not the case," Griffin said, leading her to the beach and leaving her two crew members to fend for themselves. "I'm Daniel Dravot and this is my private island. You're safe here."

"That's a huge relief after what we've just been through. I'm Eunice Huffnagle." She gestured to her two crew members standing a respectful distance away with Dumah and the curious tribespeople. "Willie is my ship's captain, and Sam is first mate."

"Eunice Huffnagle," Griffin said. "What an unusual name."

"I was named after my great-aunt. She went insane one night and killed her mate." Kate cut her eyes to Nick.

"Your boat looks like it's sustained significant damage," Griffin said. "You don't have your great-aunt on board, do you?"

"Goodness, no. We were attacked by pirates," Kate said. "They came out of nowhere on speedboats and just started shooting at us with machine guns. Luckily, no one was hurt. We have to call the coast guard right away."

"There's no point. There's nothing the authorities can do."

"But those pirates are still out there, waiting to ambush somebody else."

"It's a big sea with a thousand islands, all of it infested with pirates. You escaped. Consider yourself very, very lucky."

"So it's just open season on the tourists."

"Only the ones who stray far from civilization and flaunt their wealth and vulnerability."

He regretted the remark the instant he made it. Insulting a woman was probably not the best strategy for getting her into bed. But, to his relief, she didn't seem offended. She shrugged his comment off.

"I wanted to get away from it all and experience the true Indonesia, not sit around in one of Daddy's hotels. So I rented this little boat. What's the point of having lots of money if you don't spend it?"

"So true," Griffin said, trying to sneak a peek down her silky top. "How did you get away from the pirates? Surely you couldn't have outrun them."

"Sam blew up their boat with a rocket-propelled grenade launcher."

Eunice said it in a casual, offhand sort of way that made it seem as if she was referring to a common yacht accessory.

"Really?" Griffin looked over her shoulder to Sam, who nodded.

"Her father is very protective," Sam said. "You should see what she takes with her when she goes camping."

"I may be rich, showy, and irresponsible," Eunice said, "but I'm never vulnerable."

Griffin laughed, truly laughed, for the first time in ages. Eunice was his kind of woman: sexy, smart, and sassy. He hadn't met anyone like her since he'd fled the United States. And he intended to make the most of the opportunity that had fallen into his lap, right where it belonged.

"You still must be pretty shaken up after such a terrifying experience," he said to her.

"To be honest, I couldn't stop shaking until you took my hand to help me out of the boat."

Holy crap, Griffin thought. It kept getting better and better. He had a sure thing, and she wasn't even ugly. She was pretty. Okay, so maybe her hair was sort of chopped off, but it was probably hard to get a good cut in Indonesia.

"I hope you'll let me be of even greater comfort to you," he said. "I insist that you stay here as my guest for a few days. That will give your crew a chance to clean up your yacht and make absolutely sure there isn't any serious damage. You will find the true Indonesia right here, on this remote paradise, along with the finest amenities, a world-class chef, and the best wine cellar in the region."

Eunice Huffnagle flicked a look at her yacht and then at her crew while she considered his invitation, and Griffin seized the opportunity to watch a drop of sweat roll down her chest and disappear into her cleavage. Ordinarily he prided himself on his self-control, but he'd been on the island way too long, and he was afraid to look down and check himself out for fear he was busting out of his shorts.

Eunice turned back to Griffin. "Thank you, Mr. Dravot, I would be delighted. I've never spent the night on an uncharted desert isle before."

"We're on all the navigational charts."

"Shhhh." Eunice looped her arm around his and pressed her breast against him. "Don't ruin the fantasy."

"Call me Daniel," he said, and led her away.

27

Griffin loaded Kate into the golf cart and drove her down a narrow sandy trail, about fifty yards inland from the beach, to his house.

"We have electricity from solar power," he said. "Plus gas-powered generators in a pinch. Freshwater is collected in cisterns, and there's a backup desalinization system. There's also a working farm where we grow rice, fruit, and vegetables, till the land with water buffalo, and raise pigs for slaughter."

"But do you have HBO?" she asked.

"We have all the comforts and conveniences of your yacht," Griffin said. He pointed to the small mountain that was in the dead center of the island. "I've got satellite dishes and radio antennas on top of that mountain. And I have a satellite phone, in case I want to have a pizza delivered."

She gestured to the wooden effigies staring out at them from alcoves carved into the mountain. "What are those?"

"Dead people. It's a Torajan tribal thing. When someone dies, they carve a likeness of him out of jackwood, use pineapple fibers for his hair, and dress him in the deceased's clothes and jewelry. The effigy hangs out at the funeral like an invited guest and then gets stowed with the coffin in this big cave, sort of a Torajan mausoleum, in the mountain. Once the coffin and body fall apart, the bones are gathered up and stuck up there on the mountain face with the effigy. It has something to do with them believing their ancestors all came to earth by climbing down some giant bamboo ladder in the cosmos. Maybe this helps them climb back up. But I'd rather not have them staring at me while I eat."

His large two-story house was on stilts, with big picture windows and verandas under a massive bamboo roof that reminded her of the bow of the Bugis schooners she'd seen in Benoa Harbor.

"Then why did you build your house so most of the windows face the mountain and not the sea?"

"I was required by the government to honor tribal customs, which demand that all homes face north, in the direction of Puang Matua, the creator of all things who built the first tongkonan, or master's house, in heaven."

"You believe that stuff?" she asked.

"No," he said. "The only thing I believe in is money."

"Then we have something in common," she said. "How many people are on your island?"

She wanted to know how many people she'd be up against if she ended up having to take Griffin against his will.

"A dozen, including me," he said. "There are eight members of the tribe, the chef and his wife, who runs the house, and Dumah, who I suppose you could call my property manager."

And head of security, Kate thought. She could tell by the way he scrutinized them as they approached the island and by the telltale bulge under his shirt where he hid his gun. So far, it seemed that Dumah was her only real obstacle, and she was confident she could neutralize him.

"Can I see the rest of the island?" she asked.

"Of course."

He drove her past the terraced rice paddies to the river, where a herd of water buffalo rolled in the mud, and then down to the eastern cove, where his fifty-three-foot yacht and a single-engine high-winged seaplane were tied to a long, narrow dock. The seaplane was like the small aircraft she'd taken to Mount Athos, only this one had two pontoons mounted under the fuselage and wasn't being used as a henhouse.

Two more options for a quick escape, Kate thought. If Willie could fly a turboprop, she could probably handle a seaplane.

"A sport yacht and a plane," she said. "You get around in style and with speed."

"We're remote, but with those little toys I'm never far from the action."

"I'm sure a man like you gets as much as he wants," she said. "What do you do for a living?"

"Absolutely nothing," he said as he steered the golf cart back to the house.

"Me neither. Rich parents?"

"Even better. *Dead* rich parents. I shrewdly invest their money and live off the proceeds."

"Maybe you could teach me a thing or two about that."

"There are all kinds of things I could teach you," he said, his leering smile and suggestive inflection making it clear where his thoughts were going.

"I'm filled with anticipation," she said. Gak, she thought, what a creep!

Griffin pulled up to the house and led her past the totem of water buffalo horns to the front door, which was surrounded by carvings of vines of some kind, and over the door were the words "Not God, Not Devil, But Man." He told her about the horns, how they and his herd of water buffalo were important signs of wealth and power respected by the Torajans. Moreover, they encouraged prosperity for all those symbolically under his roof.

She gestured to the sign. "What's that?"

"A reminder to keep humble."

"And the vines?"

"Fast-growing waterweeds, a Torajan symbol of fertility."

"You've got a lot of weeds and horns on your place," she said. "So much for remaining humble."

"There's a difference between being humble and stating an indisputable fact," he said.

"Which is that you're loaded in more ways than one."

Griffin sent her another suggestive smile. "You're very perceptive."

Just stick a fork in my eye, Kate thought. It would be less painful than this.

The interior of the house was modest but elegantly colonial, almost what she imagined the Raffles hotel in Singapore must look like, based on Nick's description. There was lots of rattan furniture and white paneling that stood out against the polished dark hardwood floors. The hot, humid air was pushed around to good effect with ceiling fans, the blades fashioned to resemble palm fronds.

Griffin showed her his library, which was windowless and filled with first editions. It was two floors tall, with a winding staircase to the second level, and ladders on rails made it possible to reach the highest shelves. Man-size leather armchairs were spread throughout the room. Antique side tables and old-fashioned reading lamps had been placed beside the leather chairs. An ornate mahogany desk was tucked into a back corner. There were only two items on the desk. One was a phone that Kate assumed was the satellite phone. The other item was a reinforced computer case that looked sturdy enough to withstand being run over by a truck or tossed off a cliff. Presumably the computer was locked up inside the case.

"I have first editions of Rudyard Kipling's entire body of work, as well as novels by Ernest Hemingway, Somerset Maugham, and John Steinbeck, to name a few. The room has an environmental control system to protect the books from the moisture in the air," Griffin told her.

She didn't care about the books. She was focused on the laptop in the gorilla-proof case. It was probably how he contacted his bank, and it might be possible to find his codes buried somewhere on the hard drive.

"You don't strike me as the bookish sort, Daniel."

"I had cancer as a child and spent years in and out of the hospital. There wasn't anything to do but read, and all they had around were the old classics. Those books took me away from that bleak hospital to wonderful, exotic places full of adventure and intrigue. I vowed that if I beat the cancer, I would find one of those places and make it mine. I did and I have."

Kate didn't know why Griffin collected old books, nor did she care, but she knew he'd never had cancer. His father had been a salesman for Kirby Homes, which built subdivisions throughout the western United States. Derek's mother was a stay-at-home wife and an alcoholic. Many years later, the couple invested their modest life savings with their son and he'd cleaned them out, too, along with everybody else who trusted him.

"'I did and I have,'" she said. "That's what you should have written over your front door. I might just write it over mine, if I ever stay anywhere long enough to call someplace home."

"You don't have a home?"

"I went to boarding school in Massachusetts, which was like going to a Siberian prison. I didn't read anything then and I don't now," Kate said. "I vowed that when I turned eighteen, I'd break open my trust fund, travel the world, and spend as much of Daddy's money as I could doing it."

Good job, she thought. Her fib was every bit as good as his fib.

"It's the best revenge," he said.

That might have been the first honest thing he'd said to her, considering what he'd done to his parents, who were now living in Tampa on food stamps.

He showed her his game room, his home theater, his Western-style bathroom, and his gourmet kitchen, where he introduced her to his personal chef, a Balinese man who'd studied at Le Cordon Bleu and Lenôtre in France.

One room wasn't included in the tour. The door to the room was closed, and it was obvious he didn't want her to see what was inside. Once everyone was asleep, Kate planned a nocturnal tour of her own, and that unopened door would be her first stop.

Griffin took her past his bedroom, which he made sure to identify for her, to the guest room, which had a four-poster bed with mosquito netting and a window that faced the mountain and the audience of the dead.

Her Vuitton bag was already waiting for her on a small rattan bench.

"You've had a rough morning," Griffin said. "You're welcome to relax here, if you like. My chef will prepare lunch whenever you're ready."

"The beach looks absolutely irresistible," she said. "Mind if I do some sunbathing and take a swim?"

"Do whatever you like, Eunice. You have the run of the house and the island," he said, stepping out and closing the door behind him.

Kate gave up a small sigh of relief. All her worries about seducing Griffin, luring him to the boat, and taking him back to the United States were for nothing. That part was going to be easy. The challenge would be finding the money. And stealing it back.

Dumah was waiting for Griffin downstairs. "I checked out her yacht when I dropped off her crew. It's a mess, but I think it's seaworthy. She wasn't kidding about the grenade launcher. It's a Russian RPG-7V2."

"See? There's nothing to worry about."

"How can you say that? What kind of woman carries around an RPG-7V2?"

"My kind," Griffin said. "Did you search her suitcase?"

Dumah nodded. "Nothing but clothes and toiletries."

"Enough clothes for how long?"

"Two or three days," Dumah said.

If Eunice's crew knew her well, and could make assumptions about her likely behavior, then the amount of clothes they packed for her was a very good sign. Griffin didn't want someone who would hang around. He was a slam, bam, thank you, ma'am kind of guy.

"Tell the chef to slaughter a pig," Griffin said. "We're having a feast tonight."

28

Nick and Willie cleaned the yacht, put sheets up over the broken windows, and sliced some fruit and made tropical cocktails to enjoy on the flybridge.

"I could get used to this," Willie said, sipping her drink.

"This is entirely fake," Nick told her.

"It feels real to me."

"You're being suckered by your own con."

"It's not mine, it's yours. I'm just playing along. And I'm game for more. There must be other rich international fugitives that need to be taken down."

"Derek Griffin is in a league of his own."

Which reminded Nick of the meeting on the beach. There was something about the fake name that Griffin chose for himself that was nagging at him. Where had he heard of "Daniel Dravot" before?

Nick grabbed the binoculars and scanned the island. Kate was in a bikini on the beach, lying facedown on a towel and letting Griffin untie her top and smooth suntan lotion on her shoulders, back, and sides.

"She's really working it," Willie said. "You don't need binoculars to see what's going down."

"She's just doing her job."

"Yeah, but looks to me like she's enjoying it. You aren't gonna fly off in a jealous rage, are you?"

"Not in the immediate future."

"You should have let me be the honey trap. Being that you already rejected me, the least you could do is give me a shot at the bad guy."

"Kate has more experience with criminals."

"Yeah, but I *am* one. And I have experience with men. Her, I'm not so sure about."

Nick swung his attention back to the island. Kate had retied her bikini top and was wading waist deep in water with Griffin watching from the beach. She turned and waved at Griffin, dove in, and headed for the boat, slicing through the water using a killer freestyle stroke.

"I have to give it to her," Willie said. "She sure can swim."

Nick stepped down from the flybridge, got a towel ready like the dutiful manservant he was supposed to be, and was standing on the swim deck to meet Kate when she emerged from the water.

"How's it going?" he asked, draping the towel across her shoulders.

"Seducing him is going to be easy," Kate said.

"So I've noticed."

"His only security is that guy Dumah, and I don't see him as much of a threat."

"Did you happen to see half a billion dollars lying around?"

"No, but Griffin's laptop is in his library. At least the case is there. And the case is built to survive a nuclear war, so I'm guessing the information we need is in the laptop. How hard could it be to crack?"

"Impossible without the password that unlocks it. Tell me what you saw, especially anything that seemed meaningful to him."

Kate told him about the mountainside burial ground, the water buffalo horn totem, the waterweed carvings, and the inscription above the front door. She also told him about the environmentally controlled library of first editions and Griffin's ridiculous story about how he developed his interest in old books.

"Eureka," Nick said.

"What eureka? You've figured something out?"

"Something big." He looked past her to see Griffin standing impatiently on the sand. For a guy who'd stolen half a billon dollars, Griffin turned out to be a very easy mark himself. "What was your excuse for swimming out here?"

"To let you know you're welcome to dine with the household staff at six P.M. tonight."

"Where will you be eating?"

"I'll be having a private dinner with Griffin, and then I'll spend the night at the main house. You and Willie will spend the night on the boat. It all works to our advantage, because later tonight I'll slip into his room and suggest we take a skinny dip. That's when I'll bring him to the boat, willingly or otherwise, and we'll make a quiet getaway. Mission accomplished, quick and simple. Now tell me what you know."

"What about the laptop?" Nick asked.

"I'll go back for it after we have Griffin on board, not that having it will do us much good without the password, which I don't think he's going to tell us."

"It's 'Sikander' or 'Sikandergul.' That's what I figured out."

"How do you know that?"

"I'll tell you later," Nick said.

"No! I want to know now!"

"You need to go. You've talked too long to the help already, and I don't want Mr. Dravot to get suspicious." He lifted the towel away from her, nodded stiffly as if accepting an order, and went up to the flybridge.

"Jerk," Kate murmured under her breath.

Nick smiled down at her, and she dove into the water and swam back to shore.

Kate and Griffin were the only guests at dinner, sitting cross-legged on a bamboo mat on either side of the low table on his torchlit veranda under a crescent moon. They each had a glass of wine, a bowl of white rice, and the requisite dish of sambal in front of them. There were no eating utensils. Kate would be eating with her hands again, Balinese-style. Just fabulous, she thought. Another opportunity for sambal to run down her arm and drip off her elbow into her lap.

"You mentioned you left Bali because you wanted to experience the real Indonesia," Griffin said. "So everything we're eating tonight came from this island, even the salt and seasonings, and I asked Chef to prepare babi guling."

Kate took a sip of her wine. "I hope that's nothing barbaric, like someone's head."

"The Toraja were the headhunters. Our chef is Balinese. Entirely different tribes."

"That's a relief," she said. "I'll sleep much better tonight knowing I won't be served for breakfast."

"Not breakfast," Griffin said. "Possibly dessert, if I'm lucky."

Ugh! Arrogant cretin, Kate thought. Slime-coated fungus. Diseased monkey butt.

"Luck won't have anything to do with it," she told him, licking a drop of sambal off her finger. "Tell me about our dinner."

"Babi guling is an entire pig, stuffed with spices and herbs, roasted on a spit for six hours, and basted in coconut water to caramelize the skin so it's deliciously sweet and crispy."

"Yummy. And you made this special meal for me?"

"It's not often I get such an interesting guest."

"You flatter me."

"I'm trying," Griffin said.

Kate smiled, doing her best to continue to look interesting and maybe even mysterious.

"I'm fascinated by your property manager," she said. "He seems so local. What tribe is Dumah from?"

"He's one of the Bugis, a seafaring people who terrorized the islands of their enemies, arriving by boat in the darkness. It's where the fear of the bogeyman comes from, at least around here."

"Should I look for him under my bed before I go to sleep?"

"You don't have to worry about the bogeyman coming for you tonight."

"I hope not. I feel so naked without my grenade launcher."

That was the God's honest truth, Kate thought. She'd barter her appendix for a Glock.

"I'll do my best to make you feel secure," Griffin said.

They ate the pig and Griffin told stories about Indonesia's history, the wars fought over control of the spice trade, and the difficulties during the Dutch occupation of the islands. For dessert, the chef served his own homemade recipe for dodol, a candy popular in Indonesia. The pieces of dodol were glutinous globs of rice and cane sugar that looked like saltwater taffy and tasted like a pencil eraser.

"Yum," Kate said, choking down a glob of dodol. "Very special."

They walked along the beach after dinner, and Kate admired the swaying palm fronds and gently lapping waves, but her focus was on the yacht. Lights were on, and Nick and Willie were at the dinette, obviously having chosen not to eat on the island.

"It's a shame about the damage to the yacht. You can kiss your security deposit goodbye," Griffin said.

"And let them fix the boat and rent it out again? No way."

"What other option is there?"

"I'll buy the yacht from them and keep the bullet holes intact as a souvenir of my Indonesian adventure."

"It's not over yet," he said.

She held his arm tight against her and looked into his eyes with her best attempt at a mischievous smile. "I think you may be right."

A half hour later when they returned to the house, Kate stood in front of her bedroom door and faked a yawn. "I know it's still early, but I guess the excitement of the day has caught up with me," she said. "I can barely keep my eyes open." She pressed her body against his and gave him a soft, lingering kiss. "I'm asleep on my feet."

"Would you like me to check under your bed for the bogeyman?"

"No, but if I wake up scared in the middle of the night, I hope you won't mind if I come running."

"Not at all," he said.

She slipped into her room, closed the door behind her, and ran to brush her teeth and gargle with Listerine.

It wasn't entirely an act. Kate *was* tired. Radiating hot sex was almost as exhausting as engaging in it. She had to rest up for a seduction, a kidnapping, and an escape into international waters in a bullet-riddled yacht. So she sprayed herself with DEET, drew the mosquito netting closed around the bed, and slipped under the sheets. Getting infected with malaria or dengue fever from a mosquito bite wasn't part of her plan.

According to the old-fashioned wind-up clock on the nightstand, it was 10 P.M. She set her mental alarm for 3 A.M. and stared through the netting at the view out her window. The moonlight made the wide white eyes of the effigies on the mountain seem to glow, and the effect was made even more dreamlike by the blur of the netting.

Kate awoke at 2:45, alert and ready for action. She lurched out of bed, pulled on bikini bottoms and board shorts, and slipped eyebrow tweezers and a slim metal pick into her pocket. There were sixteen ways she could kill a man with the tweezers and she could use the pick to open all kinds of locks. She was armed and ready. She laced up running shoes and quietly crept out of her room. She intended to go right to Griffin's room, but she found herself drawn to that one door he'd refused to open during their tour.

Kate went down the hallway to the door, which was across from the library, and tested the doorknob. Locked. She took the pick out of her pocket, worked it into the keyhole, and easily popped the lock. It wasn't Fort Knox, but she was proud of herself anyway. She eased open the door and peeked inside.

It was a state-of-the-art surgical suite. She didn't know the purpose for all the slick electronic equipment, but she recognized the lights, the operating table, the defibrillator, the IV stands, the oxygen tanks, and the shelves of iodine, alcohol, and other medical supplies.

The strange discovery made her think of all those James Bond movies with megalomaniac villains who had secret and outrageously elaborate island lairs, from *Dr. No* to *The Man with the Golden Gun,* and of the opening of *Diamonds Are Forever,* where 007 finds the leader of SPECTRE undergoing plastic surgery in a high-tech operating room in a cave full of molten mud.

Those movies, which had seemed so bizarre and over-the-top on screen, didn't seem so far from reality now. All that was missing were Griffin's plans for world domination, and a set of steel teeth and a razor-rimmed hat for Dumah, and she might as well be James Bond herself.

A hand clamped onto her shoulder, and she fought her instinctive reaction to take down whoever was behind her, leaving him with a broken right foot, a crushed larynx, and slivers of his nose driven into the frontal lobe of his brain. Instead, she let out a girlie shriek and whirled around, flailing her arms in a panic, to face Dumah, who stared at her with a face as wooden as the effigies'.

"What are you doing here?" Dumah demanded.

Kate looked over Dumah's shoulder and saw Nick Fox standing in the doorway of the library, grinning at her and holding Griffin's laptop case. She narrowed her eyes at him for a nano-moment and then she moved on, playing her part.

"This is so embarrassing," she said to Dumah. "I was trying to find Daniel's room."

"It's at the other end of the hall."

"My mistake," she said. "I have no sense of direction. What on earth is this room behind me used for? It looks like some sort of medical room."

Dumah looked back at her. "It's in case anyone gets seriously injured."

"Are you a doctor?"

"No," he said.

Nick slipped out of the library and disappeared down the hall, on his way to whatever window he'd used to sneak into the house. Unless he'd been ballsy enough to just walk in the front door, which, knowing Nick Fox as she did, Kate thought was entirely possible.

"What good is a hospital room on an island with no doctors?"

"You ask a lot of questions," Dumah said.

Too many, she thought, but she needed to give Nick time to get away.

"I'm naturally curious," Kate said. "Did you say Daniel's room was this way?"

Griffin stepped into the hall wearing pajama bottoms. "What's going on?"

"She was sneaking around," Dumah said.

Kate raised her hand. "Guilty as charged. I woke up and went looking for you, and I made a wrong turn." She leaned in close to Griffin, and whispered, "I'm feeling all hot and sticky. I thought you might like to join me for a skinny dip and dry me off afterward."

"Go back to bed," Griffin said to Dumah. "I can take it from here."

. . .

Kate and Griffin made their way single-file down the narrow trail of hard-packed sand. The vegetation was thick on either side of the trail, and the darkness was alive with the mating calls of countless insects and reptiles. Kate was on high alert. She doubted Nick had had time to row back to the boat, and she didn't want to inadvertently stumble onto him or the dinghy. Probably he'd pulled the dinghy into the bushes and was waiting in the shadows for her to show with Griffin.

Griffin led her off the trail and onto the sandy beach. And without any preliminary warm-up, he dropped his pajama bottoms.

"Your turn," he said, standing there naked.

Good grief, Kate thought. Who does this? Who just ups and drops his pants? The man was totally lacking finesse. And what was she supposed to do now? Was she supposed to look away or was she supposed to stare and compliment him on his woody? Okay, forget the woody. She was at a crossroads. Should she stick to the original plan? Or should she punch Griffin and go looking for Nick and his dinghy? Truth is, she felt odd about smacking Griffin when he was in his present naked, engorged condition. It wasn't something they'd covered at Quantico.

"Earth to Eunice," Griffin said. "Are you going to get naked, or what?"

Kate was weighing her options and looking at her feet, which she preferred to sizing up Griffin's Mr. Stiffy. As she saw it, her options weren't great. She could get naked, or she could sucker punch him. "Oh, hell," she said, and she smashed her fist into his face.

Griffin went down to the ground like a sack of sand, there was a flash of light in the trees behind him, and—*phoonf!*—a rocket shot out of the trees, passing so close to Kate that she could feel the heat on her cheek. It streaked across the water and slammed into the yacht, blowing it to bits in a concussive burst of flames that knocked her off her feet.

Bits of burning rubble rained down on the water, and Kate stared at the wreckage in openmouthed horror, worried that Willie had been on the boat. *No,* she told herself. You don't know that for sure. Don't even go there. There's no time for that kind of grieving. Find the guy who shot off the rocket and take him out. And then find Willie.

Kate got to her feet, with Griffin a beat behind her, looking dazed, his nose dripping blood.

"Who?" Griffin asked. "What?"

Five men burst out of the trees, their weapons aimed at Kate and Griffin. One of them had her RPG slung over his shoulder. They were a scruffy-looking group in sandals and mismatched pants and shirts. They had knives in sheaths on their belts, bad haircuts, and leathery skin. The guy with the RPG had elaborate tribal tattoos on his arms and face. His skin was dark but his features were Asian, and a scar slashed the length of one cheek.

"Now we're even," the guy with the scar said.

Oh, crap, Kate thought. The pirates.

Griffin clasped his hands over his privates, as if his balls were worth something in the world of pirate plunder. For all Kate cared, the pirates could do whatever they wanted with Griffin's balls. She was focused on the scarred guy. He was the man who'd blown up the boat. He was the man who might have killed Willie. He was the man she was going to kill at the first opportunity.

29

"Did you really think we would just run away?" the pirate asked Kate. "What kind of men would we be?"

Kate was unarmed except for her eyebrow tweezers, wearing nothing but a bikini and board shorts, up against five men with assault rifles. They wouldn't be expecting her to strike. So she figured she'd have an advantage . . . for a few seconds. She ran various scenarios through her mind. She could wait for the pirate to get close, stab her eyebrow tweezers into his carotid artery, then use his body as a shield as she picked off his friends with his gun.

"Who are you people?" Griffin asked.

"Wealth management consultants," the pirate said, dropping the RPG on the sand, rolling his shoulders, working out a kink. "You can call me Bob."

Kate almost gave a snort of laughter. Bob? Was he serious? Bob? Really? Okay, so his name was Bob. Fine. She was still going to kill him. She just had to decide on a course of action. She could grab Bob and break his neck with one sharp twist. She could jam her eyebrow tweezers between two particular vertebrae and shut him off like a flashlight. Or she could take his knife from his belt and bury it deep in his gut. Okay, let's get real, she told herself. That stuff mostly works in the movies, but real life not so much. Maybe her dad could pull it off with tweezers, but she suspected she at least needed a screwdriver.

Griffin dabbed at his nose, trying to stop the blood flow. "I'm going to bend down and put on my bottoms."

"No, you're not," Bob said. "You're going to stand there naked so we can laugh at you."

"I'd rather be shot," Griffin said. And he bent down and pulled up his pajamas.

Bob pressed a gun against Griffin's forehead. "What makes you think I won't give you what you've asked for?"

"You can't ransom a corpse."

Bob grinned. "I see you understand how my wealth management program works."

A sixth pirate dragged Willie out of the woods, shoving her into the clearing. Kate sucked in air, not sure if she was going to burst into tears of relief or coldcock Bob out of pure rage. She pulled herself together and managed to do neither.

"We found her when we boarded your boat, which by the way was a big disappointment," Bob said to Kate. "No jewelry. No money. No six-month supply of Cristal champagne and caviar. For a spoiled bitch, you don't know much."

"I know you're a disgusting pig," Kate said, back in character. "What about Sam? Wasn't he on the boat as well? Do you have any idea how hard it is to find a mate who can cook?"

"You've got the pig part right," Bob said. "But I rarely kill servants. I do, however, occasionally kill their masters. Your man is alive, too. He wasn't on the boat, but we know he's somewhere on the island. We won't hurt him unless he puts up a fight."

No problem there, Kate thought. Nick wouldn't put up a fight. Nick would sweet-talk Bob into giving up the gold fillings in his teeth.

"I didn't hear them board," Willie said to Kate. "I didn't know they were there until one of them came up behind me and put a knife to my throat."

Four more of Bob's men led Dumah, the chef and his wife, and the bewildered Torajan household staff down to the beach at gunpoint. Bob spoke to them in Indonesian, his inflection more like that of a car salesman making a pitch than a pirate warning his captives. Dumah nodded at Bob, said a few words to the rest of the staff, and they all turned and walked away as if there was nothing interesting left to see.

"What just happened?" Griffin asked, bewildered. "Where are they going?"

Bob turned to Griffin. "I told the villagers I had no quarrel with them, they were free to go back to their daily lives, and if they didn't try to intervene in our wealth management transaction, they wouldn't even notice that we were here."

It made sense to Kate. Their loyalty was to themselves and the island, not to the rich guy who'd leased their land. It apparently made sense to Griffin as well, who accepted the explanation with a nod.

"What did you say to Dumah?" Griffin asked.

"I asked him how loyal he was to you. He said, not at all. So I gave him your yacht and wished him a good life. He is a Bugis and a mercenary, like me. He knows not to betray us to the law. We would find him and kill him and every member of his family."

"But what about betraying me?" Griffin said. "Doesn't that count for something?"

"No," Bob said. "Not really."

"Isn't he worried about me coming after him for stealing my yacht?"

Bob laughed, said something in Indonesian to the others, and they laughed along with Bob.

"You really know nothing about our people or this country," Bob said to Griffin. "And you take us for fools. Don't you think we know you are hiding from someone or something?"

Griffin avoided looking at Kate. "Are we going to stand on the beach all night, Bob, or can we go back to the house and begin the negotiations?"

Bob told two of his men to take Willie to the mountain cave where the Torajan tribe buried, then visited, their dead, and to make sure she didn't escape. The Torajans went back to their homes to sleep. The Balinese chef and his wife were sent back to their kitchen to begin preparing an early breakfast for Bob and his men, several of whom watched over the couple to make sure nothing bad got slipped into their food. Kate and Griffin were force-marched back to the house.

"Nice place you had here," Bob said, standing in the foyer, stressing the past tense in the sentence. "Where is your satellite phone?"

Griffin gestured to the doorway. "In the library."

Bob went in first, followed by Kate and Griffin, and then the rest of the pirates. Kate was doing mental rehearsals, denying any knowledge of the missing laptop, when she realized the case wasn't missing. The laptop case was on the table, beside the satellite phone. Nick must have slipped back into the house and returned the laptop . . . or at least the case.

Bob tossed the satellite phone to Kate. "You have one call, princess. Choose wisely. It should be someone who values your life and is also very rich. Tell whoever it is that I want three million dollars in three days or you die."

Kate punched in the numbers and got her father's voicemail. His greeting was simply a confirmation of his phone number. He didn't give his name.

"Dad, it's me . . . Eunice. I've been taken hostage by pirates, and it's not nearly as fun as it sounds. They want money. Three million dollars in three days or they'll kill me."

Bob took the phone from her. "You will deliver the ransom in American dollars in a watertight case that floats. You will drop it from an aircraft into the sea at the following coordinates." Bob rattled off some numbers. "You will see a boat there. If I find any tracking devices in the package, or see any aircraft or boats following us, I will feed your daughter to the sharks." He disconnected the call. "I hope your father frequently checks his voicemail."

"That's not what you should think about," she said. "Ask yourself what kind of man gives his daughter an RPG and what he would do to anyone who hurts her."

"I'll try not to piss my pants," Bob said, gesturing to two of his men. "Take her to the cave."

Kate was muscled out of the library at gunpoint, shoved down the hall and out of the house. She was led across the scrub grass, past the huts of the Torajan tribespeople, and then up the winding path to the narrow cave entrance, where the two armed pirates stood guard. One of the guards pushed Kate into the mouth of the cave and motioned her forward.

"Go," he said. "You go there."

Kate picked her way through a rocky, twisting passageway, moving toward a flickering light. She rounded a corner and entered a wide cave, about twenty feet high at its highest point, lit with candles and honeycombed with tombs. The tombs were stuffed with crude, crumbling caskets that were spilling bones onto altars. Offerings of clothes, jewelry, walking sticks, and dishes filled with cash and loose change had been set on the altars. And it was all guarded by wooden effigies of the dead.

When Kate stumbled in, Nick and Willie were sitting on a rock ledge in the dim light, their clothing damp with sweat from the hot, humid air trapped in the cave, eating caviar and crackers from a silver dish on a wooden crate.

Nick smiled when he saw her. "Sit down and have some caviar. I liberated it from the house when I returned the laptop. I also took this to celebrate." He produced three tin cups and a hand-blown glass bottle filled with amber liquid, which he placed on the crate. "This is Balvenie Fifty, a single malt Scotch whisky that's been sealed for half a century in an oak sherry hogshead. Only eighty-eight bottles were produced, and they sell for thirty-five thousand dollars each."

He filled the cups and everyone took one.

"How did you get in here?" Kate asked him.

"Back door. Fairly easy to get in. Impossible to get out without some sort of ladder."

Kate sat on the rock ledge beside Nick. "What are we celebrating?"

"Our tremendous good luck," Nick said. "Everything is going our way."

"Our yacht has been blown up, we don't have Griffin or his money, and we're being held captive in a Torajan mausoleum on an island controlled by a dozen armed pirates," Kate said.

Nick tasted his whisky and nodded approval. "Griffin will beg to leave the island with us when we escape."

"Good to know you think we'll escape," Willie said. "I hadn't pictured this part of The Big Adventure." She knocked back her whisky and gasped as it burned down her throat. "Yow!"

Kate took a sip and savored the delicate blend of oak, peat, and honey flavors that had been in a cask since John F. Kennedy was president. It was the best Scotch she'd ever tasted and probably ever would taste. She just hoped it wasn't the *last* Scotch she ever tasted.

"What happened in Griffin's house?" Nick asked.

"Bob put a gun to my head and handed me a satellite phone. I called my father and left a three-million-dollar ransom demand on his voicemail. He has three days to drop the money at sea or I'm dead. I'm not sure what happens to you two in that situation, but I'm sure it's not good."

"But you really called the international security company you two work for," Willie said, "and they're going to send a strike team to rescue us."

"No," Kate said. "I called my father."

"Does he have three million dollars?"

Kate shook her head. "We're on our own here."

Willie poured herself another shot of Scotch. "You better know what you're doing," she said to Nick, "because I don't want to meet my maker in these stupid khaki shorts you made me wear."

"What about Griffin?" Nick asked Kate.

"I assume he's negotiating his own ransom since he's got nobody that he can call to pay it," Kate said.

"That's perfect for us," Nick said. "He'll have to access his account with his laptop to move the money to Bob's bank, or arrange to have the cash withdrawn and delivered to him, all of which will leave a digital trail on the hard drive that we can follow later."

"Assuming we can get our hands on his laptop again."

"We will," Nick said.

"And that you're right about his password."

"I am," he said.

"What makes you so sure it's 'Sikander' or 'Sikandergul'?"

"Because Daniel Dravot was a character in Rudyard Kipling's *The Man Who Would Be King*. And because of the quote from the book that Griffin put above all those water buffalo horns in front of his house."

"I didn't know you were such an avid reader," Kate said.

"I haven't read the book, but I loved the movie," Nick said. "Sean Connery and Michael Caine star as two nineteenth-century con men and soldiers of fortune, Daniel Dravot and Peachy Carnehan. They hatch a plot to become kings by teaching modern warfare techniques to one of the uncivilized mountain tribes of Afghanistan. Then the plan is to lead them to victory over their adversaries. Once the tribe is dominant, the two men intend to betray the king, take his throne, and lord over the dynasty they created."

"I don't understand," Willie said. "What does that have to do with Derek Griffin?"

"In one of the early battles, Dravot is hit in the chest with an arrow but doesn't bleed. That's because he has a bandolier hidden under his shirt that stops the arrow from hitting his flesh. So now the tribe thinks Dravot is a god and they basically make him their king. They give him a collection of gold and jewels that Alexander the Great, who they call Sikander, left with them centuries before in a sacred city they call Sikandergul. The problem is, Dravot begins to believe his own hype. His buddy Peachy wants to sneak out of there right away with the treasure, but Dravot wants to stick around, enjoy being a god for a while, and take one of the chieftain's beautiful daughters as his lover. But when Dravot goes to bed the girl, she freaks out and bites his lip, drawing blood, revealing to everyone that he's not a god."

"Not god, not devil, but man," Kate said, repeating the quote inscribed above Griffin's door.

"That's bad news for Dravot," Nick said. "Everybody in the tribe feels suckered, so they force Dravot out onto the middle of a rope bridge across a deep gorge and then cut it down. Dravot falls to his death and they beat the crap out of Peachy, who crawls back to civilization with Dravot's decapitated head in a burlap sack."

"You could learn a lot from that story," Kate said.

"I have," Nick said. "Griffin's password."

"I'm lost," Willie said.

"Griffin thinks his own life is tragically mirroring Dravot's," Kate said, "that he's a king with a vast fortune who is stuck in the middle of nowhere with a bunch of uncivilized natives."

"Aha!" Willie said. "And like Dravot, a big part of his undoing is his desire to nail a woman. I almost feel sorry for the guy."

"You shouldn't," Kate said. "He's a crook, and he's sleeping in his own bed while we're sitting in a cave full of corpses."

"A short-term situation," Nick said. "Twenty-four hours from now, we'll be on our way to the Indian Ocean in a seaplane with Derek Griffin and his money. We just have to figure out how to escape."

Kate thought that should be easy for a man who managed to talk his way out of prison by convincing the deputy director of the FBI not only to let him go but let him continue to commit massive frauds and help him do it. Compared to that, how hard could it be to escape from an island overrun with pirates in the middle of Indonesia?

"No problemo," she said. "Pass me the caviar."

30

Part of Kate's training as a Navy SEAL involved learning to adapt to adversity, to be able to rest and recharge in virtually any environment, no matter how extreme or unpleasant it might be, whether she was on an ice floe or lying on gravel in the open desert. So she figured she could manage to spend the night in a humid cave.

Willie was on her Really Big Adventure and up for anything. She'd just spent six weeks in jail, so she looked like she was going to be fine. She'd gone on a grave-robbing spree, snatching scraps of material off altars to the dead to make a pillow.

Kate suspected it would be different for Nick Fox. He appreciated his comfort and rarely settled for anything less than the finest accommodations. To her surprise, Nick stretched out on a slab of rock, put his hands behind his head, and went to sleep. He might as well have been reclining on a chaise in their villa in Bali. Damn,

Kate thought, you have to give credit where credit is due. The man can adapt.

Unlike Willie and Nick, Kate wasn't ready to go to sleep. She wanted to explore a little and size up the guards at the mouth of the cave. She retraced her steps to the cave opening and looked out. The two Javanese men were standing on the ledge, their guns slung over their shoulders and their backs to the cave opening. They were looking out at the view and smoking kreteks, Indonesian clove cigarettes that made a crackling sound when the guards inhaled.

"Yoo-hoo," Kate called. "Can I bum a smoke?"

The men jerked to attention as if they'd been electrocuted. The guard nearest her swore in Indonesian and shoved her back into the cave, wagging his finger at her.

"Do not go here," he said. "This is very bad behavior."

Kate smiled to herself. They were lazy and untrained. They thought their guns and knives were all they needed to keep their prisoners in line. This was a good thing for her and unfortunate for them.

In the morning, Kate and Willie were taken down to the house, where they sat on the scrub grass outside and were served rice pancakes and fruit for breakfast by the exhausted-looking chef and his wife. Bob emerged from the house wearing some of Griffin's clothes and sporting a panama hat. He was obviously ridiculing Griffin, who sat frowning on the veranda. The pirates gathered around, amused by the caricature, none more so than Bob himself, who couldn't stop smiling.

"You've got quite a setup here," Bob said to Griffin. "But there's one thing missing that would truly make it paradise. You know what that is?"

"Your absence?" Griffin said.

"Women! Surely you didn't come here to build yourself a monastery. Or are you just waiting for the right one to miraculously drift ashore?" He ambled over to Kate. "Is she the one?"

"Leave her alone," Griffin said.

Bob ignored him and grinned at Kate. "What if your father doesn't come up with your ransom? Would you stay here in paradise if this fool paid for you?" He looked over his shoulder at Griffin. "What do you say? Would you like to buy her from me?"

"I'm not for sale," Kate said.

"Of course you are," Bob said. "You won't marry a man unless he's rich, unless he can give you the things you want, and Daniel here is loaded. Well, not quite as much as he was before I came along."

"That's enough, Bob," Griffin said.

Bob glanced at Griffin. "Who are you to tell me what to do?"

"The man who has the fifty-year lease on this island. I'm not some rich tourist passing through. Her father pays and she's gone. But after I pay, you'll still have to deal with me."

"Not if I kill you," Bob said.

"And risk enraging the Indonesian authorities who'll be deprived of their generous bribes? And what about them?" Griffin gestured to the Torajan villagers who stood in front of their huts, watching the show unfold. "Their tribe was dying before I came along. Who do you think pays for the condos in Sulawesi where their families live now? If you kill me, they've all got to come back here to this rock. They won't be too happy with you about that."

"You think that scares me?"

"It should," Griffin said.

There was a reason Griffin was so successful in his business, Kate thought. He could be tough. And he wasn't stupid.

The Torajans mined the salt from the sea, using a system as old as the tribe. The process was simple. Water was lugged from the sea in buckets and poured onto swaths of sand that baked in the sun. Later, the thin layer of dried sand that was saturated with salt was shoveled into baskets. Torajan women carried the baskets on their heads to a bamboo hut, where they were emptied into a crude wooden sieve lined with mesh. Seawater was poured on the sand, dissolving the salt and carrying it out through the mesh into wooden channels leading to outdoor troughs. The water eventually evaporated, and the salt that remained was gathered up with carved coconut shells and put into new baskets.

The tribe kept a small amount of the salt for their own use but sold the bulk of it to wholesalers. It didn't bring in much money, but it was reliable income apart from whatever they were paid by Griffin. More important, it was a tradition and a ritual, one they weren't willing to give up just to sweep Griffin's floors.

"I wouldn't want you to attempt an escape out of boredom," Bob said to Griffin, Willie, and Kate, "so I'm going to let you work on the salt flat."

For the rest of the day, Griffin lugged seawater to his designated patch of sand, and Kate and Willie scooped up layers of dry, salty sand into baskets, carried the baskets into the hut, and poured the sand into the sieves. Kate played the spoiled heiress, complaining and periodically abandoning her job to stagger off in search of shade. In truth, she was keeping a head count of the pirates, trying to get a sense of how many men were on the island and how well armed they were. Her estimate was about a dozen, not counting how many were on Bob's mother ship that was anchored on the other side of the island. No way to get a count of them. All of the men had automatic weapons and knives. None of the men looked especially smart.

Late in the afternoon, Griffin, Willie, and Kate were given a dinner of rice, dried fish, and fruit, which they ate outside in silence. After dinner, Kate and Willie were led back to the cave and Griffin remained at the house.

Nick was waiting in the large chamber beyond the boulder. He had whisky and fresh fruit set out on a flat rock, lit by candlelight. "Welcome home," he said.

Kate poured out a shot of whisky. "The pirates are searching the island for you."

"They're not searching very hard, and I can't blame them. There are only two ways off the island, either on the boat they are using to go back and forth to their Bugis schooner, or on the seaplane they think none of us knows how to fly. So while you two were relaxing on the beach today, I scouted the island."

"How many men are guarding the dock?"

"None. And I only saw two men out on the schooner. I've counted a dozen men on the island."

"Me, too."

"I have a plan," Nick said.

Kate sipped the whisky. "Mine's better."

"You haven't heard mine yet."

"I don't have to. You are a con man. I'm a trained soldier. The escape is a military op, that's *my* bailiwick. We should make our move at two A.M. by overpowering the two guards. Willie will head for the seaplane and get it ready for flight while I get Griffin and you steal the laptop. Unless it's too risky to get the laptop. The laptop is a bonus, not a necessity. We'll have Griffin and his passwords, and if we can't figure out which bank he's stashed the money in, then Diego de Boriga can squeeze the name out of Burnside. All we have to do is get Griffin to the seaplane." Kate turned to Willie. "Can you fly it?"

"Sure," Willie said. "A plane is a plane."

"This one takes off and lands on water."

Willie shrugged. "I'll pretend it's a runway."

"That doesn't fill me with confidence," Kate said.

They all knocked back another whisky.

"Okay," Kate said. "I'm feeling more confident now."

"Your plan is actually the same plan as mine, with one key difference," Nick said. "I'll get Griffin while you make the run for the laptop. The con isn't over. You have to look at the long game. If we want Griffin to come with us willingly, we need to stay true to the characters we're playing. Eunice Huffnagle wouldn't be leading an escape, but the guy her father hired to protect her might."

"Good point," Kate said. "Okay, we'll switch jobs."

"We're also going to need a distraction to keep the pirates occupied while we make our escape."

"I've got that covered," she said.

Nick smiled. "Then we're good to go."

31

The first thing Nick and Willie saw when Kate nudged them awake at 2 A.M. were two unconscious pirates stripped to their underwear and lying side by side on the ground, bound and gagged with garments pilfered from the dead. Kate stood over the men, one AK-47 slung over her shoulder, the other one propped up beside her.

"You took them both out on your own?" Willie asked Kate.

"I didn't want to wake you." Kate held out the second AK-47 to Willie. "You might need this."

Willie looked the gun over. "I'm more a buckshot kind of girl. You want to walk me through this?"

"It's easy. Here's the safety catch and the selector for semiautomatic or fully automatic fire. As you can see, it's got a pistol grip. All you have to do is point and shoot. You've got thirty rounds."

"Ignore what she just told you," Nick said. "You don't need to know any of that."

"She does if she's carrying a weapon," Kate said.

"Carry it, but don't use it," Nick said. "If you shoot at people, they usually shoot back."

"What if the pirates start shooting at me?" Willie asked him.

"Duck and run," Nick said.

"And if I'm cornered?"

"Surrender," he said. "Having a gun is a good way to get shot, which is why I don't ordinarily carry them."

He reached for Kate's AK-47, but she swatted his hand away.

"Eunice Huffnagle wouldn't carry an assault rifle," Nick said.

"Fine. Great. Wonderful," Kate said, rolling her eyes. "Take the gun. I don't need it anyway."

They picked their way around the boulders and followed the winding route to the mouth of the cave, where Nick grinned at the two wooden effigies dressed in the pirates' clothes and standing on the ledge. From a distance, and in the darkness, they would easily pass as the guards.

"Nice," Nick said to Kate. "I assume this is your work?"

"I tried to make one of them smoke a cigarette but it wouldn't stay lit."

Kate looked at the compound below. She could see two armed pirates patrolling the main house, but otherwise there didn't seem to be anyone around.

"Everybody's asleep and nobody's expecting any real trouble," Kate said to Willie. "You should be able to make it to the plane without a problem. Be careful."

Willie disappeared into the shadows, and Nick and Kate crept down to the house. Not a lot of action going on. The two guards were patrolling the outbuildings at the back of the property, talking and laughing. Nick pointed to a guest room veranda, and they silently scuttled across the lawn and climbed up onto it. Kate eased a window open, and they slipped inside the empty room. Nick closed the window, and they crossed the room and moved into the hallway.

"Okay," Kate whispered. "You get Griffin, and I'll get the laptop."

She watched Nick until he disappeared around a corner, and then she headed down the hall to the library. The door was open and she could see the laptop on the table. Unfortunately, Bob was sleeping in an armchair beside it, and he wasn't alone. Three other pirates were asleep in the room, two on chairs, one on the floor. They were all snoring.

Not gonna happen, she thought, and she scratched "Take the laptop" from her to-do list. She moved across the hall to the operating room, eased open the door, and stepped inside. When she closed the door behind her, the windowless room became pitch-black. She'd thought ahead and taken matches and a candle from the cave. She lit the candle and set it on the operating table, and in the dim, wavering light she disconnected the oxygen tank from the anesthesia machine. She carried the tank to the far wall, bunched some towels around it, and soaked the towels with iodine and alcohol. She opened the tank valve just a bit, allowing it to leak oxygen, and left a trail of spilled iodine and alcohol from the tank to the operating table. She was about to ignite her makeshift firebomb when she heard a commotion in the hallway.

She recognized Bob's voice, and it wasn't hard to tell he was furious. There were more voices, more feet running, more yelling in Indonesian. She blew her candle out and listened at the door. People were being hustled her way, and she heard Nick's voice in the mix.

"How was I supposed to know you wanted to stay?" Nick asked.

"Because I live here, you idiot," Griffin said. "I've already paid my ransom. I'm just waiting around for you to go."

"We'd be on our way if you hadn't raised the alarm," Nick said. "It was Eunice who insisted I come for you."

"My new best friend is playing it smart," Bob said. "His ransom was a retainer for my ongoing protection from people like me."

"Your escape could have jeopardized that arrangement," Griffin said.

Kate gave her head a shake. If she didn't have bad luck, she wouldn't have any luck at all. She'd underestimated the possiblity that Griffin would turn, that he'd work out a deal of his own that would make it more attractive for him to stay than to escape with them.

Bob gave an order in Indonesian to his men, and she heard everyone moving outside. Probably this wasn't a good sign. Like when they shot Nick they didn't want to get blood splatters on the wallpaper. Time for the big diversion, she told herself. Time to blow the operating room to smithereens.

She broke the candle in half, so what remained was about an inch tall. She lit the candle, and set it on the floor at the end of her liquid fuse. She figured she had maybe five minutes to make her play, whatever it was going to be, before the explosion.

Willie reached the point on the path where the forest met the beach. Still hidden in the brush, she paused to see if there was anybody on the sand, or on the dock, or visible on the schooner anchored in the cove. The seaplane and a speedboat rocked gently on the swells and bumped against the dock, making the wood slats creak.

She took a deep breath, hung tight to her AK-47, and dashed

across the sand and onto the dock. She jumped into the speedboat, set her rifle on the floor, and yanked a bunch of wires out from under the cockpit dashboard. Good luck chasing us now, she thought. She turned and choked down a scream. A man dressed in black stood in the stern of the boat. The black paint on his craggy face made his eyes huge, horrifying, and unnaturally white. And he was pointing the AK-47 at her chest.

Kate made as much noise as she could climbing out of the guest bedroom. First she threw her suitcase out, then she jumped down after it. She fussed around for a couple beats, thinking the pirates were the most inept band of kidnappers to ever have walked the earth. When they finally rushed out of the darkness at her with guns drawn, she had her suitcase in hand. She made a quick show of being startled, and then wasted no time getting herded to the front of the house, worried she wouldn't be in place when the OR blew.

Nick was standing in the grassy area where they'd had breakfast, his back to the sea. Bob was next to him, casually holding his gun at his side. The pirates and tribe members stood to one side, as if watching a performance in a park. The Torajans seemed intrigued, but distant from it all. They knew that none of this involved them, that they were mere observers, like the effigies of their ancestors looking down from the mountain. They were here before this little drama unfolded and they'd still be here long afterward.

Nick shook his head in disbelief at Kate. "You went back for your bag?"

"It's Louis Vuitton. Besides, you didn't expect me to wear this for the next three days, did you?"

Griffin didn't expect her to wear anything at all. Griffin wanted her dead. If Eunice's father paid her ransom and she was set free, her father and the United States government would undoubtedly exert enormous pressure on the Indonesian authorities for an investigation into the kidnapping. And the Indonesians would comply because a story like this would be very, very bad for tourism. The wealthy would take their vacation dollars, and their resort investments, to some other tropical locale. And that meant things could get very bad for Griffin. The U.S. didn't have an extradition treaty with Indonesia, but the local authorities could arrest him, put him through a show trial, and lock him away in one of their hellhole prisons, even though he had nothing to do with the crime. He'd be sacrificed to the Gods of Tourism.

There was only one way out of this. He'd fork over the ransom money himself and get Bob to kill Eunice and her crew. Bob would be very rich. And Griffin could keep his island and get some long-term protection out of the deal, too.

"We need to talk," Griffin said to Bob.

"We can talk after I kill this guy," Bob said to Griffin, pointing his rifle at Nick.

"It's rude to point a gun at someone," Nick said, grabbing the AK-47 by the barrel, pivoting, and yanking it across his midsection. The move jerked Bob along with the gun, Nick elbowed Bob in the throat, took the gun from him, and whacked him in the gut with the stock. Bob went down to the ground, and Nick held the gun on him. The whole series of maneuvers took maybe three seconds.

No one was more surprised by the disarming than Kate. She thought she knew everything there was to know about Nick Fox, but she had no idea where he'd learned to do *that*.

The two guards behind her pressed their guns to her head and all the other pirates were taking aim at either her or Nick.

"That was a big mistake," Bob said, doubled over in pain and trying to catch his breath. "You have five seconds to drop the gun or the girl dies."

"If she dies, so do you."

Bob tipped his head toward his men. "Do you think they care? The ransom is what matters to them. You can save her, but no matter what happens, you are a dead man."

That's when the house blew up. It was like dynamite had gone off in a box made of Popsicle sticks. Flaming debris rained down, there was pandemonium among Tarajans and pirates, and in the middle of the confusion Kate took out the two pirates holding her at gunpoint. She snatched one of their rifles and pointed it at Griffin. "Grab my suitcase and run for your seaplane."

"We'll never make it," Griffin said.

"You can die right here, or you can run. Your decision. You have one second."

"He has less than that," Nick said, grabbing Kate's suitcase, ramming Bob's gun into Griffin's back. "Run!"

They all ran hell-bent for the cove, with the pirates shooting blindly into the darkness in their direction, bullets shredding the brush and pocking the ground around Kate and Nick and Griffin. Griffin stumbled and Nick scooped him up under the arm and kept him moving.

"We need to find cover," Nick said.

"We'll get pinned down," Kate said. "You run ahead with Griffin and hope Willie has the plane ready to go. I'll stay behind and hold them back for you as long as I can."

Nick looked at Kate. "Is the laptop in the suitcase?"

"Yes. *Go!*"

He shoved the suitcase at her. "*You* go."

"No way."

"You're both nuts," Griffin said. "Give me the suitcase and I'll go and you can both stay here."

"Sounds like a plan," Kate said, handing over the suitcase. "Keep running until you get to the plane and don't look back," she said to Griffin.

Griffin took off, and Nick grabbed Kate and kissed her with a lot of tongue and his hand on her ass.

"Just in case we get overpowered I didn't want to die without doing that," Nick said, breaking from the kiss. "And in the interest of world peace, if we don't die I suggest we forget the whole kiss and ass grab ever happened."

Kate didn't think she was likely to forget it. It had been, hands down, a fabulous kiss. And after the dust settled, Kate was going to give the kiss some thought, because Kate was feeling emotions she wasn't supposed to feel . . . at least not with Nick.

She moved to take her position on the opposite side of the trail so she and Nick could take the pirates down in a cross fire, when Griffin suddenly reappeared, running toward Kate in a blind panic.

"Help!" Griffin said.

"Fire in the hole," someone yelled from behind Griffin, and a grenade sailed over Griffin's head.

Nick, Kate, and Griffin hit the ground, and an instant later there was an explosion that brought an end to the gunfire from the pirates. Nick looked up to see a man in black limping toward them from the trail leading to the seaplane. The man in black had a rifle slung over his shoulder and was holding another grenade. Behind the man, and on either side of him, a dozen other dark figures fanned out in the trees toward Griffin's blazing compound.

"I see you started the party without me," the man said.

He pulled the pin on the grenade and lobbed it in the same direction as the previous one.

"Daddy!" Kate said, scrambling to her feet, running to Jake. " 'I knew you would come for me," she said, hugging him. "You are definitely getting my vote for Dad of the Year."

"I have a lot of years to make up for," he said. "Are you okay?"

"I'm fine. I just wasn't sure if you'd be able to make it in time."

"I have lots of friends in the neighborhood." He waved his arm toward the men on either side of him, who now surged ahead, opening fire on the retreating pirates. "And they were glad to help, especially if it gave 'em a chance to shoot at pirates."

Kate gestured to Griffin. "Can you take him and the suitcase back to Mexico?"

"Mexico?" Griffin stood. "What the hell is really going on here?"

"Diego de Boriga sends his regards," Jake said. And he punched Griffin in the face, sending him back down to the ground.

"This face punching thing must run in your family," Nick said to Kate.

"About Mexico?" Kate asked her dad.

"It'll be no problem, honey," Jake said. "I was doing extraordinary renditions back when they were still called foreign abductions. You're not coming with us?"

"It'll be less risky if it's just the two of you," she said. "We'll make our own way back."

"Willie has the plane fired up and ready to go," Jake said, looking at Nick. "You surprised me, Fox. Instead of saving yourself, you stayed to fight beside my daughter. For that, you will always have my respect."

"I never abandon my crew," Nick said.

"Then we've got something in common." Jake studied his daughter. "Are you sure you're okay?"

"Never better," she said. "That was fun."

She kissed her dad on the cheek and headed down the trail with Nick.

Jake watched her go and smiled to himself. "That's my girl."

32

Thirty-six hours later, Derek Griffin woke up on the floor of a cinder-block prison cell and squinted into the harsh blast of sunlight that blazed through the barred window. The air was hot as a pizza oven and smelled like rotting carcasses. He sat up, slid over to the wall beside the stainless steel sink, and leaned against it to get out of the light and assess his situation.

The last thing he remembered was being on the floor of a boat, looking briefly into the black-painted face of the man who'd hit him on the island, and then getting jabbed in the neck with a syringe that knocked him out again.

He had a skull-splitting headache that made it hard to focus his eyes. His throat was raw, his lips were chapped, and his body felt as if it had been run over by a truck, twice. His clothes, the same ones he'd been wearing on the island, were drenched with sweat. He rubbed his face and felt two days' growth of beard.

His first thought was that he was in an Indonesian prison, but the air was too dry, the texture of the light was wrong, and the stainless steel toilet was Western-style. Then he remembered what Eunice, or whoever that bitch *really* was, had said to the man in black face paint.

Can you take him and the suitcase back to Mexico . . .

Griffin grabbed hold of the sink, pulled himself to his feet, and almost collapsed again from light-headedness. He turned on the faucet, held his face under the lukewarm water for a long moment, then drank from the stream, his head crooked at an angle that nearly got him stuck in the sink. It wasn't until after he'd maneuvered his head out from under the faucet that he saw the tin cup on the rim of the sink.

Across from him was a cinder-block shelf with a thin mattress on top that served as a bed. He went over to the bed and sat down on it.

"Hey, Derek, are you awake over there?"

The voice came from the other side of the wall and he recognized it immediately. Neal Burnside.

"Yeah," Griffin said. "You in a cell, too?"

"The lap of luxury, isn't it?"

"Where are we?"

"Somewhere in Mexico, guests of Señor Diego de Boriga."

Griffin remembered the name. It was the last thing he'd heard before he woke up here. "Who is he and what does he want with us?"

"There's no point lying to me," Burnside said.

"Because you're my lawyer and we have attorney-client privilege?" He said it derisively, knowing full well that Burnside was probably the reason he was sitting in that cell. Burnside was the only person on earth who'd known where he was.

"Because we're prisoners of a brutal Vibora drug lord who invested his mob's money with you and wants it all back."

Griffin had never met Diego de Boriga, but then a drug lord probably wouldn't introduce himself as one, or reveal that his money was dirty, to someone he thought was a legitimate investment banker.

"I had no idea I was laundering anybody's drug money."

Not that it mattered. Griffin never cared where the money came from, whether it was from little old ladies or from mob bosses, as long as it kept coming in.

"You told him where to find me," Griffin said. "You ratted me out."

"Of course I did," Burnside said without a trace of guilt or regret in his voice.

"I would never have asked for your help to go into hiding if I'd known you'd tell anybody who asked where to find me."

"Not anybody, just Mexican drug lords ready to take a blowtorch to my balls to get your home address."

"I thought you were a man of principle."

"I am, and my basic, overriding, number one principle is personal survival."

"What makes you think he won't kill us both now?"

"I'm a pretty good judge of character. For instance, I knew you were a crook the second you walked through my door."

"That's because everybody who walks through your door is a crook, including you."

"I know you hate me right now, but I still consider myself your lawyer. I am looking out for your best interests. What we are facing is like a trial, with Diego de Boriga as judge, jury, and executioner. You need to let me do the talking for both of us."

"You sold me out once before, how do I know you won't do it again?"

"You don't," Burnside said. "But what other choice do you have?"

On Nick's orders, Willie flew them from Dajmaboutu to a secluded bay near Jakarta where Nick had underworld contacts. In return for Griffin's seaplane, the contacts fabricated replacement fake passports for Nick, Willie, and Kate, complete with Indonesian customs point-of-entry stamps that matched the date of their actual arrival. Nick accessed funds from his Shanghai bank account and bought three first-class tickets on separate flights on different airlines back to the United States.

Seventy-two hours after the events on Dajmaboutu, a tanned but tired Kate O'Hare met her boss, Carl Jessup, at a McDonald's off the I-10 freeway in Indio, California, and gave him Derek Griffin's laptop computer. There were a couple bullet holes in the thick, protective casing, but otherwise it was fine.

They ordered Big Mac Extra Value Meals, and while they ate, Jessup booted up the computer, punched in the password "Sikandergul," and used the restaurant's free wireless access to transfer $500 million from Griffin's Cayman Islands bank account into the U.S. Treasury's coffers.

Kate and Jessup celebrated the successful covert recovery of the stolen money with two large McFlurries.

Later that same day, Griffin and Burnside were hosed down and given clean clothes. The lawyer didn't know whether that was a good sign or a very, very bad one.

Once they were dressed, Char took them at gunpoint to the house for an audience with Diego de Boriga. Boriga was relaxing in the shade on a chaise, sipping a sangria. He was dressed in a Ringspun Kyuzo panther glitter T-shirt, black skinny jeans, and Diesel sneakers. He reeked of Dolce & Gabbana men's cologne, which prevented the pervasive stench of rot in the air from reaching his nostrils.

"Sit," he said, gesturing to the two chairs across from him. "I'm sorry I wasn't able to see you earlier, Mr. Griffin, but I was engaged in some other business. I trust you have recovered from your long journey in the meantime. I am Diego de Boriga. Does that name mean anything to you?"

"He didn't know who you were, or anything about your money, until I informed him of his predicament," Burnside said.

"I wasn't talking to you, was I? If you answer for Mr. Griffin again, Char will slit your throat. Nod if you understand."

Burnside nodded.

Diego shifted his gaze back to Griffin. "Do you know who I am?" he asked Griffin.

Griffin didn't want to insult the man's ego by not knowing who he was, but he also didn't want to start their conversation by contradicting Burnside and, perhaps, irritating the drug lord.

"I do now," Griffin said, "but I didn't know who you were before I got here or that you'd invested money with me."

"Are you familiar with the Central California Farmworkers Children's Education Fund?"

He was. They were one of the many nonprofits whose cash he managed, invested, and completely pilfered. He felt the safest reply was just one word:

"Yes."

"That was mine. By that, I mean it was Vibora profits as well as the life savings of every man, woman, and child in the village of Boriga. We gave it to you for safekeeping and growth, but you stole it all."

"If I'd known it was yours, I would never have taken it."

"That's your first lie," Diego said. "Tell me another, and I will pluck out one of your eyeballs."

"I can give you all of your money back," Griffin said. "With interest."

"You already have," Diego said, and lifted a towel on the chaise beside him to reveal Griffin's laptop computer. "I may even rename my new estate Sikandergul in your honor."

Griffin went light-headed, as if he'd experienced a sudden and profound loss of blood. Five hundred million dollars, he thought. *Gone*. All those years of diligent embezzlement and fraud. All his careful planning. All his extraordinary risk. All for nothing. He was completely broke, homeless, and facing prison time in the United States and, perhaps, Indonesia as well, if he was ever caught. How could it have gone so wrong so fast?

"As you can see, Griffin is a ruined man," Burnside said, not able to contain himself any longer. "I think we can also agree that you've been made whole on your losses, and richly compensated beyond any reasonable measure for the insult, the despair, and the misery that you and the people of Boriga felt as a result of his betrayal. The suffering and humiliation he faces now will be an everlasting torture that's deeper and more agonizing than any physical pain you could inflict."

Griffin was convinced this was true. In fact, he was tempted to ask Char to slit his throat right there. But his fear of death was greater than his fear of poverty.

"You've had your vengeance and retribution," Burnside said to Boriga. "Is there really any purpose served by punishing Griffin any further or holding me in any way accountable for his actions? You're an intelligent, honorable man. You know in your heart that there's no reason not to let us both go free."

Burnside was confident that this would end like all of his other trials. He'd get to walk out of the courtroom no matter what the jury, in this case Diego de Boriga, decided about his client. His reasoning was simple. It was Griffin who'd committed the crime. Burnside was just his lawyer. Yes, he'd helped his client avoid justice, but isn't that what a good lawyer is supposed to do? Diego would certainly understand that and not begrudge him for bending the law on his client's behalf. Wouldn't Diego expect the same level of representation for himself? Of course he would. So Burnside felt pretty good about his chances. He was far less certain about Griffin's odds.

"You make a very persuasive argument, Mr. Burnside," Diego said.

"Thank you."

Diego nodded to himself and slapped his hands on his thighs, making a decision. "Very well. You may go."

Burnside smiled to himself. *You are a superstar, baby. Doesn't matter if the trial is in federal court or a drug lord's living room, you're the lion king amid a herd of zebras.*

"Excuse me?" Griffin said, blinking hard. It was not the outcome he was expecting.

"My men will blindfold you, drive you to a remote location, and set you free."

"How do we know you won't execute us?" Griffin asked.

"As Mr. Burnside pointed out in his eloquent argument, I am

an honorable man. I keep my word. Where you go after you are released, or how you get there, is your problem. But if you ever speak of me, or tell anyone that we have the money Mr. Griffin stole, I will slaughter you and anyone you've ever loved, including pets. How does that sound?"

"Very generous," Burnside said.

Diego smiled. "That's what people always say about me."

Kate and Nick were watching on monitors in the surveillance room on the second floor of the house. Kate had watched covert shakedowns and stings before. This one was especially satisfying.

Nick was sitting in the chair beside Kate and gave her a nudge. "Sweet, isn't it? And the fun isn't over yet."

33

Char put hoods over the prisoners' heads, bound their wrists with plastic zip ties, and led them to a panel van parked in the compound. Burnside and Griffin climbed inside and sat down. The door slid shut with a heavy clank. The truck left the compound and they rode over the bumpy, rutted roads in silence.

Burnside was relaxed, basking in his success, but Griffin was shaking, convinced that they were being taken for execution to the pit where the bodies of Diego's enemies were left to rot.

The truck came to a stop fifteen minutes later. The rear door was opened, and Char pulled them out, stood them in the sandy dirt on the shoulder of the road, and cut the zip ties around their wrists with a knife.

"You are being watched," Char said. "Do not remove your hoods for five minutes after I have driven off or you will be shot."

"Understood," Burnside said.

Char got into the truck and they heard him drive away. Burnside began to count off the five minutes, sixty seconds at a time, in his head. The relief that Griffin felt at not being executed gave way to worry as the enormity of his bad situation hit him full force. He was stuck in the middle of Mexico without even a peso in his pocket.

"How are we supposed to get home?" Griffin asked.

"Shut up, or I'll lose count."

"You can just walk through the nearest U.S. border crossing and go back to your life, but what about me? I'm a wanted fugitive. I'll have to stay here and live like a peasant."

That was true, but Burnside didn't care what happened to Griffin now that the man was penniless. "Would you rather be dead?"

"I might as well be."

"Where there's life, there's hope."

Griffin yanked off his hood. He didn't give a damn if the five minutes were up or not. Let the bastards shoot him. He squinted, temporarily blinded by the harsh sunlight, before he was able to see the large sign directly in front of him. It read: *El Pollo Loco coming soon to this location.* Just past the sign a dirt road cut across a vast expanse of graded desert and the foundations for future structures mapped out with wooden stakes. And beyond the staked property was a broad boulevard lined with several big box stores and scores of fast food franchises. Palm trees dotted the sand-and-asphalt commercial landscape.

Two patrol cars raced up the road toward them, lights flashing, sirens silent. Behind the cars, there was a sprawl of housing developments, green grass, and more palm trees. Rising above it all, just a few blocks away, was the tower of the Fantasy Springs Resort Casino, the tallest building for miles.

Burnside pulled off his hood and turned around, taking all of this in just as the two Indio Police Department cruisers slid to a stop. "We aren't in Mexico and we were never prisoners of the Viboras," he said.

"We've been conned," Griffin said. "I was played from the first moment Eunice Huffnagle showed up on my island." He gave his head a very small shake. "It was brilliant."

Nick, Kate, and their crew watched it all unfold from the window of the presidential suite at the Fantasy Springs Resort Casino. The only thing they couldn't see from this distance were the expressions on the faces of Derek Griffin and Neal Burnside as they were taken into custody by the police, following an anonymous call from Kate.

Kate knew that by the time the two men reached the Indio police station, agents from the local FBI field office would be there waiting for them. Griffin would definitely go to prison, perhaps for the rest of his life. As for Burnside, she supposed there was a chance that he might avoid prison for aiding and abetting Griffin's flight from justice, but he'd almost surely lose his license to practice law. So Burnside was finished, too.

"We did it," Nick said, passing out glasses of champagne to his crew. "We got back half a billion dollars in stolen money and nailed the guys responsible, all as a result of your unique skills and hard work."

Kate clinked his glass. "And on behalf of all the victims of Derek Griffin's crimes, we thank you."

"It was the best role of my career," Boyd said. "My one regret is that I don't have anything for my reel."

"My regret is that I didn't get to be the honey trap," Willie said.

"I would have gotten some mileage out of Griffin before he got carted off."

"I don't have any regrets," Tom said.

Chet nodded. "Me neither. You can call me anytime."

"So what's next?" Willie asked.

"That's up to you," Kate said. "Our job's done."

Nick checked the time. "We need to leave. You guys better get going. The two of us will finish covering our tracks."

Tom, Chet, and Willie left, and Kate and Nick stayed behind.

"You did good," Kate said. "It was an amazing con. And so far as I know, you didn't steal anything."

"Yeah, it doesn't feel right. It's like something's missing."

Kate pulled a small gift-wrapped package out of her tote bag, and handed the package to Nick. "A memento."

Nick tore the paper off the package and grinned. He was holding a first edition copy of Rudyard Kipling's *The Man Who Would Be King.*

"This is perfect," he said. "I love it. You stole this from Griffin's library when you went back for the laptop, didn't you?"

She nodded. "I thought you should have it."

He flashed her the thousand-watt smile. "Do you realize what this means?"

"Yeah, I'm a thief."

"Honey, that's such a turn-on."

He reached for her, and she jumped away.

"Stand down," Kate said. "My hands are lethal weapons."

Nick backed her against the wall and leaned into her. "I've got a better lethal weapon than you do," he said. "Wanna see it?"

"No!"

Good lord, she could feel his lethal weapon pressing against her belly. It was big and hard. And as much as she hated to admit it, his big, hard weapon was exactly what she needed. She looked down and gasped because it was so perfect.

"Is this for me?" she asked.

"Absolutely," he said. "Take it if you want it."

"I want it," she said. "I really, really want it."

It was a Toblerone bar. Giant size.

"It's more a symbol than a memento," Nick said, handing her the Toblerone. "So where does this leave us?"

"It leaves us waiting for our next assignment from Deputy Director Bolton," she said. "I go back to being an FBI agent and you go back to being a fugitive on the run from the law. But I should warn you, I've been reassigned to head up the manhunt, so stay out of trouble."

"We'll see," he said.

It was late at night and Lula and I were hunting down Salvatore Sunucchi, better known as Uncle Sunny, when Lula spotted Jimmy Spit. Spit had his prehistoric Cadillac Eldorado parked on the fringe of the Trenton public housing projects, half a block from Sunucchi's apartment, and he had the trunk lid up.

"Hold on here," Lula said. "Jimmy's open for business, and it looks to me like he got a trunk full of handbags. I might need one of them. A girl can never have too many handbags."

Five minutes later, Lula was examining a purple Brahmin bag studded with what Spit claimed were Swarovski crystals. "Are you sure this is a authentic Brahmin bag?" Lula asked Spit. "I don't want no cheap-ass imitation."

"I have it on good authority these are the real deal," Spit said. "And just for you I'm only charging ten bucks. How could you go wrong?"

Lula put the bag on her shoulder to take it for a test drive, and a giraffe loped past us and continued on down the road, turning left at Sixteenth Street and disappearing into the darkness.

"I didn't see that," Lula said.

"I didn't see that neither," Spit said. "You want to buy this handbag or what?"

"That was a giraffe," I said. "It turned the corner at Sixteenth Street."

"Probably goin' the 7-Eleven," Spit said. "Get a Slurpee."

A black Cadillac Escalade with tinted windows and a satellite dish attached to the roof sped past us and hooked a left at Sixteenth. There was the sound of tires screeching to a stop, then gunfire and an ungodly shriek.

"Not only didn't I see that giraffe, but I also didn't see that car or hear that shit happening," Spit said.

He grabbed the ten dollars from Lula, slammed the trunk lid shut, and took off.

"They better not have hurt that giraffe," Lula said. "I don't go with that stuff."

I looked over at her. "I thought you didn't see the giraffe."

"I was afraid it might have been the 'shrooms on my pizza last night what was making me see things. I mean it's not every day you see a giraffe running down the street."

My name is Stephanie Plum, and I work as a bond enforcement officer for Vincent Plum Bail Bonds. Lula is the office file clerk, but more often than not she's my wheelman. Lula is a couple inches shorter than I am, a bunch of pounds bigger, and her skin is a lot darker. She's a former streetwalker who gave up her corner but kept her wardrobe. She favors neon colors and animal prints, and she fearlessly tests the limits of spandex. Today her brown hair was streaked with shocking pink to match a tank top that barely contained the bounty God had bestowed on her. The tank top stopped a couple inches above her skintight, stretchy black skirt, and the skirt ended a couple inches below her ass. I'd look like an idiot if I dressed like Lula, but the whole neon pink and spandex thing worked for her.

"I gotta go see if the giraffe's okay," Lula said. "Those guys in the Escalade might have been big game poachers."

"This is Trenton, New Jersey!"

Lula was hands on hips. "So was that a giraffe, or what? You don't think it's big game?"

Since Lula was driving we pretty much went where Lula wanted to go, so we jumped into her red Firebird and followed the giraffe.

There was no Escalade or giraffe in sight when we turned the corner at Sixteenth, but a guy was lying facedown in the middle of the road, and he wasn't moving.

"That don't look good," Lula said, "but at least it's not the giraffe."

Lula stopped just short of the guy in the road, and we got out and took a look.

"I don't see no blood," Lula said. "Maybe he's just takin' a nap."

"Yeah, or maybe that thing implanted in his butt is a tranquilizer dart."

"I didn't see that at first, but you're right. That thing's big enough to take down an elephant." Lula toed the guy, but he still didn't move. "What do you suppose we should do with him?"

I punched 911 into my phone and told them about the guy in the road. They suggested I drag him to the curb so he wouldn't get run over, and said they'd send someone out to scoop him up.

While we waited for the EMS to show I rifled the guy's pockets and learned that his name was Ralph Rogers. He had a Hamilton Township address, and he was fifty-four years old. He had a MasterCard and seven dollars.

The EMS truck slid in without a lot of fanfare. Two guys got out and looked at Ralph, who was still on his stomach with the dart stuck in him.

"That's not something you see every day," the taller of the two guys said.

"The dart might have been meant for the giraffe," Lula told them. "Or maybe he's one of them shape-shifters, and he used to *be* the giraffe."

The two men went silent for a beat, probably trying to decide if they should get the butterfly net out for Lula.

"It's a full moon," the shorter one finally said.

The other guy nodded, and they loaded Ralph into the truck and drove off.

"Now what?" Lula asked me. "We going to look some more for Uncle Sunny, or we going to have a different activity, like getting a pizza at Pino's?"

"I'm done. I'm going home. We'll pick up Sunny's trail tomorrow."

Truth is, I was going home to a bottle of champagne that I had chilling in my fridge. It had been dropped off as partial payment for a job I did for my friend and sometimes employer Ranger. The champagne had come with a note suggesting that Ranger needed a date. Okay, so Ranger is hot, and luscious, and magic in bed, but that doesn't totally compensate for the fact that the last time I was Ranger's date I was poisoned.

The champagne had been left on my kitchen counter yesterday, and I was saving it for a special occasion. Seemed like seeing a giraffe running down the street qualified.

Lula drove me back to the bonds office, where I picked up my car, and twenty minutes later I was in my apartment, leaning against the kitchen counter, guzzling champagne. I was watching my hamster, Rex, run on his wheel when Ranger walked in.

Ranger doesn't bother with trivial matters like knocking, and he isn't slowed down by a locked door. He owns an elite security firm that operates out of a seven-story stealth office building located in the center of Trenton. His body is perfect, his moral code is unique, his thoughts aren't usually shared. He's in his early thirties, like me, but his life experience adds up to way beyond his years. He's of Latino heritage. He's former Special Forces. He's sexy, smart, sometimes scary, and frequently overly protective of me. He was currently armed and wearing black fatigues with the Rangeman logo on his sleeve. That meant he was most likely filling in for one of the men on patrol.

"Working tonight?" I asked him.

"Taking the night shift for Hal." He looked at my glass. "Are you drinking champagne out of a beer mug?"

"I don't have any champagne glasses."

"Babe."

"Babe" covers a lot of ground for Ranger. It could be the prelude to getting naked. It could be total exasperation. It could be a simple greeting. Or, as in this case, I'd amused him.

Ranger smiled ever so slightly and took a step closer to me.

"Stop," I said. "Don't come any closer. The answer is *no*."

His brown eyes locked onto me. "I didn't ask a question."

"You were going to."

"True."

"Well, don't even think about it, because I'm not going to do it."

"I could change your mind," he said.

"I don't think so."

Okay, truth is Ranger *could* change my mind. Ranger can be very persuasive.

Ranger's cellphone buzzed, he checked the message and moved to the door. "I have to go. Give me a call if you change your mind."

"About what?"

"About anything," Ranger said.

"Okay, wait a minute. I want to know the question."

"No time to explain it," Ranger said. "I'll pick you up tomorrow at seven o'clock. A little black dress would be good. Something moderately sexy."

And he was gone.

ABOUT THE AUTHORS

JANET EVANOVICH is the #1 *New York Times* bestselling author of the Stephanie Plum series, the Lizzy and Diesel series, twelve romance novels, the Barnaby and Hooker novels and Trouble Maker graphic novel, and *How I Write: Secrets of a Bestselling Author*.

Visit Janet Evanovich's website at
www.evanovich.com
Facebook/JanetEvanovich
or write her at
PO Box 2829
Naples, FL 34106

LEE GOLDBERG is a screenwriter, TV producer, and the author of several books, including *King City, The Walk,* and the bestselling Monk series of mysteries. He has earned two Edgar Award nominations and was the 2012 recipient of the Poirot Award from Malice Domestic.

www.leegoldberg.com

ABOUT THE TYPE

This book was set in Minion, a 1990 Adobe Originals typeface by Robert Slimbach. Minion is inspired by classical, old-style typefaces of the late Renaissance, a period of elegant, beautiful, and highly readable type designs. Created primarily for text setting, Minion combines the aesthetic and functional qualities that make text type highly readable with the versatility of digital technology.

BEFORE

THE HEIST ...

THERE WAS

THE CAPER!

Enjoy this never-before-published mini-adventure featuring

KATE O'HARE and NICOLAS FOX!

FBI Special Agent Kate O'Hare took a firm grip on her Hazelnut Macchiato Grande and wedged herself into the backseat of the black Suburban. Her shoulder-length brown hair was pulled up into a ponytail, and she was wearing a navy polyester suit that could survive a nuclear blast without wrinkling. She was sharing the seat with two Sasquatch-size agents from the local Seattle office, and she was debating the wisdom of the Starbucks stop. Okay, so Agent Kruger had been up all night with his two-year-old daughter and had desperately needed coffee, but jeez Louise, Kate thought, this was freaking frightening. She was sitting thigh to thigh with two men holding scalding-hot liquid in paper containers, with a driver who thought he was trying out for NASCAR.

"Hey, we've got coffee here," Kate yelled to the agent behind the wheel. "If it spills on one of these guys next to me, he isn't going to be able to have a family."

The driver glanced in the rearview mirror. "We're not too sure if they should reproduce anyway."

Kate had spent the night hastily acquiring a Seattle-based task force, and this morning she'd flown from her home base of L.A. to Sea-Tac, where she'd been picked up by the A-team. A guy named Levine was at the wheel, and Kruger was riding shotgun. Mo Smitt and Andy Munder were flanking her. She was following a lead that Nicolas Fox, the slick international con man and thief she'd been chasing for three years, was in Seattle, running a scam. The lead was more than speculation. She had confirmed visuals, and she had a handle on the scam, thanks to her cousin Cindy. Cindy lived in Seattle, and two days ago she'd spotted Kate's picture on a city bench.

"You're not going to believe this," Cindy had said, "but there's a real estate agent here who's a dead ringer for you. And she's in business with a smoking-hot guy. I'm standing here looking at an ad on a bench in front of a bus stop. I'm sending you a picture now."

Moments later Kate had pulled the ad up on her email. The headline read: "Our Listings Don't Sit on the Market, They Sell! Call Us NOW!" Under the headline was a full-color picture of the Realtors, Eustace and Irma Haney. Eustace was Nick Fox, looking like sex in a suit, wearing a tux, his bow tie unfurled carelessly at his open collar, his mischievous smile making his brown eyes sparkle. Irma was next to him, sporting a face lifted from Kate's driver's license picture and Photoshopped onto the body of an outrageously big breasted woman in a black dress with a plunging neckline.

After round-the-clock computer work and several phone calls, Kate put it together. The CFO at a big health insurance company had been quietly released from his work obligations while federal officials pored over the company books. The CFO had disappeared from sight, off on a six-month cruise. And like the brilliant opportunistic thief that he was, Nick had swooped in, posed as a Realtor, and sold the CFO's $3.5 mil house out from under him. Closing was scheduled for three o'clock this afternoon.

Kate checked her watch. It was almost noon. "Are we sure Nick is in the real estate office?"

"There's a guy with a scope on the roof across the street," Mo said. "He's watching Fox. Positive ID."

Levine stopped at an intersection and gestured to an ad on a bench backboard. "That's him, right?"

Kate gaped at the ad. It was the first time she'd actually seen it in person.

"Holy crap," Levine said to Kate. "That looks like you next to him."

The four men leaned forward, looking from the ad to Kate and back to the ad. All four men gave a simultaneous bark of laughter.

"Nice picture of you," Mo said, smiling wide.

"It's been Photoshopped off my driver's license," Kate said. "Nick Fox humor. The man is evil."

"Sort of a shame," Levine said. "I kind of had a thing for Irma."

"Are those ads all over the city?" Kate asked.

"Pretty much," Levine said. "Out in Bellevue too."

"The names are familiar," Kruger said. "I know them from somewhere."

"Nick thinks it's fun to use names from old TV shows," Kate said. "According to my dog-eared copy of *The Complete Directory of Episodic Television Shows,* Eustace Haney was the con man in *Green Acres* who sold Eddie Albert and Eva Gabor their dilapidated farm."

A driver behind the Suburban leaned on his horn, and Levine moved through the intersection.

"Are agents in position on the scene?" Kate asked.

Mo nodded. "We've surrounded the building and can secure the block in thirty seconds."

"Tell them to stay out of sight. Nobody moves until I give the order. I don't want to spook him."

The Suburban sped south on 1st Street through Pioneer Square, which was the original heart of the city and only a block east of Puget Sound. It was a skid row neighborhood of nineteenth-century Romanesque brick and stone buildings that was slowly being gentrified with art galleries and coffeehouses.

Levine parked in the red zone at 1st Street and South Washington, positioning the Suburban so that it was kitty-corner from the ground-floor offices of Jet City Realty. Mo took Kate's macchiato and handed her a pair of binoculars. She trained the binoculars on the first-floor reception area, where Nick was talking on his cell phone. Then he slipped his phone into his pocket and moved out of view.

"Yep, that's him," she said. "And he looks clueless."

Kate gave the binoculars back to Mo and slipped a Bluetooth headset into her ear.

"I'm going in," she said.

"Alone?" Mo asked.

"I'm not alone. I have a whole task force behind me."

"What if he's armed?"

"He doesn't use guns," Kate said.

"He might if he's cornered."

"Then I'll have to shoot him before he shoots me."

Kate climbed over Munder and exited the Suburban. She crossed the street, tuning in to Mo communicating with the other agents, telling them to hold tight. There was another black Suburban in the alley half a block down, and a few agents posing as civilians on the sidewalk. They acknowledged Kate with a glance, and she glanced back and walked into the real estate office.

The walls were stripped to show off weathered old bricks. The reception desk was a tall counter in front of a glass partition with JET CITY REALTY etched into it. Behind the glass were cubicles where the Realtors worked.

The receptionist was a sleek blond woman in her thirties whose eyes went wide when she saw Kate. "Mrs. Haney!" she said. "What a wonderful surprise. I thought you were still in Florida recuperating from your goiter reduction. Goodness, the doctors did an amazing job. Your neck looks terrific. And I see you had the wart removed from your nose as well."

Kate could hear the other agents laughing in her earpiece. It would take all her self-control not to shoot Nick on sight.

"And you learned all this from my husband?"

"He's been terribly worried about you."

"I'll bet," Kate said. "Where is my little love bug? He doesn't know I'm back, and I want to surprise him."

"He's in his office. It's the third one on the left, past all the cubbies."

Kate walked the short corridor and whispered an order into her Bluetooth to seal the building. She drew her Glock and tried the doorknob to Nick's office. Locked. She stepped back and put everything she had into a well-placed kick to the left of the doorknob. The door splintered at the jamb and flew open into the room. There was a desk, desk chair, and file cabinet in the room. No Nick. She could see that the single window to the street was locked from the inside.

People were spilling out of their cubicles into the corridor.

"What was that crash?" someone asked.

"Mr. Haney's door," someone else said.

And then someone took a good look at Kate and screamed, "Gun!"

People dove under desks, ran for the front door, and shrieked in panic.

Kate took her badge out of her back pocket and held it above her head for everyone to see. "FBI," she said. "Relax. I'm looking for Haney. Where is he?"

"He never said anything about you being in the FBI," the receptionist said to Kate. "Are you sure you aren't one of those crazy jealous wives? You don't want to kill him, do you?"

"It's a tempting thought, but no," Kate said. "I don't want to kill him."

"I saw him go into his office," a woman said. "He went in and closed his door, and I didn't see him come out."

Kate looked behind the desk and around the file cabinet. She cautiously opened the closet door. The closet was empty, the floorboards had been removed, and a ladder led down into the basement.

"He must be in the basement," Kate said to the agents listening in on Bluetooth. "I'm going after him."

"That's not a basement," Mo told her. "It's the first floor. In the 1890s, to stop the constant flooding, the city built a retaining wall along the shore and raised the streets downtown. The second floor of every building became the new street level, and everything below was covered up."

"So what the heck is down there now?"

"It's a maze," Mo said. "Most of it was sealed and condemned over a hundred years ago. A lot of it was buried. But the part right under Pioneer Square is open for tours, and the homeless use the rest of it for shelter in the winter."

Kate rummaged through Nick's desk drawers, grabbed a mini flashlight keychain with the Jet City Realty logo on it, and climbed down the ladder. Walls were visible in the dusty darkness. Windows had been bricked over. Doorways were open. Thick wood beams supported the street above and were braced against the buildings.

Kate heard the sound of footsteps muffled by more than a century's worth of fine dirt that had sifted down onto the original street, and a flash of light turned a corner about thirty yards in front of her. Kate ran toward the light, gun in hand, trying not to stumble over the bricks and fast-food packaging, beer bottles, soiled mattresses, and remnants of campfires that littered the passageway. Every so often, glass cubes embedded in the sidewalk above cast sunlight into her underground world.

"He's down here," Kate said to Mo. "Cover all exits."

"We don't have the manpower. There are dozens of ways out of there. Every building and manhole cover for blocks is a potential exit."

Kate swore and came to a fork in the underground road. Which way did he go?

She pulled the Bluetooth out of her ear and switched it off. She didn't want Mo and everybody else listening in.

"Nick," she yelled.

"Hey, Kate," Nick yelled back, somewhere in front of her, lost in the darkness.

"How did you know I was coming for you?"

"If you want to be inconspicuous, drive a Ferrari, not a black Suburban with tinted windows." His reply was relaxed and amiable, as if they were two old friends catching up on the phone.

Kate listened carefully, hoping she could place him. "Only you would think a Ferrari is subtle."

"Sometimes being intentionally conspicuous is as good as being invisible. If you'd arrived in a Ferrari, you'd probably have me in handcuffs right now."

"It's not too late."

All of his talking had helped her pinpoint him. She took the path to her right and moved as quickly as she dared toward his voice without turning on her flashlight and revealing her position.

"You'd look good in a Ferrari," he said.

"You'd look good in handcuffs," she said.

"Do you imagine that often?"

"Not as often as I picture you in a jail cell."

Kate saw a shaft of daylight illuminating Nick on a ladder at the far end of the underground street. He blew her a kiss and climbed out. The daylight shut off like a candle being blown out. She switched her Bluetooth back on and worked it into her ear as she ran toward the ladder. "He's up above."

"Which street?" Mo asked.

"I don't know. There are no signs down here."

She came to a ladder leading to a manhole cover. She eased the cover up slowly and peeked out. No cars came rushing at her. She was under a park. She pushed the manhole cover aside and climbed out into the sunlight. There were homeless people lazing around and some skateboarders surfing the railings and flying over steps. No sign of Nick.

She jogged to the nearest street and saw Nick staring at her. Not in the flesh, unfortunately, but from a bus bench advertisement. Nick looked as handsome as ever, but someone had drawn a mustache under his Realtor wife's nose with a Magic Marker.

"O'Hare, are you there?" Mo asked in her ear. "What's your 10-20?"

Kate sat on the bench and sighed. It would be a while before she lived this one down. She glanced at the street sign.

"South Main Street," she said.

Right at the corner of Humiliation Boulevard.